THE SCREAMING EAGLES

Iron Mike MacDonald was in charge of the squad they called the Bad Boys. None of them were the sort to be interested in history, but that is what they made... The 101st Airborne Division had been nicknamed 'The battered bastards of Bastogne' after the German breakthrough into the Belgian Ardennes. Now on Christmas Eve, 1944, Iron Mike's men are ordered out on a desperate mission to save what's left of their crippled division. They must link with Patton's Fourth Armored by the 26th, the day the Germans launch their last all-out offensive. It's the Screaming Eagles' last chance...

The Screaming Eagles

by

Duncan Stirling

Magna Large Print Books
Long Preston, North Yorkshire,
BD23 4ND, England.

British Library Cataloguing in Publication Data.

Stirling, Duncan
    The screaming eagles.

    A catalogue record of this book is
    available from the British Library

    ISBN   978-0-7505-2881-8

First published in Great Britain 1983 by Arrow Books Ltd.

Copyright © Duncan Stirling 1983

Cover illustration © Mary Evans' Picture Library

The moral right of the author has been asserted

Published in Large Print 2008 by arrangement with
Eskdale Publishing

Magna Large Print is an imprint of Library Magna Books Ltd.

Printed and bound in Great Britain by
T.J. (International) Ltd., Cornwall, PL28 8RW

'We're the Eagles, MacDonald's Eagles, crooked, cunning and cruel!'

The motto of Captain 'Iron Mike' MacDonald's Bad Boys squad 1944

A NOTE FROM IRON MIKE

'*The battered bastards of Bastogne*' the Allied press called us back in December 1944. It was the usual corny bull of the time. Most of the Screaming Eagles of the 101st Airborne Division, trapped in that one-horse Belgie township of Bastogne, paid little attention to the sort of crap that Ike's PR people, nice and safe in Gay Paree, habitually dreamed up for us. Mostly we were too busy trying to save our necks from the Krauts. Of course, we *did* know we were heading for the history books; I mean there was nobody like us. And I guess the grandkids of those same Screaming Eagles (now mostly white-haired old gents, if they're still alive today) read about that 'historic defence' in their highschool textbooks. That is, if modern kids still read books. But even the ones who don't read them surely know what our commander General McAuliffe said when the Krauts asked him to surrender at the height of the siege? Hell, it is part of the American legend, isn't it? It was one short hard word – '*Nuts!*'

But I wonder if even those surviving

Screaming Eagles know the real role that my Bad Boys squad (as we used to call the bunch of assorted crooks, conmen and goof-offs under my command back in 1944) played in that great 'historic defence' of the textbooks?

I suspect they know nothing of it, for to my knowledge, no records were ever kept. It is, in essence, part of the Secret History of World War Two. Well, thanks to Mr Stirling, here it is, for the very first time, in the shape of *The Screaming Eagles. I liked it!* I hope you do too.

Michael 'Iron Mike' MacDonald,
Maj. Gen. US Army retd.
Arlington, Va. Spring 1982

PRELUDE TO BATTLE

'Bastogne must be eradicated, Bayerlein, if we are going to cross the Meuse. It will be a running sore on our lines of communication. It must be deal with. In the name of our Führer Adolf Hitler, Bayerlein, I command you – KILL BASTOGNE!'

General von Luttwitz to General Bayerlein,
commander Panzerlehr Division,
Saturday 16 December 1944

Soon it would be dawn. One by one the hard winter stars were beginning to disappear. The cruel silver light was giving way to the dull grey of a new day at war. Again that icy wind straight from Siberia was beginning to howl through the snow-heavy firs which marched up the hillsides on both sides of the narrow Belgian road like spike-helmeted Prussian guards. To the front the horizon flickered a silent pink as the fires of the great retreat still burned.

In their foxholes on both sides of the road, the 'wet-lips', the green reinforcements thrown into the great new battle this very morning, waited anxiously, shivering with cold and fear. All that day they had seen the panic-stricken, broken men of the frontline outfits who had been hit first by the Kraut surprise attack streaming back to the rear, abandoning their equipment as they came, and all with the same stammered frightened phrase on their blue twitching lips, 'The Krauts are coming ... the Krauts are coming...'

Now for over an hour, the road had been empty of them. That could mean only one thing. To their front now there were only Krauts. The next lot of men coming down from the hills – which were inside Germany – and along this frontier road would be dressed in the field-grey of the *Wehrmacht;* and they would be shooting when they did so. Now this was the frontline!

Six o'clock. In the hills the guns had started to rumble again. Now green youngsters forgot their cold, their misery. Red, green and white signal flares had begun to curve into the grey sky. Somewhere to the right a machine-gun started to chatter faintly. 'One of our BARs,' a frightened rookie stated hopefully. The platoon sergeant in charge of the hastily erected roadblock, the only veteran among them, shook his greying head sadly. 'No,' he said laconically, 'Kraut … genuine Kraut.' He flashed a look at the woods to their front and told himself it wouldn't be long now.

Six-thirty. They could hear a faint rusty squeak coming from the other side of the hills. Most of the scared youngsters pretended they hadn't heard the new sound and no one dared ask the grizzled noncom what it was. Instead they crouched there fearfully, hearts thudding, hands gripping the icy stocks of their weapons suddenly wet with sweat.

Sergeant Rice looked at his watch and did a quick calculation before rapping out his orders, as he rose from his foxhole and walked deliberately to the centre of the road, tommy-gun held at the port. 'Now hear this, you bunch of shavetails,' he said, trying to make himself sound more confident than he felt, his breath fogging the air in a great grey cloud. 'What you can hear is Kraut tanks. Now, don't youse guys go pissing yer pants! A trained infantryman who keeps his nerve can cope with tanks, too,' he added hastily, seeing the sudden terrified looks on their pinched, youthful faces. 'We've got a daisy chain of Hawkins grenades strung out across the road and the first Kraut tank that hits it will block the whole goddam road. So what'll they do then? I'll tell you guys,' he answered his own question. 'They put in their infantry, coming in from both flanks to try to winkle us out of these nice warm holes of ours.' Instinctively he raised and cocked his tommy-gun, as the sound of tanks grew closer. 'Now if you all keep your heads, they won't get us out of these holes because on account of the fact that a guy running to the rear with his back to the enemy is more likely to get plugged than one who sticks it out in his hole with only his head showing. Got it?'

There was no answer. All their eyes were fixed on the horizon, at the point where the tanks must soon come.

Sergeant Rice spat angrily into the ankle-deep snow. 'Well, you heard what I had to say. Now I'll tell you guys just one more thing. Twenty miles back up this road there is a little Belgie one-horse town called Bastogne. Bastogne is Corps HQ and the Corps Commander General Middleton, who is an old drinking buddy o' mine, has empowered me personally to shoot any one of you shavetails who gets up outa his hole and starts to bug out. Get it? Shoot ... *dead!*'

And with that, Sergeant Rice, who had never met General Middleton in all his life and had another quarter of an hour to live, stalked to a position directly behind the road and took up his stance, tommy-gun at the ready, eyes searching the horizon with every now and again a quick glance towards the trembling skinny backs of his handful of youngsters.

The star shell exploded with a sharp crack directly above the roadblock. Immediately the faces of the scared young GIs were bathed an eerie glowing ice-white. 'Stand to,' Rice cried desperately. 'Here they come!' He raised his tommy-gun as the first black monster came rumbling down the hillside, snapping pines as if they were matchsticks, churning up a great white wake of flying snow.

Now the flares were exploding all round the roadblock. Red, white, green, they blinded the defenders in their glowing brilliant light. Rice flung up his free hand to shade his eyes. The tank was rattling towards the barricade now. Behind it white-clad infantrymen came

14

scurrying through the snow, burp guns held tightly to their hips. 'Shoot the pricks, for Chrissake!' Rice yelled frantically, and raising his tommy-gun, fired a wild burst at the advancing infantry.

A German went down abruptly. Another stopped, face contorted with agony under the white helmet, his hand clawing the air as if climbing the rungs of an invisible ladder. A third pitched noiselessly into the snow.

The tank gunner pressed his trigger. An angry red-and-white morse of glowing tracer sped towards the barricade. Lead stitched a crazy pattern in the snow, running in a wild zigzag to the lone noncom standing there. Rice yelped with pain. A red-hot poker had been suddenly plunged into his right knee. He dropped into the snow, his kneecap shattered, still firing as he went down.

Now his greenhorns were returning the enemy fire, their bullets whining off the thick armour plate of the white-painted tank rattling towards the barricade, its cannon spitting fire.

A sudden crump. The tank rose in the air for an instant, then came abruptly to a stop as thick white urgent smoke poured from its ruptured engine. Next moment it disintegrated, ammunition exploding in its ready-locker, tearing it apart before zigzagging aimlessly into the sky.

'Hurrah!' A hoarse cheer rose from the defenders, and everywhere the German infantry dropped to the snow, as pieces of steel hurtled lethally through the air.

'That's the way, boys,' Rice gasped through his pain; and a grey mist wavered before his tear-filled eyes and threatened to engulf him as he knelt there, his blood dripping steadily into the snow. 'Now keep them Krauts up there occupied … fire at will… You–'

The rest of his words of encouragement froze on his lips. Three white-painted monsters were ploughing their way effortlessly through the snowy fields to the right. They were so huge they seemed to fill the whole sky. 'Tigers,' he quavered. 'Oh, my God, Royal Tigers!'

The leading tank fired. Scarlet flame stabbed the grey. There was a huge rush of racing air as if an express train was hurtling into a station. A tremendous explosion. Rice, lying helpless on the bloodied snow, felt his lungs burst, as the flimsy pathetic barricade disappeared into the huge explosion. Just as he died, he saw the first tank poise itself over the foremost of the foxholes and slowly and deliberately begin to grind its tracks round, its twin exhausts belching smoke, digging its way deeper and deeper into the crumbling earth, burying the GI who occupied the foxhole in a trench filled with his own blood. Then, mercifully, all went black and Sergeant Rice had fought his last battle.

'Schrecklich, mein lieber Bayerlein,' Corps Commander von Luttwitz commented, adjusting his monocle and staring down at the man crushed flat into the middle of the tank's tracks, as if he had been made of cardboard, *'aber das ist Krieg.'*

Bayerlein, his face still tanned from his days in the desert with Field Marshal Rommel, nodded his agreement. 'War,' he told himself, *'is* terrible, very terrible indeed.' He looked up the road at the wrecked Mark IV tank, its crew now a black putrid paste in its fire-red turret; the American sergeant with his guts ripped open, the viscera swelling out of the yellow flesh like a giant scarlet sea-anemone, the dead GIs squatting in their foxholes, already turning black like some rotting sprout stumps left in a worker's winter allotment, and told himself that even after five years of war at the front he would never get used to the sight of death in battle. Then, the complete professional that he was, he forgot the Americans and turned to his somewhat gross Corps Commander, who affected a monocle in the Prussian fashion, and asked, 'What's the drill now, General?'

'Bastogne and the Meuse, as planned, Bayerlein,' von Luttwitz snapped promptly. 'My signals people have just intercepted a

17

typically careless Ami radio message. At last they are beginning to react to our new counter-offensive here in the Belgian Ardennes. Eisenhower's HQ in Paris has alerted his only two reserve divisions, the 82nd Airborne and the 101st Airborne. They are located somewhere in France.'

Bayerlein nodded. 'I have heard of the 82nd, fought them in Sicily and Italy to be precise. But this 101st–' he shrugged and left his thoughts unspoken.

'Not to be worried about particularly, Bayerlein,' von Luttwitz answered easily, watching his soldiers begin to loot the bodies of the dead youngsters, yelling in triumph to each other when they found a bar of sticky, sugar-sweet Ami chocolate or a pack of Lucky Strikes. 'They fought in Normandy and in Holland with heavy losses, but without any great success. They call themselves the Screaming Eagles from their eagle divisional sign, but they are not to be greatly feared. After all,' he looked hard at the smaller general through his monocle, 'what can a parachute division, armed only with light weapons and hardly any transport do against such a fine and well-trained division as your Panzerlehr, eh?'

Bayerlein knew he was intended to be flattered by the statement but he did not rise to the bait; he was too concerned to know his next objective. So he said woodenly, 'I presume, General, that I shall be asked to see these ... er ... Screaming Eagles off.'

'Exactly, my dear Bayerlein,' von Luttwitz boomed. Now his men were attempting to remove the dead Amis' fine boots in order to replace their own shabby, battered 'dice-beakers', as they called their jackboots. Two of them had slung a dead Ami over a tree and had lit a fire under his feet, trying to thaw the boots out so as to pull them off more easily. Soon, he knew from past experience, they would be quarrelling about who should have the precious boots. 'It is Intelligence's guess that these Screaming Eagles fellows will be sent to Bastogne, the last remaining road and communications centre before the River Meuse. Now if the Amis win the race to the damned place, or can hold it with whatever forces they may have there already, we are in trouble.'

Bayerlein understood. The road network within the snow-bound Belgian Ardennes was poor. Key towns such as Bastogne would have to be captured if the great German Army, now driving into Belgium in this last-ditch attempt to throw the Amis back into the sea, was to succeed.

Von Luttwitz's face hardened. He set the monocle more firmly in his right eye and stared down the long, straight road that led to the West – and the unknown. 'Bastogne must be eradicated, Bayerlein,' he rasped, his voice suddenly harsh and worried, 'if we are going to cross the Meuse. It will be a running sore on our lines of communication. It must be dealt with.' Suddenly his voice shook with emotion. 'In the name of our Führer Adolf Hitler, Bayerlein, I command you – *kill Bastogne!*'

Book One:
INTO THE CAULDRON

Bastogne, which had been untouched when the troops moved in, wore that ghostly air of desolation which had come to many European towns in the war. In the still night air a man walking past the ruins could smell the sickly-sweet odour of the untended dead.

Lt. Col. L. Critchell,
101st Airborne Division

Day One:
Sunday 17 December 1944

'All right, yer lucky buggers, step forward and have yer greenbacks at the ready,' Limey called out of the side of his cunning mouth, his sharp, bright-blue eyes taking in the faces of the 'fly-boys' and a handful of older men from the COM Z who crowded the dingy little French bar. 'This is yer chance, mates. Yer'll never get another like it to beat Kovalski, the human metal-grinder!' With a dramatic flourish, he indicated Corporal Jerzy Kovalski of the 101st Airborne, known to his buddies of the Bad Boys squad as Polack, who was leaning his massive bulk across the zinc-covered bar awash with beer suds, watched by an apprehensive French madame in rusty black silk who looked as if she feared her whole *établissement* might collapse under that tremendous weight at any moment.

Polack gave the others a gold-toothed grin, and almost as if he was hardly aware of what he was doing, he picked up one of the razor blades he had prepared for his little demonstration and neatly bit off its end. With apparent enjoyment, he started to crunch the metal.

At his table at the far end of the crowded bar, loud with the tinny music of French *bal musette* and thick with cigarette smoke, Polack's running mate Pfc van Houten-Gore shuddered and said, his pale, intelligent face set, 'I wish that he wouldn't do that, for heaven's sake, even if it is a trick! My God, he could cut off his tongue.'

Big Red, the Bad Boys' sergeant, took a deep pull at the weak French beer, muttered his usual 'Gnat's piss', and said in his big deep bass, 'Polack wouldn't miss it. That big lug never says much anyway, and when he does half of it's in Polack so yer can't understand him.' He ran his big hand through his mass of bright red hair and grunted, 'For Chrissake, give me a pull of that rye you've got stashed in yer hip pocket, Dude. This frog beer is undrinkable!'

Dutifully van Houten-Gore, product of Phillips Academy and Yale, and scion of one of the richest families in the Hudson Valley, pulled out his pint of black-market rye and handed it to the noncom. Like the rest of the Bad Boys squad, he seemed to have been solidly on KP ever since they had come out of the line in Holland the previous November. Perhaps with the aid of the rye, he could sweet-talk Big Red into arranging a three-day pass for him in Paris this Christmas away from those nauseating kitchens always

24

heavy with the stench of 'shit on shingle'.

Now a crowd had collected around the big Polish-American and the undersized English-man Limey, who surprisingly enough had found himself in the US Army after having 'deserted more times than you lot of Yanks have had good dinners', as he was wont to boast. Confidently the Englishman in his oversized, laced jumpboots faced his audience and said, 'All right, gentlemen, here's the time to put yer money where your mouth is. My friend here is prepared to eat *anything*, and I repeat *anything*, for a small wager. Show 'em Polack.'

Like an obedient performing animal, Kovalski picked up a beer glass and took a deep bite at it. It crunched in his mouth and with seeming pleasure, he swallowed a large piece of glass, while the black-clad madame clapped her pudgy, beringed hand to her forehead as if in despair.

Polack's audience was impressed, yet as always at such demonstrations there was someone who doubted the big Pole's ability. In this case, it was a big fat noncom of the Army Air Corps. 'A greenback says, your guy can't chew that ashtray over there.'

Dude gulped as the noncom picked up a tin ashtray, filled to over-flowing with wet cigarette ends and handed it to a grinning confident Limey.

'You're on mate,' he said, slapping down a

dollar to match the sergeant's, 'but it'll cost you another buck if he's going to eat the butts.'

Dude pulled the rye bottle out of Big Red's paw. 'For God's sake, give me a drink. I'm going to puke in a minute!'

Smiling stupidly, the Polack raised the nauseating ashtray and was about to drain its contents, when the door of the little French *estaminet* flew open. Framed there against the background of dirty snow stood a crowd of drunken infantrymen, led by a massive first-sergeant with a nasty livid bayonet scar running down the side of his craggy face. All of them wore the big red number one patch of the US Army's premier infantry division, the First.

The first-sergeant's face contorted into a mean smile. 'Now looky heah, boys,' he said to the men crowded all around him, 'ain't that just like the Geronimo jerks – eating butts out of an ashcan in a Frog whorehouse. Screaming Eagles, they call themselves,' he sneered. 'Christ on a crutch they look like a bunch of lame ducks to me.'

Quietly Big Red nudged Dude. The Dude nodded, and as Big Red clutched a bunch of five franc pieces in his hamlike fists to make a primitive pair of brass knuckles, he knocked off the neck of the bottle of rye, turning it into a deadly, frightening weapon.

As always it took Polack some time to

register what was being said to him, even insults. He stared at the scar-faced first-sergeant and then at his divisional insignia. 'You're from the Big Red One,' he said at last, as if he had established a fact of some importance.

'Jeez, it can really speak,' the first-sergeant sneered, so taken up with the giant at the bar that he did not notice the little man with the oversized jump boots sneaking up on his right, billiard cue hidden carefully behind his skinny back.

'I think you're pulling my pisser,' Polack said uncertainly.

'D'ya hear that guys, the big jerk thinks I'm pulling his pisser,' the first-sergeant jeered. 'Brother, ain't he quick on the uptake?'

The men behind him roared with laughter.

At his side, Limey nodded.

Big Red and Dude returned the nod.

Limey hesitated no longer. He raised the cue. With all the strength of his skinny arms he brought it down on the first-sergeant's shaven skull. The noncom yelped with pain as the cue shattered on the back of his head and went down on his knees, yelling 'They've murdered me, guys ... murdered me. *Get the bastards!'*

The fat madame screamed and ducked hastily as a bayonet flew through the room and stabbed the wall just above her head.

The light splintered and went out, and suddenly all was cursing chaos, with khaki-clad soldiers sprawled and rolling on the glass-littered floor, punching and kicking each other, breath coming in short hectic gasps, while the madame screamed and screamed and screamed.

A whistle shrilled urgently. Outside there was the squeal of brakes. Boots clattered on the *pavé*. 'All right you guys, now knock it off,' a harsh voice cried. 'I said – *knock it off!*' As if to emphasize his command, the big MP framed in the doorway raised his .45 and fired a quick shot into the ceiling. That did the trick.

Limey dropped his billiard cue and shoved his hands quickly into his pockets. He leaned against a broken table and started to whistle aimlessly, as if he were just an innocent spectator. The fistfuls of French francs fell from Big Red's massive fists, while Dude quietly placed the broken rye bottle, dripping with blood, on the littered bar behind him. The madame lay slumped across it in a dead faint.

Only Polack failed to react to the MP's command, remaining where he was, with an unconscious Big Red One man raised high above his head, caught in the white beam of the MPs' torches, as if he were a ballet dancer illuminated at the high point of a *pas de deux* by the arc-lights of the theatre.

'Drop that man,' the MP sergeant commanded. 'Now move it, you big dum-dum!'

'Yes sir.' Polack, as always, reacted to any command given in a firm authoritative manner. He let the unfortunate Big Red One soldier drop. He slammed to the floor. His nose split like an over-ripe fig. Blood spilled everywhere.

Big Red groaned aloud. 'Now they'll really have our asses,' he moaned and held up his hands as if waiting for the handcuffs to be slapped on them.

But for once Big Red was mistaken. Instead of being arrested, the Airborne troopers were shoved outside into the freezing evening air. There two two-and-a-half open trucks were waiting, the drivers gunning their engines, while in the back drunken Screaming Eagles cursed and moaned, watched by keen-eyed MPs armed with shotguns. Big Red looked at the MP noncom who led them through the double line of MPs. 'Hey what is this?' he cried, as the men on the trucks recognized the senior NCO of the Bad Boys squad and began to give him the Bronx cheer and cry drunkenly, 'You'll be sorry!'

'What is it?' the hard-faced, gimlet-eyed MP echoed, as the guards lowered the tailgate to allow the four running-mates to board the leading truck. 'Ain't you guys heard? The balloon's gone up at the front... Youse Screaming Eagles is needed up there... They're gonna drop you personally in old Adolf's own backyard.' He laughed maliciously. 'That should take all yer piss and vinegar outta ya – for good!'

'Famous last words,' the little Englishman said in a hollow voice and lowering his head like a condemned man, he allowed himself to be shoved up into the deuce-and-a-half...

'Kay, so the shit has really hit the fan, men,' Captain 'Iron Mike' MacDonald said in that precise West Point manner of his, as he strode along the ranks of his Bad Boys, the sauce-hounds, crooks, rapists and general misfits who General Taylor, the divisional commander, had handed to him to discipline and make soldiers of. 'And what are you bunch doing? I'll tell you!' he rasped, his hard blue eyes flashing fire and making even Polack quail. 'You're out, beating the daylights outa of our own men, though' – he lowered his gaze so that his sorry-looking soldiers couldn't see the sudden look of merriment that flashed momentarily across his harshly handsome face – 'sometimes I wonder if you could say the Big Red One belongs to the US Army.'

Then he dismissed the bar-room brawl and got down to business. Outside, the suddenly alerted camp blazed with lights in spite of the blackout regulations, and paratroopers scurried back and forth, loading weapons and gear onto the waiting trucks. 'Yesterday at dawn the Krauts struck our lines in the Ardennes and although the situation is very confused up there, it seems as if General Middleton's Eight Corps has taken a bad beating. Not too put too fine an edge on it, there seems to have been a big bugout at the front with our guys falling back everywhere.'

Legend

———————— Original Frontline,16 December 1944

– – – – – –German Penetrations

———————▶ German Attacks

He took up the pointer that Big Red held out to him and tapped the large map of France and Belgium spread out on the blackboard in the centre of the lecture hall, with its old pot-bellied stove glowing a dull

31

purple underneath a pin-up poster of Betty Grable that showed her 'million dollar' legs to best advantage. 'According to Intelligence, the Krauts have broken through on a 60 mile front between Monschau – here in the north – and Echternach – here in the south. They're obviously heading for the River Meuse. Now if they can seize bridges across it, we've got no reserves to stop them. It'll be 1940 all over again,' he added, his handsome face with its cleft, determined chin, suddenly very grim.

'Christ, not another bleeding Dunkirk, sir,' Limey moaned. 'I just couldn't stand any more of that blood, sweat and tears bit!'

But for once, Limey's peculiar British humour raised no smiles, for even the Bad Boys, whose principal war aims were getting drunk and laid, sensed the tragedy of what had happened at the front this day.

'Now in order to keep moving fast in this kind of arctic weather,' Iron Mike continued, 'the Krauts need to capture the key road and rail centres up there in the Ardennes. Already they've got the Belgie border town of St Vith – here – pretty well surrounded, and Intelligence believes that their next objective is going to be Bastogne here, not a dozen miles from the Meuse. Capture Bastogne and they control the whole road network to the river, and fellers' – Iron Mike's hard eyes swept the ranks of his Bad Boys, while outside NCOs cried hoarsely in the freezing night: 'Come on, you drivers, roll 'em! For Chrissake, let's get this goddam show on the road now ... *roll 'em!*' – 'we can't let the Krauts do that.'

'So what role have the Bad Boys been assigned for this caper?' Iron Mike asked the question that had been worrying even dull-witted Corporal Kovolski. 'I'll tell you. We've picked a beaut. We're going to spear-head the Division into Bastogne. General Middleton's HQ was there yesterday, so the Division has got to get there, but fast, just in case he's bugged out, or worse, he's already been captured in the attempt to get away.'

His Bad Boys beamed in sudden relief. This was the kind of assignment they liked, away from the prying eyes and discipline of the divisional staff; but their relief was short-lived.

'Before you guys start shooting your wad,' Iron Mike said warningly stretching up to his full six foot two, 'let me tell you exactly just how we are going to carry out that spearhead op.' He tapped the map once again. 'Along the River Meuse from Liège to Belgium's border with France, there are three bridges across the river from north to south – at Liège itself, Dinant and Huy. Now the closest of those bridges to Bastogne is the one at Huy. I have suggested to the commanding general that the Division should use the Huy Bridge and he has agreed that it sounds the best bet for getting to Bastogne in the quickest possible time. But there's a catch,' he looked squarely at his men, their faces hollowed to death's-heads in the poor light of the hut. 'The Krauts, for all we know, might have worked a flanker on us and already be approaching that bridge – it's only guarded by a handful of rearline troops and a coloured anti-aircraft battery at present. So our problem is to find out the situation at the Huy Bridge so that *if* it has been captured by the Krauts, we can inform Division and they can pick an alternative. The problem therefore, is this – how do we get to Huy in double-quick time?'

He let his question sink in for a few moments. 'It's outlaw country out there, fellers, I can tell you. The Krauts are reported to have dropped paras all along our lines of communication. The roads are bogged down with guys bugging out from the front and we've heard reports that Frogs and Belgies who side with the Krauts are sniping our rearline columns – and of course, our Division and the 82nd are crowding the roads to try to make it to the front. So to get to Huy is one helluva problem, and as I have said before we've got to get there pretty damn quick, especially with the CG (Commanding General) breathing down our necks.'

'We *are* paratroopers, sir,' Dude volunteered hesitantly, 'though I guess most fields are pretty well socked in in this kind of lousy Frog weather.'

'That they are, soldier,' Iron Mike agreed, 'but we have been fortunate to find that Orleans field is open. 96th Troop Carrier Squadron is ready and willing to take off.'

'But then, sir, that's solved it,' Big Red said hastily.

Iron Mike frowned. 'In a way, fellers, it has, but not in the way you might think.'

The Bad Boys looked at their CO, puzzled. 'How do you mean sir?' Limey ventured, always quicker off the mark than the others.

Iron Mike sucked his teeth. 'The 96th are not a paratroop-carrying outfit. They're' – he hesitated for only a fraction of a second – 'a glider-towing unit.'

'*Glider-towers!*' the Bad Boys echoed in astonished unison.

Iron Mike hung his head, as if in shame.

Now they had left the snow-bound, war-torn countryside below them and were flying through the night at 2000 feet, the only sound the muted throb of the Dakota towing the two Waco gliders that contained the Bad Boys squad. Sitting in as co-pilot next to the Army Air Corps pilot, all that Iron Mike MacDonald could see by peering through the perspex of the cockpit were the small blue formation lights on the top wing of the Dakota and the reddish glow of the exhaust arresters. They might well have been all alone in the dark world, though he knew that out there somewhere to the east were German fighters, braving the worst winter weather in forty years to support their victorious ground troops. Any moment a Focke-Wulf 190 could come barrelling out of the shifting cloud, cannon and machine-guns thumping, and that would be that; for their Dakota tug carried no weapons and as for the two Wacos, they were only held together by 'string, glue – and a prayer,' as one of the Army Air Corps had cracked just before take-off.

Iron Mike dismissed that particularly worrying thought from his mind and turned to the pilot, peaked cap set on the back of his wavy hair and wearing sun-glasses for some unfathomable reason. 'What's our expected time-of-arrival over the DZ (Dropping Zone), Major?' he asked. The pilot was already a major though he didn't look a day over eighteen.

'Zero six hundred, just before dawn at this time of year. Though', the youthful pilot added, not taking his eyes off the faint shadow of the Dakota to the front, 'I don't know if we're gonna be able to hit the designated DZ.'

'You mean the dark?'

'Yeah,' the major said, shifting the wad of gum from one smooth boyish cheek to the other. 'Ops picked a high plateau just to the west of Huy, but I'd give myself a fifty-fifty chance of finding it under these conditions and with a total blackout down below. Still,' he said with forced cheerfulness, 'we can always land on the Meuse. You can always make out a river.'

Iron Mike shot the pilot a look of alarm. 'The way my boys are loaded, they'd sink like bricks.'

The comment left the pilot unmoved. 'Yeah, I guess they would at that, Captain.'

That put an end to their conversation and Iron Mike sank into a mood of gloomy apprehension.

Back of the Waco, the mood of his Bad Boys was equally sombre. Big Red was quietly vomiting into his helmet, clasped between his knees. Polack chewed stolidly on his 'mascot', a piece of glass, mechanically cleaning his toenails with his trench knife. 'My ma back in Pittsburgh allus sez ya ought to be clean in both body and mind when ya going on anything like dis,' he had explained when the others had protested at the stink. Only Limey, the little runt of an Englishman, and Dude were inclined to conversation as they sailed steadily eastwards at 150 mph. But even the ever-cheerful little Cockney was gloomy and apprehensive, and a little ashamed that veteran Screaming Eagles should be going into action in a glider. 'It's typical Kate Karney, natch, Dude, sending trained paratroopers into battle in a bit of plywood and canvas like this. Don't yer know – it ain't got a prop. A right old Snafu (Situation normal, all fucked up), 'if you ask me.'

Dude nodded his agreement, all thoughts of trying to read the *Iliad* in the original Greek, which he always brought along with him to calm his nerves on a combat jump, vanished. 'Yes, and do you realise, Limey, we ain't even got parachutes?'

Limey swallowed hard and said hastily, clutching the Dude's arm in fear, 'Don't even think things like that, Dude, will yer!... No good'll come of it, Dude, I tell yer. And the shame of it, if it comes out in the Division that real old Geronimo blokes like us ever went in a glider.'

Dude raised a weak smile and then he, too, gave up any attempt at conversation. Thus the Bad Boys sailed on silently through the night into the unknown, while far down below Agent Sleeper Three, of the organization left behind by the Germans at the time of their great retreat three months before, recognized the unmistakable sound of the Dakota, caught a fleeting glimpse of the two gliders, and began tapping out his urgent message to the Reich.

Now it was an hour before dawn and the Dakota tug was steering lower and lower, with the two glider pilots fighting their controls as they started to hit the thermals rising from the unseen ground below. In the Wacos more and more of the Bad Boys began to vomit into their helmets as the light canvas and wood planes hit turbulence and even the imperturbable Polack started to look apprehensive and a little green.

'Do you think the Dakota pilot has spotted the DZ?' Iron Mike asked through gritted teeth, as the hot green bile flood his throat nauseatingly and the glider fell a sickening fifty feet.

'Sure,' the young major said cheerfully, 'or else he's going into crash land.' He pressed his throat mike and called, 'Hello Baker Charley One, what gives up there?'

Iron Mike leaned sideways so that his head was pressed to the pilot's earphones and he could hear the strangely metallic voice of the Dakota pilot replying. 'Something funny out there... Caught a glimpse of flame ... like those darned buzz bombs the Krauts are using on Antwerp... Don't want to tangle with one of those... Look, there it is again!'

Iron Mike strained his eyes. To their immediate front but higher than the gliders the darkness was stabbed by a sudden dagger of scarlet flame and then it was gone almost immediately. He flashed an anxious look at the young major who was still chewing his gum mechanically. 'A Kraut flying bomb?' he queried.

The major shook his head, not taking his eyes off the controls as the Waco came lower and lower and in the rear the Bad Boys forgot their churning stomachs, now aware too that something strange was happening. 'Don't think so, Captain. I've seen those things flying towards Antwerp and their after-burners don't give off any–'

WHAM... WHAM... The rest of his words were drowned by the chatter of 20mm cannon. Like angry red hornets a swarm of tracer shells hissed through the darkness towards the Dakota. 'Jesus H. Christ!' the pilot called as a great black silhouette, tracing a blazing flame behind it, raced across their front at an impossible speed. 'Jets ... Kraut fighter jets!' He grabbed the controls, the sweat glistening like a film of grease on his forehead, as the glider rocked wildly in the departing plane's turbulence. 'Now the shit really has hit the fan!'

As always when here was a prospect of violent action, Iron Mike was detached and absolutely cool. He thrust on his helmet and as the unknown attackers came roaring in again cried over his shoulder, 'Helmets on, everybody... Get ready to bale out!' Behind there was feverish activity as the Bad Boys

40

poured the vomit from their helmets and grabbed for their packs.

Not a moment too soon. From left and right two frightening, racing shapes hurtled towards the Dakota. Cannon chattered. Tracer shells hissed through the darkness. The tug staggered violently as if it had run into an invisible wall. A sudden burst of purple flame. Horror-stricken and awed, the men in the Waco saw how the Dakota's right engine had started to rip away from the plane's wing and the tug began to bank heavily to the left.

'Hell fire!' the young pilot cursed fervently as the glider trembled violently, almost jerking the controls from his sweating hands. 'Cast off... Oh, for God's sake, cast off man, while there's still time!'

Now the Dakota, flying only on one engine, trailing thick black oily smoke behind it, began to go into a shallow dive, dragging the two Wacos behind it, as the German jets zoomed up high into the darkness, ready to come hurtling down for the kill.

Abruptly the tug pilot's voice came crackling over the major's earphones. Hurriedly Iron Mike placed his head close to his. The pain in the Dakota pilot's voice was all too apparent. 'I'm gonna cast off... Most of the crew have bought it... Badly hit myself...' The strangled phrases came out in harsh, hectic gasps and Iron Mike, not normally an

41

imaginative man, could visualize the dying pilot fighting his plane as it went down to its inevitable doom.

'Here the bastards come again!' the major yelled, as the two sinister black shapes came hurtling in at 600 mph. Bright vicious lights crackled the length of their clipped wings. The Dakota staggered again. In the garish light of the exploding shells, Iron Mike could see lumps of metal ripped off the tug's side and float away into the darkness. A flower of silk erupted. Someone was trying to bale out of the Dakota. To no avail! The cannon-shells tore the unknown crewman's body to shreds and, transfixed by horror, Iron Mike could see the trapped man writhe and twist for a few moments before he hung limply in the shrouds, dead.

A sudden great lurch. Grimly the major hung on to the controls as the towline was swept away and the Waco bounced a good fifty yards into the air. A jet howled away to their right. They had escaped destruction in a mid-air collision by inches. Close by the 20mm cannon chattered frenetically once again. The Waco's perspex cockpit shattered into a crazy glistening spider's web. Splinters of plastic sprayed Iron Mike's face. An icy wind flooded the cockpit.

The major reacted immediately. He dropped the Waco's nose. 'Going down,' he grunted through clenched teeth. 'Come hell or high water.'

'On a wing and a prayer?'

'Yeah, Captain, on a goddam wing and a prayer. Here we go!'

Another burst of shells stitched a lethal pattern the whole length of the fuselage. The Bad Boys ducked abruptly. The plane was filled instantly with the acrid stink of burnt explosive, as the Waco trembled violently under the impact.

'Feet up,' Big Red yelled, taking over. 'Grab hold of each other!'

'But I don't love the Dude,' Limey cracked, but no one was listening to his peculiar brand of British humour at this particular moment.

Hurriedly the men raised their high-laced jump boots from the deck and heads bent, clasped each other to take the shock of impact. The Waco sailed lower and lower. To their front the Dakota went into its final dive, carrying its dead and dying crew with it. Iron Mike and the struggling pilot watched horrified as it smacked into the snow fields below, exploded, scattering blue sheets of burning fuel for hundreds of yards before disappearing altogether in a mass of searing, all-consuming flame. Then all thoughts of the men below vanished as the jets came hissing in once more, cannon firing. This time they were not having all their own way. Desperately the two pilots of the much slower Wacos manoeuvred their

43

engineless craft, while in either cockpit, Iron Mike and Second-Lieutenant Willard, his second-in-command, pumped off burst after burst from their carbines in a pathetic attempt to put the German pilots off course.

The jets roared past them, shells exploding harmlessly above them, while the young major in Iron Mike's plane fought his Waco down in grim silence, his gaze fixed almost hypnotically on the altimeter. The trembling glowing green needle hit 400 ... then 300 ... 250.

In one last desperate attempt to finish them off the Me 292s came howling in at an impossible speed, guns blazing. Again the lethal morse of the tracer shells cut the darkness, but again they overshot their much slower targets and then they were gone, zooming high into the dawn sky, bright-red lights flashing from their after-burners, to vanish for good.

Now they were alone, apart from the other Waco circling somewhere in the darkness, and the only spot they could identify was the flickering, fitful light of the burning Dakota. The young major, eyes narrowed to slits against the biting wind, tried to find a suitable place to land, as they came down to 200 and then 100 feet.

Holding on with one hand, Iron Mike freed his .45 and, seizing it by the muzzle, began to systematically to smash away the shattered perspex so that the pilot could see better. 'Thanks,' the hard-pressed pilot gasped, and cursed, 'Come on you sonuva-bitch, raise that tail,' as he pulled hard at the tail to slow the glider down even more.

Iron Mike leaned forward. To his right he could make out a long stretch of spiked firs, an impossible place to land the stricken Waco. Then his heart leaped and he cried joyfully, 'Beyond that wood at two o'clock, see it!'

The pilot nodded, hardly daring to speak now as the glider seemed to hang there in mid-air, ready to go into a final fatal stall at any moment.

'Beyond it, there's what looks like open fields. Anyway the snow seems smooth and uninterrupted–' Iron Mike broke off abruptly. Down below ahead of them the other Waco had suddenly appeared. At full speed it was racing for the firs, flames crack-ling the length of its fuselage.

'Holy cow!' the young major cried in alarm. 'It's Pete ... he's gonna buy it, the poor sonuvabitch!'

'No ... he might yet do it!' Iron Mike yelled back over the howling wind, as the Waco dropped lower and lower and the firs came closer by the instant. 'He's going to do–'

The words died on his lips. He gasped fer-vently. The Waco's undercarriage smashed into a stand of the snow-heavy trees. It snapped like matchwood. The Waco's sleds came tumbling down. It staggered like an ancient truck; then, with startling suddenness, turned clean over, hit the ground nose-first, and was instantly a sea of flames. Straining his eyes to the utmost, Iron Mike peered down at the burning glider as his own swooped on towards the fields in silence, save for the ghostly sound of the rushing wind. No one got out of the flaming wreck. Their daring mission not even started, and already he had lost half his command.

Suddenly the Waco's nose dropped alarmingly as fresh splinters of perspex struck them in the face like razor-sharp particles of ice. With all his strength the young major jerked back at the controls the sweat glistening like pearls on his forehead. 'Lift up, you whoreson!' he cursed through gritted teeth. *'Up for Chrissake!'* Desperate he twisted the controls to the right. Equipment slithered the length of the plane. The men held on for dear life. Viciously the pilot kicked the rudder. For one alarming moment Iron Mike, bathed in sweat now, hardly dared to breathe as the glider refused to respond and the snow-covered ground raced up to meet them at a terrible speed. Then, in the instant that it seemed a crash was inevitable, it answered the controls.

The pilot breathed a heart-felt sigh of

relief, and freed one hand for an instant to wipe away the sweat dripping into his eyes. Now they were less than 100 feet from the ground. To the right Iron Mike caught a vague silver glimpse of a river and tall white cliffs. Perhaps it was the Meuse, but this was no time for such considerations. In a matter of seconds they would be hitting the deck. 'You're doing a swell job, Major,' he gasped.

'We aim to please,' the major grunted, and then abruptly as the Waco yawed frighteningly to the right, he yelled in a sudden frenzy of alarm. 'Cover your face!'

Iron Mike flung up his hands to protect his eyes. Not a moment too soon. The Waco's nose fell. It went into an impossible dive. With a stomach-churning loss of height, it slammed into the snow-covered field. Next instant it rose high into the air to plummet to the ground again. Now it started to slither across the field, throwing up a house-high wake of white behind. The men hung on grimly as it continued its wild progress, seemingly unstoppable, shimmying madly from side to side.

The knuckles of the young major's hands, gripping the controls, were white with the strain of fighting the plane. A fierce rending sound filled it; the horrifying shriek of wood. By a miracle they missed a vast stump of a tree sticking out of the snow. A wing came off and fell behind them like a huge leaf. The

Waco swung round in a wild circle, snow whirling upwards in a crazy white fountain. And then, with a tremendous loud-echoing crash, the Waco smashed into the side of an ancient stone byre, its remaining wing crumpled up like a banana skin. They were down!

Iron Mike opened his eyes. Like a boxer coming out of a knockout, he shook his head slowly trying to drive the numbness out of his brain. Behind him someone was saying over and over. 'Never again ... never again...'

Iron Mike felt the copper-taste of blood in his mouth. He spat cautiously into his hand. A few particles of perspex fell onto the palm, all of them tinged a faint pink. So far so good. He had not been injured internally. Perhaps his gums had just been burst by the force of the impact. He turned his head wearily to look at the confusion of the shattered fuselage, with holes ripped everywhere in the canvas. 'Everybody all right?' he queried.

'Yo! ... yo! ... yo,' the replies sang out from the men, trying to free themselves from the jumbled mess of equipment and wreckage.

Iron Mike nodded his approval and turned to the young major. He was still slumped over the shattered controls, trapped by his harness, his head hanging at an odd angle.

'Hey, you okay?' Iron Mike asked.

There was no reply.

Anxiously, Iron Mike reached out and

touched him with fingers that felt like thick, clumsy sausages. He jerked him upwards. 'Come on,' he grunted. 'Let's get the hell outa here. We don't know wh–' The words died on his lips. He gave a horrified gasp. The shattered control shaft had transfixed the young major: all the front of his chest looked as if someone had thrown a handful of strawberry jam at it.

Slowly, almost reluctantly, Captain MacDonald lowered the dead pilot. It seemed that everything was going wrong with their mission right from the outset...

Some twenty-five miles away from where the Bad Boys now found themselves, General Bayerlein did not share Captain MacDonald's depression. Carefully sipping the hot grog, allowing the steam to warm his frozen face, he walked among the scraggy trees, splintered and smashed where his tanks had barged their way through for the night's laager, listening to the sounds and words as his HQ awoke to a new day of battle.

Deep in the heart of the wood they had lit big fires and now the skinny young men – not the veterans he had commanded against Montgomery in the Desert, but full of the self-sacrificing patriotism of the New Germany all the same – lined up patiently with their canteens for the morning's soup. He watched their rough-bearded young faces in

49

the ruddy glow of the fires and told himself that, inexperienced as they were, they would pull it off. The Amis had been running panic-stricken for forty-eight hours now; there was no reason why they should stand and fight today. With a flourish he finished the last of his rum-and-hot water, feeling its fire surge deep into his bowels. His eyes sparkling, he turned to his adjutant, young Captain von Eberfeld. 'Well, Heinz, it's about time we got moving again.'

The young aristocrat, with the gleaming black and white enamel of the Knight's Cross of the Iron Cross dangling at his throat, nodded his agreement. *'Jawohl, Herr General,'* he barked standing to attention.

Bayerlein smiled and patted him on the shoulder. 'Not so formal, my dear boy, not so formal. Yet all the same I suppose this is a historic occasion in a way. The last day that the Amis were able to hold territory to the east of the River Meuse, one more day to the end of the Ami presence in Europe.' He turned up his collar and pulled his fur earcaps down over his face. 'Tomorrow at this time, *mein Lieber* Heinz, Bastogne will be ours – and that will be that.'

'Tomorrow morning at this time,' Heinz echoed, as if in response to some formal toast.

Together they strode towards the waiting staff car, as engine after engine broke into noisy life.

It was dawn on Monday, 18 December 1944…

Day Two:
Monday 18 December 1944

Now there was no mistaking the rumble of the heavy guns to the east, muted a little by the sad flakes of snow drifting down yet once again. Even the clatter of the refugees' carts as they trundled westwards, laden high with the peasants' pathetic possessions, could not drown that ominous sound. Everywhere the Belgians flicked their whips at their slow ponderous oxen or skinny-ribbed, drooping nags to urge them to greater speed. The Boche were coming again. They *had* to clear this last town and cross the Meuse before it was too late.

Morosely, big bluff, bespectacled General Middleton stared out of the window of the tall red-brick building which housed his HQ. But his eyes were not on the long column of drab civilians, but on the men in khaki who straggled with them westwards or squatted in the gutters, heads sunk in hands in abject defeat. Many of them were without helmets or overcoats, some even without weapons.

He knew why. They had fled from the front of his broken corps. They belonged to the big 'bug-out', as the GIs were now calling it, and it was no use sending out his officers to round them up in order to form a stopline in Bastogne. As soon as the officer went back inside again, they would bug out once more.

Behind, in the big, echoing operations room, the staff officers came and went hurriedly, telephones jangled, typewriters clattered, while operations officers called out the latest situations to the clerks working the maps. *'Krauts coming down the Wiltz road, map reference... Fire fight on the heights beyond Noville road... Enemy advanced recon coming from Height...'* The alarming reports came flooding in from all sides and without even turning to look at the big situation map of Bastogne and area, covered with a rash of red marks indicating the enemy, Middleton knew that the Germans were rapidly surrounding him and that soon he'd have only one approach road left from the west, the *route nationale* that ran from Huy to Bastogne.

'Sir.'

Almost reluctantly Middleton took his gaze off a bareheaded tech-five who squatted on the curb, toying with a paving stone. Opposite him there was an abandoned wineshop and Middleton knew instinctively what was going through the soldier's mind. In five or ten minutes he'd fling the rock through the window of the shop, and then the drinking and general looting would begin. Time was running out fast in Bastogne. He turned.

It was Robson, his G-2 Intelligence, his face flushed excitedly, eyes sparkling behind his pince-nez which made him look a little like some Mid-Western schoolteacher. 'Yes, Major?'

'They're trying to hit us on the flank, sir.'

'Where?' Middleton snapped, forgetting about what was going to happen outside in the street soon. What available forces he had left were deployed in a semicircle to the east of the Belgian town. If the Krauts tried to outflank him to south-east or north-east in order to cut off that vital road from Huy, he was sunk.

'From the south-east, sir,' Robson answered promptly. 'We've got an identification too. It's Bayerlein's Panzerlehr!' He looked up at the big corps commander, as if he expected a pat on the back for his swift identification of the attacking force.

He was disappointed, however. Instead Middleton groaned. 'Holy mackerel, that's all we need! One of the best divisions in the whole of the *Wehrmacht*, Led by a guy who learned the job from Rommel himself... All right, shoot the works. *Where?*'

'They're going up the road to Longvilly – at speed.'

53

'What we got up there, Robson?'

'A combat team manning a road barrier about 1000 yards to the west of the village.'

Middleton mused for a moment. Outside the sound of the German guns grew increasingly louder. Soon, he knew, he would have to evacuate his Corps HQ. He could never allow himself to go into the bag; that would be a tremendous victory for the Krauts. 'Where in Sam Hill is he getting his strength!' he cried and then pulling himself together, rasped, 'All right, Robson, here's your chance to win yourself a good medal. There's no more use for G-2 Intelligence here. We know all we need to know about the Krauts, namely that they've got us with our dong in the wringer! So, Robson, I want you to take my Corps defence company and those two 105mm self-propelled guns out back there and get on up that road to Longvilly. Those guys guarding the road block are gonna need all the goddam muscle they can get.'

Robson swallowed hard. He knew better than most at Corps HQ just how bad the situation up front was. He had just been given a suicide mission. For a moment Middleton thought he was going to refuse the order; then Robson muttered weakly. 'As you say, sir.' He touched his hand to his cropped head in a weak ineffectual salute and left Middleton staring at the map of

Bastogne covered with that ugly rash of blue and red marks. The one thought now uppermost in his mind: Where was the 101st Airborne Division?... Would the Screaming Eagles make it in time before the Krauts hit Bastogne in strength?...

Wearily the survivors of the Bad Boys trudged along the high bank of the Meuse, every few minutes eyeing the pink glowing horizon to the east and the tall, stark black columns of smoke rising into the leaden grey, ominous sky. It was obvious even to Polack, who was at point, that the Krauts could not be far away now.

Iron Mike MacDonald, bringing up the main column, looked at the dead cow, its legs protruding rigidly from a bloated body so that it look like a tethered barrage balloon, lying near the brown shell hole and told himself that the enemy's long-range artillery must have already started to zero in on the western bank of the Meuse. They'd use their old trick, of course. They'd bring down interdicting fire on both sides of the bridge at Huy to prevent any attempt to defend it, while refraining from aiming directly at the bridge itself. Naturally they would want to capture it so that their armoured columns could break forth out of the rugged Ardennes into the flat, easy plain of Belgium and Northern France. Still, there was one consolation. The bridge would be kept intact for the Screaming Eagles, though, of course, the Krauts wouldn't know about that. Or would they?

But before the worried captain had time to answer that particular question, Big Red came trotting down the road from point, tommy-gun gripped in his steam-shovel of a paw as if it were a kid's toy, his breath fogging the icy air was grey cloud.

Iron Mike held up his hand.

Automatically, veterans that they were, the Bad Boys hit the dirt, weapons at the ready, eyes peering suspiciously across the snowy fields to left and right.

'Trouble?' Iron Mike asked anxiously as Big Red came to a halt, chest heaving, face a steaming brick-red.

'No sir. We've found wheels down there, sir, a White half-track and three jeeps. They belong to some guys of the 106th who are bugging out. They're looting gas from a POL (petroleum supplies depot) outfit so that they can take off even further. Hell, if they bug out much more they'll be in the goddam ocean!'

Iron Mike laughed. 'Swell, that's just what we need, Red, wheels. With wheels we can reach Huy and be on our way to Bastogne before the snow really starts. Kay, guys–' he swung round on his troopers crouching in the snow. 'Let's go!'

Five minutes later they found themselves in the outskirts of Huy. Down below lay the bridge, small and insignificant but still intact, as more and more figures poured over it, ant-like in their panic-stricken flight westwards.

For the moment Iron Mike's main concern was with obtaining the wheels which were vital to their mission now. The Bad Boys could see that the survivors milling around the POL depot were in an ugly mood and it was going to be difficult.

The best they could, they pushed their way through the frightened throng of men and past the depot's defensive force, two lone negroes manning a 37mm anti-aircraft cannon, their faces green with fear, shivering with cold.

The jeeps and the half-track were parked just outside the depot gate. Their drivers were gunning their running engines, as if fearful they would stall on them, while a big, bare-headed major argued with the bespectacled first-sergeant who was obviously in charge of the place.

'I don't give two hoots what your orders are, Top,' the major was saying in a rasping Bostonian accent, his craggy Irish face flushed with anger. 'I want gas – and I want it *fast!*' He dropped his gloved hand down to the .45 strapped to his belt.

The noncom was scared, that was obvious. Yet he stuck to his orders. 'But sir,' he protested. 'I can't give gas to anyone who ain't got a work ticket. You gotta understand that, sir. Them's orders,' he added desperately. 'Knock it off!' the major barked. 'Don't you understand? The Krauts are on the other side of them hills over there. We got to get out while there's still time. Now get outa my way and let my boys fill up.'

'Yeah,' came the chorus of agreement from his scared men. 'Move ya butt, First, and let's gas-up.'

Iron Mike looked at Big Red. The latter nodded his head significantly. Without a word, the Bad Boys broke into two groups and moved their way through the crowd of onlookers, some of whom were frying spam on their entrenching tools over little fires of sand and gasoline. They came in on the fugitives in the vehicles from left and right.

'Kay, I'm not gonna dick around with you any longer,' the major cried, pulling out his .45 and clicking back the hammer. 'I'm gonna give you to three and then by God, if you don't open up that gate, I'm gonna plug you dead – right through the middle of your goddam ugly face!' he raised the pistol, a wolfish look on his unshaven face, eyed blazing. *'One!'*

The top-sergeant stumbled back, his face ashen. 'But, Major, you can't shoot me. I'm under or–'

'Two!'

'*Major!*' the noncom cried desperately, hands held up in front of his face as if he could ward off a slug with his naked flesh. '*No–*'

The major's brutal Irish face hardened. The pistol jerked in his fist. As that range he couldn't miss. The top-sergeant screamed once, as the centre of his forehead burst apart in a welter of purple blood. His spectacles falling askew, his false teeth bulging absurdly out of his mouth, he slithered down the gate to the dirty snow.

There was a great gasp of shocked anger from the watching GIs and Iron Mike yelled, 'Why, you murdering sonuvabitch!' Instinctively he pulled his own trigger. The Irish major flew from the jeep and slammed against the barbed-wire fence of the compound, dead already as he hung there, as if crucified, the bloody mess of his shattered face sliding down to his chest like red molten wax, before his body slumped to the ground.

Next instant Big Red had sprung into the half-track's cab, ripped up the .5 machine-gun that stood on the mount above the driver and levelled it at the men in the jeeps. 'Okay, you lugs,' he growled threateningly, 'now you just freeze it nice and gentle!'

Five minutes later it was all over. While the deserters from the front watched sullenly, the Bad Boys had almost completed filling the jeeps and the half-track for the last leg of their journey to Bastogne.

His big Colt still grasped in his right hand, watching the deserters carefully in case they tried to play any tricks, Iron Mike Mac-Donald told himself that perhaps things were beginning to work out well after all, in spite of the bad start to their scouting mission. With a bit of luck they'd be through Huy and across the bridge down below there in the next half-hour or so. If there were no Germans hidden in the houses high upon the steep bank opposite, he would use the half-track's radio to contact divisional head-quarters and tell staff they could start direct-ing the 400 or so trucks bringing up the rest of the Screaming Eagles from France to Huy; the road to Bastogne was open.

The tanks of his little convoy were filled to the brim, for Iron Mike reasoned that there would be no more gas available on the other side of the Meuse. While Polack, a devout Catholic in spite of his monstrous appear-ance, draped a groundsheet over the two dead men and knelt in the snow for a moment, his big head bent in prayer, the cap-tain gestured contemptuously with his pistol. 'Clear out, you scum!' he snarled. 'If you damn well won't fight, get out of the damned way!'

Reluctantly the sullen-faced men of the big bug-out cleared a path for the little convoy. Iron Mike stood upright in the cab of the half-track and pumped his free hand up and down rapidly, the infantry signal for move out. 'All right, guys, let's–'

The command died on his lips.

From the east, three very familiar shapes were abruptly outlined a stark black against the leaden grey morning sky. There was no mistaking them. How often had he seen those ancient slow structures in the old captured German training films back in Fort Benning when he had first joined the Airborne! He had seen them preparing for the drop over Fort Eben Emael in 1940, then readying for the greatest German parachute drop of all – the attack on the Island of Crete back in '41. Yes, he recognized them all right and as he did so, his heart sank like a stone. They were German three-engined Junkers 52s, and he knew with the sudden clarity of a vision why they were now flying in their slow pedantic manner over Huy. The Krauts had beaten him to the bridge. They were going to do what they had done in Holland in May 1940. *They were going to drop paras right on the bridge itself!*

Not twenty miles away from where Captain MacDonald fumed at this sudden blow to his optimistic plans to reach Bastogne that night, General Fritz Bayerlein, commander of the crack Panzerlehr Division, ordered the driver of his half-track to halt. Behind him the advance guard of the Division ground to a stop and waited while the general, standing upright in the big half-track, studied his map, soft flakes of snow falling about his shoulders.

At that moment he was located at the Luxembourg border village of Niederwampach, 8 miles east of Bastogne. Now the last important town before the Meuse was within grasping distance. With a bit of luck he would be able to seize it that evening before rolling on to Huy, already under attack, as he knew by the Green Devils of the Parachute Army. Now it was really a matter of selecting the best road to reach Bastogne for the final attack. In essence he had three choices. He could take either of the two paved roads which would bring him to the key village of Longvilly, or he could use a secondary road that led through the village of Mageret.

For a few moments the general considered while his staff officers waited expectantly. Bayerlein knew his Amis. He often said they were born with wheels instead of legs. If they were marching out of Bastogne to meet him in battle anywhere, it would be along those two good roads where their infantry could use their vehicles and would not be forced to march. He made his decision. He'd select the road which the Americans, if they had any choice, would avoid. He indicated to his front to the straight, narrow road leading to Magaret: *'Gerade aus!'* he commanded.

'Gerade aus, Her General!' his cocky-faced Berlin driver echoed dutifully and thrust home first gear. Slowly the long convoy of half-tracks and tanks began to move forward, packed tightly together. The panzer grenadiers in their half-tracks were laughing and joking in spite of the freezing cold, their young faces confident and at ease. For two days the Amis had run away every time they had seen their tanks approach. Why should the handful known to be in Bastogne be any different? 'This night,' they joked with one another, 'we'll be sleeping in warm Ami beds, slipping their whores pieces of good German sausage!'

Time passed slowly as the convoy ground its way down the road, the snow packed high on both sides in the verges, something which pleased Bayerlein, standing upright in the leading half-track. For he had come to respect Allied air power. Even if one of their feared Jabos managed to break through the thick grey cloud that filled the winter sky, the convoy would still be difficult to spot in the deep snow. But now Ziemen, his driver, started to curse more frequently as the country lane grew narrower and narrower, reducing speed time and time again in order to get the big half-track through. 'Heaven, arse and cloudburst!' he complained, not taking his eyes off the road. 'This road is meant for cycles not tanks.'

'Keep a civil tongue in your head, Ziemen,' Bayerlein said, without hardness, for the young Berliner had been with him a long time now. 'That's why you've got this cushy number as the general's driver. You've got to suffer a little as well.'

'Transfer me to the infantry then, General,' Zieman said without conviction.

Another fifteen minutes passed. Now the convoy was moving at a snail's pace and the big grin had vanished from Zieman's face. The road had dwindled into a simple cow path. Bayerlein had made the wrong decision. Behind the half-track more and more of the tanks stalled in the thick mud beneath the snow, and Bayerlein's radio crackled with cries for help and advice. He fumed and cursed, but he knew there was no turning back. There had to be a way through. *'Tempo... Tempo,* Zieman!' he ordered through gritted teeth his face crimson with cold and anger, 'if we're going to take Bastogne this night, we've got to get through... *Tempo!'*

Captain MacDonald hesitated no longer. The three transports were circling very low over the river, down to almost 200 feet. He knew why. They were making sure that the German paras would drop right on target and not be carried away by any thermals caused by the cliff-like banks on both sides of the Meuse. In a minute they'd come tumbling out of the Junkers' sides in tight sticks, risking a broken arm or leg in order to be right on target. It was now or never, for a grim-faced Iron Mike knew that once airborne troops had dug themselves in, especially in a city, it was darned hard to winkle them out. The best defence against paras was to hit them while they were still landing.

High up on the half-track he turned back to his waiting men and the pale-faced deserters. 'Now listen you guys, I'm not asking you to fight. Scum like you would just surrender or fade away anyway. But I am asking you to save your own miserable hides.' He let his words sink in and as the first Junkers slowed down to almost stalling speed, a sure sign that she was about to discharge her cargo; he cried urgently. 'All I want you to do is to roll those cans of gas to the top of that hill there, then you can high-tail it outa here.'

'But why?' someone asked incredulously, as the first Junkers came lower and lower.

'Because we need some kind of fire-cover when we try to jump that bridge,' Iron Mike yelled back. 'Now don't ask any more fool questions, let's get this show on the road. Each two of yer grab a can of gas and start rolling it to the hilltop–' he jerked up his

Colt significantly '–or else!'

That did the trick. Hastily the scared deserters started to roll the 50-gallon cans of gasoline towards the hilltop, eyes averted as they passed the dead quartermaster and the Irish major, the blood now beginning to seep through the groundsheet they had placed upon them earlier.

'What's the deal, sir?' Big Red asked anxiously, as the jump doors in the lead Junkers were flung back and they could see the faint black, flapping figure of the dispatcher outlined against the opening.

'We're okay in the half-track, Red. The armour is at least bullet-proof. But the Joes in the jeeps would be sitting ducks. We need some cover for the guys when we try to rush the bridge.'

Listening intently Limey breathed out harshly, 'Did you say rush the bridge, sir?'

'I did.'

'Cor stone the ferking crows! Do you think I could have a quick transfer to the pay corps or someat?'

Iron Mike forced a grin though he had never felt less like smiling. 'Sorry, old buddy, we're all out of transfers at this moment.'

'Captain, they're hitting silk!' Polack's bellow cut into his words.

They swung round as one. The tiny black dots which were German paratroopers were tumbling out of the side of the slow-moving transports. Everywhere the fast-release, tri-angular parachutes which the Germans had adopted from the Russians were blossoming into silken flowers, as the paras fought their shroudlines trying to bring themselves down on the ground on both sides of the river. There was no time to lose.

'Get the plastic!' Iron Mike yelled urgently. 'Put an ounce on each 50-gallon drum and fix a two-minute time pencil! On the double now!'

'So that's it,' Dude called in admiration, tugging at the half-dozen time pencils clipped to the pocket of his combat jacket, and doubling down to where the deserters were sweating over the heavy cans. The others followed, reaching for their plastic – lumps of khaki-coloured plastic explosive that stank of bitter almonds and gave a man a headache if he breathed in its fumes too long. Swiftly and expertly, while more and more German paratroopers came floating down onto the bridge area, the Bad Boys raced from can to can, slapping on a lump of plastic explosive and sticking a time-pencil detonator into the stuff.

Impatiently Iron Mike waited, counting the Germans as they came down and telling himself that his force was outnumbered at least two to one. If he didn't surprise them now, all hell would be let loose. He could wait no longer. 'All right,' he bellowed above the drone of the three-engined machines, 'roll the cans!'

With all their strength the deserters heaved and kicked the cans into position, while the Bad Boys doubled back to their vehicles, the drivers already gunning their engines. Iron Mike took one last glimpse at the big drums of gasoline, already beginning to gather momentum as they started their downward path along the cobbled road that led down to the bridge and then he, too, followed the others to take up his position next to Big Red at the .5 calibre machine-gun in the cab of the lead half-track. He glanced swiftly around at his little force, noting just how unperturbed his men appeared, and then suddenly seized by a wild blood-lust, the blood-lust of battle, he cried 'Okay fellers, roll 'em... *Geronimo!*'

'*Geronimo!*' came back the hoarse, enthusiastic answer. A moment later they were rolling down the hill...

'*Ach, du Scheisse!*' General Fritz Bayerlein cursed as the half-track turned the corner in the tight lane and came face to face with a small group of weary-looking men in ankle-length black slickers collected around a 37mm anti-aircraft gun, stamping their feet in the icy cold. '*Das auch noch!*'

'They're only Ami niggers,' his driver sneered, as the negro gunners stared open-mouthed at the strange vehicle which seemed to have appeared from nowhere. 'Feed 'em some nuts and they'll climb back in the shitting trees, General.'

'Halt die Schnauze!' Bayerlein yelled in alarm, as the Americans roused themselves from their lethargy with *'Krauts!'* and raced to man their gun. 'In three devils' name – get us out of here!' Behind him his key staff officers raised their pistols and one hand on their hips started to aim at the flustered black men, as if they were back on some peacetime range.

The suddenly alarmed driver, eyes full of fear as the Amis began to bring their cannon to bear, desperately rammed home reverse gear and gunned the engine. Nothing happened! The slugs were howling off the metal shield of the 37mm gun in flurries of angry blue sparks, but they did not disturb the negroes. They continued their task deliberately, slowly lining up the half-track in the ring-sight.

'God in heaven!' Bayerlein cried in a frenzy of fear. 'Get the shitting thing back up the lane... *Schnell ... schnell!'*

The sweat standing out on his forehead in opaque beads, the frantic driver tried again. Nothing.

'Rock it back and forth,' Bayerlein urged as the 37mm gun thundered and the first shell howled inches above their heads making the

6-ton vehicle rock violently in the blast. 'Get us out of here before it's too late!'

But even as he yelled the words, Bayerlein knew that the driver wasn't going to do it. They had only moments left to live. *'Raus ... Raus!'* he screamed and flung himself over the side of the half-track to fall in a bundle in the deep snow. Next moment the others were doing the same, all save Ziemen who was stubbornly still attempting to free the half-track, muttering something about feeding the 'nig-nogs nuts!' as the fatal shell struck the half-track like a bat out of hell, sending it reeling into the ditch. One instant later the gas tank exploded and it became a sea of blue flame.

Buried deep in the ditch, Bayerlein groaned, and cursed his ill-luck. Now he was a commander without a command, buried in the middle of nowhere, with no radio and no wheels. His dreams of glory, of his congratulatory reception by the Führer for his bold capture of Bastogne on 18 December 1944, started to fade rapidly.

The first of the lumbering 50-gallon cans of gas went rolling down the cobbled street, careening from side to side as it struck the curb and was pushed back on course, heading straight for the first group of German paratroopers who were hurriedly freeing themselves from their chutes and scrambling to open the long cigar-shaped containers which held their heavy weapons. 'Come on … come on,' Big Red yelled, hanging on to the turret machine-gun for all he was worth, as the half-track sped down the slope after the cans in this grim race with death, the jeeps following close behind. The leading can hit one of the bridge's bollards and gave a great leap in the air. Iron Mike caught his breath. If it landed as he wanted, it would hit the group of German paras busily setting up a heavy machine-gun. It didn't. Instead it flew straight over the side into the Meuse. Next instant the time pencil detonated the charge of plastic explosive. All that happened was that a column of water leaped high into the air, quite harmlessly.

'Great buckets of blood!' Limey cursed and fired a wild burst from his grease-gun at the Germans running everywhere now on the bridge. 'You bleeding Yanks couldn't hit a piss-pot in a pox-hospital!'

Another can went thundering down the steep incline between the tall shuttered red-brick houses. It rolled and rolled and then abruptly came to a stop, right in front of the men manning the heavy machine-gun, already threading in a long belt of gleaming ammunition, ready to tackle the Americans charging down the street.

'Come on … come on, you sonavabitch, *explode!*' Dude cried frantically, as the can

71

simply lay there, dribbling gasoline from its punctured side. Nothing happened. In a second the Germans would open up and they would be easy targets in the jeeps behind.

A soft crump. A sheet of scarlet flame. Abruptly the can rose high in the air, a dramatic fiery ball of ugly blue, blazing gasoline spurting everywhere. The machine gunners were drenched in fire. Hopping and screaming like crazy men they tried to beat out the flames which rose higher and higher, clutching greedily at their limbs, turning their hands into burning black claws in an instant.

Now the cans were exploding everywhere on the bridge, and screaming paratroopers lay in pools of burning blue flame on all sides or flung themselves madly into the water far below to smack into the frozen Meuse and crumple there, like bags of wet cement.

Then the Bad Boys were in among the survivors, their faces savage, lupine, lethal in the lurid glow of the burning gasoline, grease-guns and machine-guns chattering, scything down those who still attempted to fight back, carried away by the blood-lust of battle, giving and expecting no quarter...

Iron Mike knocked down Limey's grease-gun with an angry gesture. 'All right, Limey, there's been enough slaughter,' he said wearily, the sweat tracing tiny rivulets down his smoke-blackened face. 'Let him live.'

Reluctantly the little Englishman took the muzzle of his sub-machine gun from the back of the terrified German's skull, as he lay there on the bridge, bleeding from half-a-dozen wounds. 'Yer know what they say, skipper, the only good Jerry is a dead Jerry. Besides he's gonna snuff it anyway.'

'Knock it off, Limey,' Iron Mike, shoulders bent with sudden weariness, trailed his carbine behind him on the body-littered road, the evil little blue flames flickering everywhere still, as he stumped back to the half-track. 'Dude,' he ordered, 'give me the radio. Contact me with the CG.'

Obediently Dude did as ordered, happy to be able to take his horrified gaze from a dead German, his face a black, crusted mask, two vivid, suppurating scarlet pools where his eyes should have been, his arm, the flesh broken by the heat, raised above his head in a terrible twig-like black claw.

Five minutes later he was through. 'The commanding general, Skipper,' he announced.

Hastily, Captain MacDonald grabbed the radio. 'Sir, MacDonald of the Pathfinder here.'

'The Bad Boys squad,' General Mc-Auliffe's voice crackled over the air with a metallic chuckle. 'Well?'

'We've got it, sir.' Suddenly Iron Mike felt

a fresh burst of energy surge through his body, engendered by his victory, that overcame his weariness and disgust at the slaughter which had just taken place. 'We've got what you wanted!'

'Hot shit, MacDonald! That's the best news I've heard this day. And you can betcha bottom dollar that the Screaming Eagles are glad too. They've been farting around all over Northern France in open trucks for the last twenty-four hours. They'll be glad to get their heads under cover at last. We're on our way, MacDonald. Geronimo … *over and out!*'

'Geronimo,' Iron Mike echoed excitedly, as the instrument went dead in his hand.

But his excitement vanished as abruptly as it had come. He stared across the eastern half of the city of Huy to the far horizon. Signal flares were soaring everywhere into the air and the snow-heavy sky was tinged with the dull pink of battle. They had won the first round, that was true. But the Krauts were still coming, in strength. Would a few thousand underarmed paratroopers with no heavy weapons and no armour hold back the armoured might of a whole German Army?

Suddenly Iron Mike MacDonald shuddered, as he saw a future before him which was bleak, uncertain, and deadly. Would Bastogne be the final resting place of the brave Screaming Eagles?

Day Three:
Tuesday 19 December 1944

At eleven o'clock precisely the Supreme Commander's convoy started to roll down the heights that led into Verdun, France. In front was a Staghound armoured car, behind that two jeeps laden with heavily armed MPs, the Supreme Commander's olive-drab sedan with its five stars, and at the rear four more jeeps filled with more hard-eyed, suspicious MPs, fingers on the triggers of their grease-guns, as if they expected German killers to jump out of the nearest dingy French house at any moment. Sirens howling to clear the streets of the troops moving up to the front in the Ardennes and the ambulances bringing the wounded down to Verdun's huge military hospital, the convoy swept across the bridge over the Meuse, past the station and then up the incline towards Fort Maginot, where the rest of the brass was waiting for the all-important conference this cold Tuesday morning.

The driver opened the door of the Supreme Commander's sedan. Immediately the company of MPs closed in on their chief, forming a living shield around him as he entered the old nineteenth-century barracks, dominated by the heights where twenty-eight years before German and Frenchmen had slaughtered each other by the hundred thousand for ten square miles of shell-holed mud.

His generals were all there, save Montgomery, waiting in the bitterly cold squad room heated by a single, pot-bellied coke stove: Bradley and his staff, pale and nervous, shaken still by the great German counter-attack; Patton, brash, bold and bull-headed, supported by his team of brass, all ready to make promotions and headlines out of the new threat.

Eisenhower, the Supreme Commander, his broad Mid-Western face unusually grim, was shaken too, not only by the German attack but also by the fact that the Germans were supposed to be out to assassinate him behind the lines this day. He paused at the door, clearing his throat as he took off the helmet his security people had made him wear, and stared around the semicircle of faces. 'Gentlemen,' he announced with more confidence than he felt this grey, icy morning, 'the present situation is to be regarded as one of opportunity for us and not of disaster... There will only be cheerful faces at this conference table.'

Bradley, who knew that due to his slackness and over-confidence the American Army in the Ardennes had suffered a defeat,

76

remained solemn, but his subordinate Patton exploded into a big grin. Exposing his dingy sawn-off teeth, he cried in that strangely high, feminine voice of his, 'Hell, let's have the guts to let the sons of bitches go all the way to Paris! Then we'll really cut 'em off and chew 'em up!' Some of those present smiled, others shook their head ruefully. Would Patton ever grow up?

Eisenhower frowned and shook his head. 'No, the enemy will never be allowed to cross the Meuse.'

Now Eisenhower's Chief-of-Intelligence, British General Kenneth Strong, a tall, dark-haired Scot, stepped up to the map, covered with blue and red crayon marks. Skilfully he sketched in the situation at the front. Already Manteuffel's Fifth Panzer Army had broken through, deep into the heart of Middleton's Corps, with panzer divisions racing for the Meuse everywhere. Bastogne was still in Allied hands, but it would only be a matter of hours before Manteuffel's leading armour, belonging to the Panzerlehr Division, reached the last remaining road and rail-centre east of the Meuse. 'An educated guess, gentlemen,' he concluded, 'is that the Boche will have surrounded Bastogne by early tomorrow. Thank you.' He sat down without any further comment, the perfect Intelligence officer.

Eisenhower rose and stood there in silence,

the only noise the crackle of the old-fashioned stove at the back of the room and the soft crunch of the sentries' boots on the hard frozen snow outside. Eisenhower looked at Patton, huddled in his parka, lacquered helmet with its outsize gold general's stars at his feet. 'George,' he said, 'I want you to go to Luxembourg and take charge of the battle, making a strong counter-attack with at least six divisions.' He hesitated momentarily, his face very serious, as if he felt he was asking a question which would be damnably difficult to answer, 'When can you start, George?'

'As soon as you're through with me, Ike,' Patton answered immediately.

Eisenhower frowned. 'What do you mean?'

Opposite Patton, Bradley and his staff officers shuffled uneasily in their seats. Patton was being his usual brash, over-eager self, it seemed. Behind them a couple of red-capped British officers laughed softly to themselves. Patton was showing off again. How could he move his Third Army from Northern France, 133,000 motor vehicles over one and a half million road miles, in some of the worst weather Europe had seen for a quarter of a century; then go into action against elements of three German armies? It was an impossible task.

Patton, however, was undaunted. Waving his big expensive cigar, he said, 'I left my household back in Nancy' – he meant his

Army HQ – 'in good order before I came here.'

Eisenhower nodded his understanding. 'All right, George, well when can you start?'

'The morning of 22 December,' came back Patton's answer.

Eisenhower's sallow face flushed and that ear-to-ear grin known to movie audiences all over the free world was noticeably absent. 'Don't be fatuous, George!' he snapped.

'This has nothing to do with being fatuous, sir,' Patton answered calmly, taking a puff at his cigar and letting the other officers hang on his words. He was enjoying this minor triumph, and the fact that he was the centre of attention after fighting so long in Northern France in battles that he thought no one took any notice of. Now the top brass needed him and by golly he was going to make the most of it. 'You see, I've made my arrangements and my staff are working like beavers at this very moment to shape them up.'

Hastily he explained his plan which he had worked out with his staff back in Nancy that very morning. If Ike agreed to it, all he needed to do was to make one single telephone call and the whole Third Army, half a million strong, would begin a gigantic wheel out of Northern France into Luxembourg and then into Belgium. 'I am positive I can make a strong attack on the 22nd, but only with three divisions. I cannot attack with more until some days later, but I'm determined to attack on the 22nd with what I've got because if I wait, I'll lose surprise.'

He pointed at the wall map with his big cigar and turning to his boss, bespectacled General Bradley who looked exactly like the Mid-Western schoolteacher he had once been, said, 'Brad, this time the Kraut has stuck his head in the meat grinder. And this time *I've* got hold of the handle!' He beamed at Bradley triumphantly.

With that remark the conference ended, but as they rose to go back to their various headquarters, Eisenhower wagged a warning finger at the man who had emerged the hero of this conference which would decide the fate of the United States Army in Europe. 'Remember, Georgie, the advance has to be methodical – sure.'

Patton showed his dingy teeth as he placed his glittering helmet on his thin silver hair. 'I'll be in Bastogne by Christmas,' he said confidently, then as Eisenhower turned away he lowered his head, for he was a superstitious man, and whispered fervently, *'Please, God!'*

'Kay,' General McAuliffe said without any apparent emotion on his broad, bluff face, 'the Krauts have surrounded us here in Bastogne.' He shrugged. 'So we were surrounded in Normandy and we were surrounded in Holland. Hell, the poor Kraut bastards don't know the trouble they've gotten themselves in!'

His staff listening to the general in the cellar of the Belgian schoolhouse HQ grinned, in spite of the freezing cold, the thunder of the guns outside and the rattle of the boxlike ambulance bringing yet more wounded Screaming Eagles back from the line. The Old Man was in great form, despite the seriousness of the Division's position.

McAuliffe wiped some flakes of falling ceiling plaster from his face, eyes glittering in the white, burning incandescence of the hissing Coleman lanterns. 'Now we don't know how long we're gonna be cut off up here before our own guys start to counter-attack, though any mutt can figure, with this weather and the strength of the Kraut opposition, we're gonna have to look after ourselves for – at least – the next forty-eight hours. So we've got to make provision for difficulties and shortages. Kay, let me lay it on the line, but first I'd like to make this completely, perfectly clear. We are not under a state of siege in Bastogne – I want none of that we're cut off kinda crap. We are *temporarily* separated from our own forces. Clear?'

'Clear,' came back the mumble of voices from the officers crowding the cellar and

Captain MacDonald standing to the rear nodded his approval; the Old Man certainly knew how to create the right state of mind in men who soon would be fighting for their lives.

'So let's look at the ration situation first. We've got about 10,000 troops and some 4000 Belgian civilians inside Bastogne and area. Now priority number one is the Joe in the fox-hole, freezing his butt off and doing the nasty business of fighting. He stays on full rations as long as possible. The other guys who bring up the coca-cola, and that includes us of the staff, gentlemen, plus the civvies, go on half rations forthwith.'

Again Iron Mike smiled. The gesture would be approved by the frontline Joes who always complained there was one guy in the line and five others nice and safe behind the front to bring up the coca-cola.

'Artillery. From this moment on, you limit each gun to ten rounds a day unless you have specific permission from me to use more ammo.' McAuliffe saw the looks of dismay on the faces of his staff and added quickly, 'I know, I know. Don't bust a gut. But as soon as this goddam snow clears, TAC Air will be available again and they can act as flying artillery for us... Now deserters, lay-abouts and the like. They either pop-to, or they're posted out. If they won't fight, they don't get fed, and as far as I'm concerned you can kick their butts from here to the nearest Kraut outpost. Let the enemy feed the cowardly bastards. I want none of them…'

And so it went on, with McAuliffe, hardly ever referring to notes, rapping out order after order, until finally he ended with a bold, 'Gentlemen, from here on in, it's root hog. The time for pussy-footing is over. It's kill or get killed! Thank you, you're dismissed.'

Hurriedly the Screaming Eagles' officers saluted and departed to carry out their various tasks while there was still time, throwing back the black-out curtain which masked the door of the cellar to let in the icy air and the hollow boom of the German guns softening up the frontline ready for the attack which would come as soon as dusk fell.

Iron Mike waited patiently until McAuliffe had finished his canteen of cold coffee, knowing the general deserved it; then finally he stepped into the glowing, bright-white circle of light cast by the Coleman lantern around the ration crate which served as the general's desk. 'Captain MacDonald, sir,' he barked, standing rigidly to attention, his hard jaw cleanly shaven, his face glowing with good health and the naked roll in the snow he had taken before he had come to HQ, 'reporting for duty.'

'At ease … at ease, Mike.' For the first time that long morning McAuliffe smiled, as if pleased by what he saw after all the haggard, weary, unshaven officers he had been dealing with over the last hours. The handsome young officer looked as if he might just have stepped out of a recruiting poster for the US army. 'Nice job, you did yesterday on the bridge. When I get round to it, I'm gonna put you in for the DSC.'

'Thank you, sir,' Iron Mike snapped, standing at ease.

McAuliffe nodded to MacDonald's class ring. 'You're a West Pointer, aren't you?'

'Yessir. Class of Forty.'

'Well, a good medal can't harm your chances of promotion, can it? If this goddam war lasts long enough, you'll end up a colonel. But no matter.' McAuliffe drained the rest of his cold coffee and pulled a face. 'Now I know I promised your guys twenty-four hours off after what you did at the bridge. But now the situation has changed drastically. So it's no-can-do. I'm afraid I've got to send them up the line. I need every goddam rifleman I can find up there. I've even got negroes up there acting as riflemen, so you can see just how strapped I am for anyone who can fire a M-1.' He crooked a finger at the immaculately turned out captain. 'Come on over here and let me show you something on the map.'

MacDonald did as he was commanded. Together they bent over the map spread out on the packing-case table. 'Now I don't need to tell you that my front is as full of holes as an Eyetie cheese. I've spread my Eagles in groups to cover the roads with sizeable gaps between them. Naturally I'm hoping that the Krauts are gonna stick to the roads because they can't move their armour across the snow-bound fields, though' – he sighed heavily like a man sorely tried – 'of course I can't be sure. The Krauts have had a helluva sight more experience of fighting in deep snow than we have.'

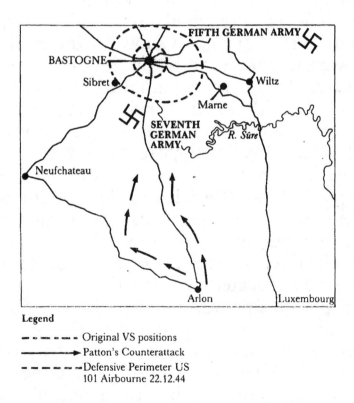

Legend

— ·· — · — · - Original VS positions

————➤ Patton's Counterattack

– – – – – –Defensive Perimeter US
101 Airbourne 22.12.44

He dismissed what was obviously a nagging suspicion from his mind and went

85

on hurriedly. 'So I've got my fortified hedge-hogs everywhere, spread as thinly as I dare, save down here on the south-west flank,' he stabbed the map with his forefinger. 'Here, where there are two main roads and a secondary one running into Bastogne from Luxembourg. Now controlling the network to the front of the village of Marvie, I've got Team O'Hara, a mixed bunch of Screaming Eagles and some armour from the 10th Armoured Division which fell back on Bastogne, what was left of it, during the big bug-out. They're good guys and I expect them to put up a good show for themselves. However, what if the Kraut does take to the fields and come up behind the O'Hara road-block, heading for the Arlon-Bastogne road or to re-enter the Wiltz-Bastogne highway? What have I got to oppose them then?'

He answered his own question, his voice angry and raw. 'I'll tell you, Mike. A bunch of no-goods, raw green kids who bugged out the first time they ever saw a Kraut, and a bunch of weak sisters as officers and senior non-coms, located here at Marvie, tactically well placed to cover either of the two roads if necessary. But my guess is that they'll high-tail it again at the first sight of a Kraut tank, and Mike, I just ain't got the men to fill the gap. I'm stretched to the limit!'

'My mission, sir?' MacDonald asked promptly.

86

McAuliffe beamed up at the tall, harshly handsome young officer. 'Good for you, Mike! It's exactly the reaction I expected from you, son. Your mission? This, knock those guys into shape. Ever since the CG picked you to look after the Bad Boys squad back in the UK, you've managed to make a mighty lot of guys who wouldn't soldier shape up. Try to do the same with those weak sisters up in Marvie before it's too late.'

MacDonald snapped to attention, back ramrod straight, keen blue eyes fixed on some far object beyond the small general's right shoulder. 'I'll do my best, sir.'

McAuliffe looked relieved. '*Your* best is good enough for me, Mike,' he said and the words came straight from the heart.

It was unearthly cold. The wind came whistling over the snow-bound fields straight from Siberia, lashing the livid, wind-burnt faces of the Bad Boys plodding through the knee-deep snow. Icicles hung at their eyebrows and every breath was like a stab to the lungs. Snow blinded them as they crawled through that vast empty landscape like a train of insignificant black ants.

Up at point with Limey, while Big Red brought up the main body, Iron Mike told himself that the very countryside breathed hostility. Never had he felt so alone and so threatened. If there were Americans up here somewhere defending Bastogne, he could see no sign of them. They might well have been the last men on earth.

The little Englishman plodding stolidly at his side seemed to read the captain's thoughts, for he gasped, shielding his mouth to prevent the icy air flooding his lungs, 'Blimey, sir, are you sure we ain't in Germany yet? We must have left the rest of our lads miles behind by now. I 'spect we'll be seeing old Adolf offering us a cup o' char any moment now.'

MacDonald shot a quick look at the compass strapped to his wrist and shook his head, wishing next moment he had not done so for the movement dislodged the snow packed on the crown of his helmet and sent it slithering unpleasantly down the small of his back. 'No, you little rogue, we're still on course. We should be hitting Marvie soon.' He narrowed his eyes to slits against the howling snow blizzard. 'Though in this goddam storm we could probably just hike by the place and never even see it.'

'Don't say that, sir. Yours truly is fair perished,' Limey moaned. 'Me north an' south is froze up and me plates o' meat ain't much better.'

'*North an' south, plates o' meat* – what the Sam Hill are you talking about?' Iron Mike broke off abruptly.

The little cockney with his plum-coloured

face and frozen white eyebrows had stopped suddenly and cocked his head to the wind, the cold and his own personal misery forgotten completely as he listened intently, as if his very life depended upon it.

'What is it?'

The Englishman did not reply. Now the main party 50 yards behind them had come to a puzzled halt too, and in spite of their frozen weariness, had dropped on one knee into the snow, weapons cocked.

Suddenly Iron Mike heard the faint creaking rumble like a door working on rusty hinges. It was coming from somewhere in the whirling white fog to their right. *'Tanks!'* he breathed.

Limey nodded, still not speaking.

Iron Mike's brain raced feverishly as he quickly calculated where exactly they could be. He concluded that if he were on course, they should be between the two main roads leading into Bastogne, one of them held by Team O'Hara, which had armour. Were those unknown tanks out there American tanks retreating – or, the alarming thought shot through his mind – were they German advancing on the besieged city?

He licked his frost-cracked parched lips. 'Bazooka teams!' he commanded, hardly daring to raise his voice.

Obediently Dude and Polack came trotting forward carrying the cumbersome 3-

inch rocket launchers, followed by two Bad Boys laden with rockets.

'There … there!' Iron Mike indicated two positions, although there was no cover in this white snowfield.

Dude and Polack dropped to one knee and placed the long tubes on their right shoulders. Hastily the loaders rammed home rockets and waited, faces tense and expectant, knowing that they might knock out a couple of the lead tanks, if they were lucky. But that would be all. The next metal monsters would cut them apart with combined machine-gun fire.

The seconds passed in anxious, nerve-tingling apprehension, the fitful wind sometimes blowing the rattle of tank tracks closer and then further away. But in the end, strain their ears as they might, the sound vanished altogether and Iron Mike gave the signal for his men to continue the hard slog to Marvie, his face set in a worried frown, as he puzzled out the mystery of the tanks. If they *were* Team O'Hara's armour retreating, then he would be out on a limb at Marvie. If they weren't, it meant that the Krauts had somehow sneaked round the flank of the men holding the road-block and that sooner or later they would be hitting the weak sisters holding the little Belgian hamlet in strength.

Marvie was a typical red-brick village of the

area, a collection of shabby two-storey houses, with piles of smoking manure heaped under every kitchen window, huddled together around the ancient Gothic church which dominated the cobbled central square, complete with the usual marble war memorial dedicated to the dead of the First World War.

In combat formation the veteran Screaming Eagles started to march into the village street and it needed no crystal ball to tell them that the men defending Marvie were a spent force. Here and there, unshaven, dirty young GIs crouched over blue-smoking fires of twigs and broken wood, trying to dry damp socks or heat cans of C-rations. Others lounged against doorways, heads wrapped in Khaki blankets like old women, eyes staring into nothing. Standing in the centre of the village square, where a 57mm anti-tank gun had been dug in, a tall officer in a dirty raincoat was arguing with a group of sullen gunners, holding a swagger stick in his hands that trembled violently.

'Jerk-offs, the whole goddam lot of them,' Big Red said in disgust and spat at the feet of a drunken soldier, bottle cradled protectively to his skinny chest, mumbling his way through 'I'm Dreaming of a White Christmas' in a pathetic imitation of the 'Old Groaner' himself.

'Yeah, Sarge,' Polack agreed in his slow

ponderous manner, 'they don't look too good. But they're only kids.'

Big Red shot him a fiery look. *'Kids!'* he snorted. 'We're all kids in this man's army, but we're soldiers, too! Sometimes Kovalski, I wonder why the tarnation you've ever joined up.'

'Cos the garbage cans froze up in the winter of '40 in Pittsburgh and–'

'–I didn't have nothing to eat.' Limey completed the phrase for him. It was the only wisecrack Polack knew and his big lumpish face drooped sullenly now that the little Englishman had spoiled the fun for him.

'Why did you have to go and say that, Limey? You know it's my joke.'

'Knock it off!' Iron Mike's hard voice cut into the conversation. 'Let's show these guys what real soldiers are. March to attention now… Come on, give them the real old Screaming Eagles' style, willya!'

Suddenly a transformation came over the weary, snow-covered men. Their shoulders straightened. Even Limey, the smallest of the lot of them, acquired a bold swagger which made him seem six feet tall, like the rest of the Bad Boys squad. They marched smartly towards the square, followed by the awed looks of the bug-outs.

'Halt!' Captain MacDonald bellowed, his voice cutting through the plaintive whine of the officer in the dirty raincoat. He turned

92

round startled.

As if he were back on the parade ground, Iron Mike, ramrod stiff, stomped forward through the snow and, swinging a tremendous salute at the sallow, unshaven major, cried, 'Captain Michael MacDonald, sir. 501st Parachute Regiment, 101st Airborne, sir!'

The infantry major swallowed hard, his adam's apple rising up his scrawny throat, as if it were being carried by a lift. Awkwardly he saluted and said, 'Major Ewell, 422nd Infantry Regiment, 106th Infantry Division.'

As Iron Mike commanded his Bad Boys to stand at ease, Limey nudged Polack and whispered out of the side of his mouth, 'Bullshit, it seems, reigns supreme, eh. Old Iron Mike's trying it on; see how far it gets him with this shower o'shit! As far as yours truly can throw them, to my way o' thinking.'

As usual the perceptive little cockney proved to be right. Major Ewell was about at the end of his tether. His lips trembled all the while and he had a bad nervous tic just beneath his right eye. Constantly he played with his swagger stick like a Greek with his worry beads. 'We were only in the line five days, straight from Stateside, when the Krauts hit us. Fall-guys we were, rotten stinking cannon-fodder. We didn't have a chance when the Krauts came out of the woods, hundreds of them, thousands of them–'

'Hold it there!' Iron Mike commanded harshly, making the black rooks nesting on the Gothic steeple rise high in the air in hoarse, cawing protest. 'You mean you ran away.'

Suddenly Major Ewell hung his head and for one awful moment Dude thought he was going to break down and cry.

Iron Mike didn't give him a chance to do so, however. Instead he rapped, 'Okay, so everybody can fail one time, especially the first time he goes into combat. But now you've got a chance, you and your men to redeem yourselves. Here, give me that fancy swagger-stick of yours.' He reached forward and pulled it from the major's nerveless hands. 'Let me put you and your men in the big picture.' Swiftly he drew a circle in the fresh snow. 'Bastogne, held by the 101st, and surrounded now. Here … here … and here–' he sketched three lines heading into the circle – 'two main roads and a secondary one, this one, leading into the town from the south-east, with here – Marvie – strategically well located to cover them. Now, Major, we, that is you and my boys, are going to hold Marvie – come what may.'

'Are we?' Ewell, raising his head, quavered.

'We are!' Iron Mike answered firmly, chin stuck out pugnaciously, 'and this is how we're going to do it.' He drew another circle in the snow. 'Marvie,' he announced, 'with here the church and the village square. Now you're going to split your company up into four groups to cover every approach into the place, with the church here acting as our OP (Observation Post) and HQ.' He forced a smile. 'We're going to make it a good old, all-around airborne defence. You'll see,' he added encouragingly, 'it'll work.'

The major gulped. 'Then I'll be getting along,' he said hesitantly.

'Yeah, do that, Major. I'll get my boys organized and have a look at that outlaw country out there from the top of the steeple.' Iron Mike waited until the major had departed, then he dropped the silly affected swagger stick into the snow, and snapped, 'Dude, take over that 57mm anti-tank gun. See that it's sighted to cover the entrance to the square. Kovalski – up into the steeple. Take a walkie-talkie with you. Get on the horn to me, immediately you see anything up there. Understand – *anything!*'

Swiftly Iron Mike rapped out order after order, as in the village the major and his noncoms started going from house to house, pleading, cajoling, threatening, even striking their men to force them into the street to take up their new defensive positions. The Bad Boys moved away at the double to their stations, leaving only Big Red and Limey and a handful of men standing there in the freezing square. He waited impatiently till the

95

Dude had moved his new anti-tank team out of earshot and had started them digging up the frozen *pavé* in order to fix in the steel trails of the 57mm cannon before he said, his voice low, hard and tense, 'Okay, fellers, you know the score here. You've seen those kids with your own eyes. They're scared, very very scared and there'll be no holding them once they start to run. It'll be a panic, the big bug-out all over again. So we're not gonna let them run.'

'How do you mean, sir?' Big Red ventured.

Iron Mike dropped his hand to his pistol significantly. 'A lot of good boys are gonna get the chop if these guys cream their skivvies and start to run, so if it comes down to cases, it would be better to shoot a few of them to encourage the others *not* to run.'

Limey whistled softly through his teeth. 'I've seen it before, sir,' he said, the usual mocking note gone from his voice. 'At Dunkirk – and it worked.'

'You're goddam right, it'll work! I want those jerks to be more scared of us than the Krauts. So Red, and you Limey, I want you to take your guys and set up your positions to the rear of them. Tell 'em you're giving them backing or something. But *if* the Krauts hit us and *if* they threaten to high-tail it out of here, shoot – and shoot to kill!' Iron Mike's face was set and determined, though he knew that what he was going to say next might well result in a court-martial and the end of his military career, let alone his high ambition of becoming a general like this father. 'And start first with their officers!' he hissed.

Big Red gasped and Limey chortled. 'Blimey, I've waited for a chance like this for ten ruddy years in the Kate Karney! Who would believe it? Mrs Smith's handsome son gets a chance to shoot a real Yank major in the back ... wonders will never cease!'

General Fritz Bayerlein beamed with pleasure. The fog that had followed the snow blizzard was thickening by the minute. Soon visibility would be down to ten metres – ideal weather for his tank attack across open fields, and now that his panzer grenadiers had caught up with his armour they would be able to go in with them and give them cover once they were inside the village and in danger from enemy rocket-launchers.

He knew, of course, that he was taking a risk – a great risk – by leaving the enemy roadblock to his rear. He would be wide-open for a counter-attack if he failed to take Marvie and got bogged down there. But von Luttwitz had been insistent. Over the radio-phone he had barked, in that curt Prussian way of his, 'Bayerlein, I can tolerate no further delay! You must push through to

Bastogne this night. Von Manteuffel is breathing down my neck and the Führer is breathing down his neck. OKW (German High Command) has given the capture of Bastogne priority number one. Now, Bayerlein, don't let me down ... take the damned place – or take the consequences!' And with that unveiled threat the radio-phone had gone dead.

It had had its effect. It had spurred him on to risk slipping crosscountry and swinging round the roadblock that guarded the way to Bastogne. That manoeuvre had been successful, too, but it had been time-consuming. Now, if he were to meet von Luttwitz's deadline, he had to capture Marvie and get back on the roads. In the deep snow of the open country, even his Tigers with their broad tracks copied from the Russians, could not make more than 10 kilometres an hour. He *had* to have those roads!

'*Herr General.*'

Bayerlein took his eyes off the ever-thickening fog and turned round.

Facing him was Captain Lange of the Special Demonstration Company. It was his job to show off the paces of captured enemy armoured vehicles for the benefit of the rest of the Panzer Corps so that they could learn the strengths and weaknesses of their foes. 'Yes, Lange,' Bayerlein rapped.

Lange, a tall, slow, cunning-eyed Rhinelander who had lost most of his chin after being hit by an AP (armour-piercing) shell in Russia, gave the little general his strange, lop-sided grin and said, 'We're ready to go, sir. I've personally recced the track up to the village – even those damned "Ronsons" will take it. Fortunately the snow isn't too deep there.'

'*Grossartig … grossartig!*' Bayerlein exclaimed happily. Everything seemed to be going according to plan, for once. 'You know what you've got to do, Lange?'

'Of course. I know those Ami crates only too well. The trick is to get as close as possible so that the enemy can't fire until it's too late. One little souvenir of this – er – glorious heroic conflict–' he ruefully touched what was left of his ruined chin – 'is sufficient for me, sir. I don't want to get my arse fried because of some damned Yankee construction failure in that lousy "Ronson" of theirs. General, I'll be in among them before they know what has hit them.'

Bayerlein clapped the skinny captain on the shoulder. 'Excellent, *mein lieber Lange,* excellent – and then those little chaps over there will finish off the job, what?' He indicated the huge, seventy-two ton white-painted Royal Tigers standing silently in the snow, their black-clad crews stamping their feet and smoking a last cigarette in cupped hands before the attack. 'Nothing will stop them.'

'Nothing will stop them,' Lange echoed and then, raising his hand to his battered peaked cap in that cynical old soldier's manner of his, he said, *'Hals und Beinbruch, Herr General!'*

Bayerlein laughed. *'Hals und Beinbruch, Lange!'*

The fog grew ever thicker.

Tension hung as heavy as the thick pearly mist over the little fortified village of Marvie. As the grey strands curled silently and mournfully in and about the houses, wreathing them in their wet dripping fingers, the men in their foxholes or dug in in the barns and cottages on the place's outskirts, started at each new sound. They peered into the swirling gloom, imagining that the stumps of trees were moving and that the snow-heavy bushes were the enemy stalking them, ready to strike the very next moment. All talk now was in subdued, hacked-off whispers. Even the chain-smokers dared not smoke in case the tiny red glow gave their positions away to the Krauts who *had* to be out there somewhere. Here and there a greenhorn's teeth chattered, not with the biting cold, but with sheer naked, unreasoning fear.

'Cor, stone the crows,' Limey whispered to Big Red as they crouched behind a BAR, that was trained at the backs of the men in the line, 'they even stink of fear!' Old soldiers that they were, they'd wrapped themselves in straw and old sacking that they had found in the barn.

Big Red nodded his agreement.

Iron Mike MacDonald was doing his second round of the tense, silent village, his legs wreathed in mist so that he seemed to float above the ground like a grey ghost. He too felt the tension and fear. Nearly every man he encountered had that typical hot, wet sheen over his eyes, and those trembling lips, as if – one and all – they might break out into tears at any moment. Even the officers constantly cocked their heads to one side in ashen-faced apprehension, fearful of hearing the first sound of the German tanks advancing upon them. At the sight of yet another greenhorn, with fear written all over his callow young face, Iron Mike clenched his fists in sudden anger. 'Christ Almighty,' he cursed to himself, 'if you are gonna attack, damn well do so!'

Up in the bell-tower of the Gothic steeple, heavy with the stink of pigeon droppings and ancient rotting timbers, Polack stared into the grey gloom. Of all the men in that place that day, he was the most imperturbable. Stolidly he stropped his razor-sharp trench-knife on the horny palm of his left hand, silently whistling an old Polish hymn between his teeth, taught to him by his tremendously pious *matka*. His slow-moving brain somehow objected to the fact that he was using a church steeple as an observation place. 'I tink, momma,' he interrupted his whistling and apologized to his mother in far-off Pittsburgh, 'it ain't a Catholic church... I tink it's one of them other ones. So it don't matter so much, does it?' Hoping that his lie had appeased the old lady of whom all the hulking, broken-nosed six-foot-three of him lived in fear and trembling, he continued his lonely vigil. As his dark-brown eyes tried to penetrate the gloom below, his ears slowly but surely became aware of the faint rumble somewhere out there in the grey sea to his right.

Down below, the Dude looked again at the five members of his anti-tank crew and told himself again they were a sorry bunch, poorly trained to the man. Just look at them. The corporal in charge was standing too close to the breech. When it came roaring back to discharge the empty shell-case, he would get the casing right in the guts. And the loader who would receive a hell of a whack in his right kneecap, if he went on kneeling like that. 'For God's sake,' he snapped in that harsh, upper-class Yale accent of his, 'Corporal, stand clear of the breech and you, loader, kneel on your goddam right knee instead of your left!'

Awkwardly the men in question did as he commanded, while the number one made a great show of pressing his eye to the rubber pad of the telescopic sight, as if he were prepared to shoot it out with a whole regiment of Tigers at any moment.

The Dude sighed and wondered again why he had not accepted the nice soft commission in the Navy which his uncle, the senator, could have obtained for him. That would have kept him in Washington and on the senatorial cocktail circuit for the rest of the war. Then he grinned, in spite of his anger at the greenhorns, and told himself, he hadn't because he was a born no-good coming from a long line of wealthy no-goods. The Bad Boys squad of the Screaming Eagles suited him fine. He was one of a bunch.

'A tank!' Polack's excited cry from above cut into his fond musings.

'What!' Dude spun round and stared the length of the square. Down there, just discernible in the thick, wavering mist, was the entrance to a country lane, used by the local peasants in better days to go to the fields.

'Yeah ... one ... no, two, *three* of 'em!' Polack yelled down from his perch in the bell-tower.

'Stand to!' Dude commanded his crew. The corporal in charge started to whimper something about 'Krauts.' 'You loader, grab another shell from the shield-rack! Come on, pop to, you slow bastard!' They all crouched down apprehensively, staring with narrow eyes at the vague entrance to the lane, their ears now taking in the rusty creaking of tank tracks, their hearts racing like trip-hammers, mouths suddenly very dry.

The grinding sound got louder and louder. Everywhere in the defensive circle thrown around Marvie, veterans and greenhorns waited for Polack's shout of identification. Were they Kraut? Or were they American? Men dared hardly to breathe, straining their hearing to its limit, trying to make out the sound. Nearer and nearer! Soon the first tank would begin to emerge from the lane and start to rumble up towards the village square.

Suddenly Polack recognized the typically high silhouette of the lead tank as it ground its way up the snowy incline. 'It's one of ours, guys,' he yelled excitedly, cupping his big paws to his mouth. 'Ours! They're Shermans!'

'*Shermans!*' The cry ran from mouth to mouth. The relief was almost tangible, as the greenhorns smiled at each other, their fear gone in a flash.

Dude rose from his crouched position behind the shield of the little anti-tank gun and stared at the first tank to emerge from the lane. Its 300 HP engine roared mightily, and the snow churned up in a white wake behind it. Slowly the smile of relief began to vanish from his face. He looked again at the unfamiliar black side-hat the man standing in the turret was wearing. US tankers wore leather helmets so that they looked a bit like football players. Why was this guy wearing a black side-hat? Was he British? But what would Britishers be doing so far away from their own Army? Then he had it with the frightening clarity of a nightmare. 'Krauts!' he shrilled. 'They're Krauts ... Polack, sound the alarm!'

He slammed his fist into the gun-layer's back. 'Open sight... Fire for God's sake!'

The Sherman braked dramatically as in the steeple above Polack started to toll the bells. Slowly, with no sound save the soft hum of its electric turret motor, the long overhanging 75mm cannon began to swing round in the direction of the lone anti-tank gun. The young loader frantically lined the white-painted monster in its crosswires.

'Come on ... come on!' Dude yelled in a paroxysm of fear as the bells tolled madly and men everywhere scrambled for cover. *'Fire!'*

CR – ACK! The 30 ton monster shook as if buffeted by a hurricane as its cannon roared. A huge volcano of stone and snow erupted only twenty yards to the front of the gun. Dude ducked as fist-sized, razor-edged shards of gleaming metal hissed through the air. The corporal next to him screamed. He dropped, clutching his face, now a mass of gore, with riddled arms that pumped blood in scarlet jets.

Next moment the 57mm gun fired. Flame sprang from its muzzle. It rose high on its trails and slammed down the next instant. The shock wave hit Dude in the face and tore the air out of his lungs so that he gasped and choked like an ancient asthmatic. There was the hollow boom of metal striking metal. The Sherman staggered. Thick white smoke started to stream from its engine cowling. A soft hideous hush. A second later and the whole rear of the tank went up in oily black-and yellow flame Captain Lange's 'Ronson' had lived up to its name, and the battle for Marvie had commenced.

Day Four:
Wednesday 20 December 1944

'They're gonna try now, sir,' the harassed staff officer called, as the red signal flare hissed into the night sky and hung there, bathing their faces in its lurid, unreal light.

Patton nodded and lifted up the big night-glasses that hung from his neck. The artillery crashed into action with a frightening, earth-shaking roar and in one great hoarse, exultant scream, the shells shot above the watchers' heads and went hurrying towards the Germans dug in further up the road. Salvo after salvo followed. Swiftly the first angry screams turned into one long baleful howl that rose and rose in elemental fury.

Now whistles shrilled to the watchers' front. Officers and noncoms rose hesitantly to their feet, crouched low as if braving a fierce storm. More reluctantly their infantry followed. Watching them in the red light, Patton knew what they were telling themselves: no one could have lived through a barrage like that. The Krauts must be all dead. His thin, cruel lips twisted in a sneer. What suckers they were, these American doughboys! Didn't they know just how deep the Krauts always dug themselves in? They would be waiting for them; they always were.

To the right, the motors of the Shermans burst into life. The stink of gasoline was wafted over on the icy night air. Soon the great drama of battle would commence. Along the whole length of the German line red distress flares began to rise into the lurid sky. Patton wondered just how badly they had been hurt by the guns.

'Move out for God's sake!' the staff officer watching next to Patton cried impatiently.

As if answering his plea, the officers of the lead companies began to plough their way across the snowy fields to both sides of the road. The tanks started to rattle after them, their rubber tracks skidding and sliding on the slick road. Patton made a mental note. American tanks needed improved tracks for this kind of winter warfare. They would be useless when it came to fighting the Russians after they had dealt with the Krauts.

Now the cries and yells and cheers of the infantry were carried back to the watchers. They advanced towards the rolling banks of smoke – 200 yards, 150. Still no reaction from the Krauts. Had the artillery barrage done the trick after all? 100 yards away – 50. Suddenly a heavy German machine-gun commenced chattering like an angry woodpecker. White tracer sliced the air. Slugs bounced off the glacis plate of the leading Sherman like golf-balls. The infantry quickened their pace, bodies leaning forward like men advancing against driving rain. There was the dry crack of a German *panzerfaust*. A scarlet flash. A trail of angry red sparks. The leading Sherman came to an abrupt halt. A great white smoke ring began to ascend from its open turret. No one got out. All along the German line small-arms fire erupted. The machine-guns swung from right to left. Fire scythed down the leading companies. Somewhere an electric mortar howled obscenely. Mortar bombs began to rain down on the GIs, cutting great gaps in their ranks.

Patton, peering through his night-glasses, muttered angrily, knowing already that the steam was going out of the infantry attack.

Another minute and they'd break, come running back, flinging away their weapons and helmets in their frantic haste.

Another Sherman was hit. Its gun drooped like a broken limb. Greedy little blue flames started to lick the length of its engine cowling. The next instant it exploded with a tremendous roar. When the sheet of flame vanished, all that was left was a great steaming brown hole in the snow and one lone bogie wheel wobbling off into the surrounding darkness. Another Sherman driver panicked at the sight. He tried to reverse and ran full-tilt into a bunch of stalled, cowering infantrymen. The 30 ton tank ran right through them, churning them to pulp underneath its flailing blood-red tracks. Next to Patton the staff officer groaned and hung his head, as if he were personally responsible.

The accident did it. As Patton had predicted, men were flinging away their weapons and streaming back to the startline while, here and there, red-faced angry officers and noncoms tried to stop them. To no avail. Now it was every man for himself. Eyes wide with fear, mouths gaping wide, muttering incomprehensible phrases, they ran past Patton's post. A helmetless top-sergeant standing 10 yards away from the general fired a crazy volley from his .45 at the retreating men. Two went down screaming. But the others did not seem to notice.

They kept on running, the wounded hobbling after them the best they could, exhibiting their shattered limbs to the general's party as they passed into the darkness beyond, as if their wounds explained everything. In disgust the top-sergeant threw his empty pistol into the bloody snow and, head bent, trailed after the rest.

Patton lowered his glasses. He had seen enough. The final attempt by Middleton's Corps to break open the road from Arlon to Bastogne had failed totally. Now, as soon as his leading divisions arrived from Northern France, he'd attack, but till then, McAuliffe's Screaming Eagles, cut off up there, would have to look after themselves.

Angrily he swung round and started back to his sedan, past the lines of wounded already being worked upon by sweating medics. By the light of flickering lanterns the orderlies pencilled in on their foreheads the morphine dosage given to each and attached red tickets to those who would be evacuated to the already crowded hospitals in Luxembourg. Patton spat out his usual phrases routinely, 'Good work, soldier... Don't worry, we'll give them hell for what they have done to you ... hell, you'll be screwing your way right through Paree this time next week, son...' But his mind was on other things. Bastogne was becoming one hell of a problem. Already it was being featured in the headlines back home. It had become a prestige objective and there would be the devil to pay if it surrendered before he could relieve it. Besides, he could not lose the glory that his Third Army would achieve when it did link up with McAuliffe's troopers. That was for sure.

'Mims,' he snapped to his sergeant-driver. 'Get me the horn to Third Army staff.'

As the sergeant hurried to obey, Patton waited impatiently, tapping his foot and listening to the fire-fight slowly beginning to die down. As always, the Krauts were not as wasteful with their ammunition as were the GIs, who seemed to think that the US Army possessed an inexhaustible supply of the stuff.

'Sir.' The sergeant's voice broke into his gloomy thoughts. 'Staff.'

'Cut out the code crap,' Patton barked as the disembodied voice back in Luxembourg City started into the normal routine for radio messages of this kind. 'Just tell me one thing. When exactly can Big Friend jump off now? Over.'

The staff officer hesitated and then stated reluctantly, as if visualizing the gleeful faces of the German radiomen who were intercepting and taking down everything he was saying, 'Zero six hundred on the day, sir, over.'

'Thank you. Over and out.'

Patton frowned as he gave the phone back to a silent Mims. It meant that it would now be exactly forty-eight hours before 'Big Friend' – his Fourth Armored Division – could start the attack and take the pressure off the 101st.

'It don't look too good, General, does it?' Mims said softly.

'It never does,' Patton agreed, slipping into his seat next to the driver. 'Okay Mims, take us back to Lux City. There's nothing more I can do here – for a while.' He slumped back, suddenly feeling very old and very tired. The staff car moved off.

Behind them, over Bastogne, the flames rose higher and higher. The all-out German attack had started and there was not one thing that Patton could do about it...

'I don't think the wet-mouths can take much more of this, sir,' Big Red said huskily, as the dawn light started to slip across the wartorn fields, reluctant to illuminate the miserable scene below, and behind them heavy artillery shells began landing on Bastogne yet again. All along the skyline over there, long funereal pillars of dead-black smoke ascended slowly to the grey above.

Iron Mike wiped the scum from his parched lips and took his gaze off one of the greenhorns, sprawled across the rusting barbed wire, arms thrown out and pierced by the cruel barbs like a khaki-clad Jesus. 'I don't think they're doing so bad, Red,' he answered, his eyes already searching the horizon for the first sign of the fresh German attack, which could come at any moment now. 'We sure as hell gave them a licking last night!'

Big Red looked at the still smoking German Shermans piled up in the lane with their dead crews sprawled all around like bundles of sodden abandoned rags. 'Yeah, I guess we did,' he agreed slowly, and fell silent.

The Germans had attacked all night. Dude and his reluctant gunners had just succeeded in knocking out the last of the Shermans when the panzer grenadiers had come swarming across the fields in their white camouflaged jackets. Crying their battle-cry *'Alles für Deutschland!'*, they had died by the score as veteran and greenhorn turned their weapons on the running figures.

For a while they had had peace. Then the heavy silence of the night had been broken by the rumble of tracks and two enormous shapes had lurched out of the gloom. They seemed to fill the whole world as they crawled closer and closer, huge cannon swinging from side to side like the snouts of primeval monsters seeking out their prey. For one awful moment, a horrified Iron Mike had thought his men would break. But he had not reckoned with Major Ewell, who had been one of the first to spring out of his foxhole as the Royal Tigers came ever nearer.

Screaming incoherently, eyes crazed with fear and wild courage, he had not run away but *directly* at the two monsters, bazooka clutched in his arms. With his chest and abdomen ripped apart by German machine-gun bullets, he had knocked out both tanks at 50 yards' range and had died in Iron Mike's arms, his intestines pulsating like an obscene grey-green, steaming snake on the snow beside him.

As Iron Mike had breathed to Big Red a little later, when the German attack had ebbed away and he had wiped the dead major's blood off his hands in the snow, 'Would you believe it, Red. Last night I was ordering you guys to shoot the poor bastard if he ran away! Now he's a goddam hero – a guy who deserves the Medal of Honor. I just don't get it!'

Neither did Big Red. But fifteen minutes later the Germans had attacked again and Major Ewell's heroic death was soon forgotten; for now his greenhorns were dying by the score.

As dawn broke, and mixed with the rumble of heavy guns pounding Bastogne to their rear, a weary Iron Mike could hear the first hoarse asthmatic cough and whine of tank engines starting up on a freezing morning, followed minutes later by the reluctant first rumble of tracks. He flung a quick look at his little command, heads just above their holes or crouched behind the barricades of shattered timber and masonry. 'All right, you guys, pop to!' he called, his breath erupting from his mouth in a small grey cloud. 'Here they come again.' He raised himself and shouted up at the steeple, its spire now holed by 88mm shellfire, 'Polack!'

Kovalski, festooned with German stick grenades that he had sneaked out to take from the bodies of the dead German panzer grenadiers, looked down from the bell-chamber. 'Sir?'

'See anything yet?'

'Just smoke, sir... They're moving out, I guess.'

'Armour?'

'Can't say, sir. But it sure does sound like it.'

'Kay, well hit the panic-button, as soon as you see 'em coming out of that wood.'

'Will do, sir.'

Iron Mike looked down at Big Red, crouched behind the bazooka, his last remaining rockets draped on the shattered stonework next to him. 'Take over here, Red. Get one of the greenhorns to act as loader for you if necessary. I'm gonna see how the rest of the boys are getting on.'

'Yessir.' Big Red replied, his beefy, brick-red face grim, not taking his gaze off his front.

Hastily Iron Mike picked up his carbine and started doing the rounds of his perimeter, face fixed in a big smile, his step jaunty in spite of his sleepless night, playing the role of commander like an actor might, trying to enthuse fresh confidence into his tired men, with a pat on the back here, a few words of encouragement there – and all the time, that slow grinding of tracks in his ears.

Five minutes later he was briefing Dude on what to do if the Germans attempted to push up the cart track into the square. Behind them the loader counted his remaining shells in a sombre voice, 'eight .. nine … ten…' Just then Polack bellowed from his position in the steeple above them – 'I can see them, sir! They're coming out of the woods now, sir!'

'Okay, Dude,' Iron Mike said quickly. 'Make every round count. Once they break into the square, we've had it. Our whole perimeter'll fold like a pack of cars.' And with that he was running to the outskirts of Marvie beyond the church where he could get a better view of the German positions.

Limey rose up from a foxhole, bazooka at the ready, a pile of what looked like soup plates stacked next to him for some reason. 'They're over there, sir,' he reported. 'At ten o'clock. Can't make them out, though… Look like half-tracks, but…'

Iron Mike was no longer listening. Throwing up his binoculars, he focused them hastily on the dark shapes emerging from the first, showering snow everywhere as they brushed against their branches.

The first one slid silently into the circle of bright, gleaming calibrated glass. Iron Mike gasped with shock as he recognized the strange clumsy-looking device behind the cab of the half-track and, standing beside it, the leather-clad, begoggled figure who looked like a World War One pilot.

'What is it, sir?' Limey asked in alarm.

For a minute he couldn't speak, as more and more of the terrifying weapons rumbled into sight. Finally he swallowed hard and whispered, 'They're flame-throwers, Limey. They're putting in flame-throwers!'

'Oh, my Christ!' Limey moaned, his skinny, cunning face turning white. *'Not that!* Remember old Porky getting caught by one back in Normandy, sir. Gawd Almighty, didn't he look a sight!'

For a fleeting moment, Iron Mike saw again that horrific figure staggering back across the battlefield, face charred to a blackened skull, with the bones showing through a brilliant white, blind and dying, one black-charred skeletal hand held in front of him as he croaked with a tongue that was almost burned away, 'Guys ... don't leave me ... please don't leave me, guys.' In the end someone had taken pity on the faceless horror. A single rifle shot had rung out and Porky had pitched to the ground dead. Nobody had spoken for a long time after that. That day they had taken no German prisoners.

Iron Mike's brain raced. He was quite sure that they'd be able to knock out two or three of the half-tracks, but there seemed to be a whole company of them. Once they had spread out, which they would, there was little chance of blasting all of them. At 75 yards they'd stop and then begin flaming the fox-holes. That would be that. Even his veteran Screaming Eagles would not be able to stand up to that terrible flame. They'd break and run. There would be no two ways about it.

'Sir,' Limey broke into his fleeting thoughts.

'Yes?'

'That low-lying ground to left-front, sir, you see it?'

'Yes,' Iron Mike answered puzzled, as more and more half-tracks emerged from the wood, the stink of their diesel engines wafting across the corpse-littered field towards the defenders.

'If we could channel the flame-throwers into that we could concentrate all we've got left in the way of bazookas and Dude's 57mm on the place. Then we could give them a real old kick up the arse.'

New hope sprang into Iron Mike's blood-shot eyes – only to vanish almost as soon as it had appeared. 'But how?' he asked lamely.

Limey's dirty face formed into a grin. *'Plates,'* he said, slapping the soup-plates at the side of his foxhole, while Iron Mike stared down at him incredulously. 'Just ordinary common-or-garden soup plates, sir!'

General Bayerlein, conducting the attack from the last half-track, watched the operator adjust the dials of his terrible weapon before crying above the rattle of the tracks, 'Pressure up now!'

He frowned. He hated flame-throwers. He had seen too often the terrible wounds they inflicted on men, wounds that were worse than those occasioned by poisonous gas in the Old War. Many were the nightmares he had had as he recalled those stricken charred men, minus eyes, nose, ears, staggering out of the smoke, streaming flame behind them. Now it was only von Luttwitz's threats of what would happen if he failed to take Bastogne that had forced him to use the damned things. He said a silent prayer that the murderous business would be over with quickly and that the Amis would surrender or flee without attempting to defend their positions.

Now the first half-track was in line with what looked to him like an Ami strongpoint, a sandbagged position built into the back of a shattered barn. The leather-clad figure in his goggles and leather helmet bent over his terrible weapon. There was a little burst of flame, like a match being struck, above the nozzle of the flame-thrower.

'He's testing the spark, General,' his own gunner said in his strangely muffled voice. 'Now watch.'

General Bayerlein tensed. Abruptly there was a mad rush of air. A vicious frightening hiss. A burning yellow rod of flame slapped out from the leading half-track. Out and out. Up and up. The noise reminded an awed Bayerlein of a thick leather strap being slapped by an old-fashioned cut-throat razor. The yellow rod curved suddenly. It started to descend. Angry blue particles of flame fell everywhere. With a clearly audible smack the flame struck the strongpoint and a dozen greedy yellow fingers leapt out to snatch at the sandbags. They burst one after another. Under a rain of sand the whole structure disappeared in a belching, hideously twisting, red-roaring, all consuming fire.

'That's toasted the Ami bastard's eggs for him!' his own gunner yelled exuberantly as a crazy figure came staggering out of the burning wreckage, the flames leaping up his body. He threw himself into a pool of melted snow, twitching and writhing in his agony, then raised himself, spine taut as bow-string, black claws appealing in vain to heaven for the mercy that did not exist this terrible dawn, and fell back dead.

The half-tracks rumbled on, heading towards the village in single file, but ready, once they had cleared the fields and were within flame-throwing distance of the enemy perimeter defences, to open up in extended order and swamp the place in one final rush.

From the rear, Bayerlein, glasses raised to his eyes, followed their progress, telling himself that naturally some of his vehicles would fall victim to the Amis' anti-tank defences, but for every one knocked out, two would get through – for, as von Luttwitz had bellowed over the radio-phone to him that dawn, 'Man, you can't expect to make an omelette without cracking eggs!' They would be the eggs.

Now his own half-track was rumbling by the flamed Ami outpost. Bayerlein caught a glimpse of what looked like the burned, shrivelled crook of a tree. But when he looked closer he saw that there was a hunk of what looked like raw meat attached to it. A little way off were the charred remnants of a foot. He turned away sickened. 'God,' he prayed to himself, 'let it be over with – *and quick!*'

But that was not to be, at least not in the manner that Bayerlein anticipated.

'Here the buggers come!' Limey hissed, as the rattling half-tracks came closer and closer, the men in them confident that they were unstoppable. 'Now we'll see if the buggers fall for it.'

Iron Mike nodded, not daring to look at the faces of his men covering the trough of ground in front of them with what was left of their bazookas. He knew instinctively what he would see there: complete and overwhelming unreasoning fear. The way the Kraut half-track had flamed the outpost had been almost too much for them, and he had his Colt in his hand ready to drive them back to their posts at gun-point. Fortunately it hadn't come to that. But he knew he wouldn't get a second chance; the next time they would run.

'Do you think they'll fall for it, Limey?' he asked as the half-track rumbled nearer and nearer, a mere 200 yards from the killing ground – if there was to be a killing ground.

'Jerries are so dumb that they've got to be told to come in out of the bleeding rain,' Limey answered with more confidence than he felt, his gaze fixed on the twin lines of upturned soup plates, flanked by dirty white tapes – the engineers' standard sign that a path had been cleared through a minefield. He licked his parched lips, noting that his breath was coming in short hectic gasps, as if he was running a race.

'How far are we gonna let them come?' one of the greenhorns asked in a frightened whisper. 'Them flame-throwers have got a range of over 75 yards.'

'Knock it off,' Iron Mike snapped brutally, and clicked back the hammer of his pistol. 'And listen – the first guy who tries to bug out gets it–'

'Sir,' Limey cried excitedly and dug his nails painfully into the officer's arm, 'They're buying it... Oh, lovely, ferking grub, the stupid sods are buying it!'

Iron Mike felt a wave of relief sweep through his taut body. They were! The line of half-tracks had changed course. Their leader had fallen for the trick. He was beginning to drive into the killing ground.

'Himmel, Arsch und Wolkenbruch!' General Bayerlein exploded, as he observed the leading half-track's change of course and knew instinctively, old soldier that he was, that the damned young fool was heading for trouble. They were funnelling their attack into a depression where it would be easy for the Amis to pick them off one by one. He grabbed the headphones from his radio operator, almost choking him as he tugged at the wires. 'Bayerlein,' he yelled above the thunder of the half-track's engine. 'What in three devils' name are you doing, man? You're walking straight into a trap, don't you see, you great horned-ox?'

'But sir,' came back the leading commander's voice, distorted over the radio, 'we've run into a mine field. We're heading through a path cut through by their engineers–'

'Straight into their anti-tank and bazooka screen!' Bayerlein screamed, not waiting for the men to finish, beside himself with frustration and rage. 'Risk the damned mines, but get out of that shitting trough at once, before it's too late...'

The sudden roaring noise like a great piece of celestial canvas being ripped apart forcibly told him that it was already too late. He dropped the headphones helplessly, realizing, with the sudden clarity of a vision, that he had failed yet again.

'Hurrah!' the greenhorns sang out as the leading half-track reeled to a stop, a great gleaming silver hole gouged in its side, dead crewmen hanging over the back like broken dolls, and the survivors running frantically for the rear pursued by bursts of flying white tracer.

Now the second one came to a halt, its progress blocked by the stricken leader. The gunner panicked. He pressed the trigger of his awesome weapon. There was a hushed intake of breath. A forked tongue of angry yellow flame flew out a good 75 yards to its front. The snow shrank, blackened and melted in a cloud of steam. Before the eyes of the watchers, the crippled first half-track glowed a deep purple in the flame. The paint on its sides began to bubble furiously.

Next moment Dude's anti-tank gun cracked again. The watchers could actually see the white blur of the solid AP shot scudding flatly across the snow to the stalled half-track. The German vehicle reeled violently, and then the fuel container exploded. The watchers caught a fleeting glimpsed of a man whirling high into the air carried upwards by the flames. Others ran screaming from the vehicle, engulfed in blue flame; they dropped on the ground, charred black and already shrunken to the size of pygmies. 'Two down,' the Englishman cried exuberantly, 'six to go!'

But already the Germans had had enough. The third driver in line panicked. With a frantic crash of gears, he swung around crazily. Behind him number four tried to get out of the way, but there was no room in the 'safe area' between the mines. The two half-tracks smashed head-on into each other. Men went flying over the sides. Others threw themselves over the best they could, running for the rear. The fifth half-track decided to back out. A burst of tracer penetrated the armoured, driving slit. The driver slumped over his wheel, dead, but his foot still pressed down hard on the accelerator. The half-track smashed right into the running men, cutting a great swathe through them, leaving a crushed pulp of severed limbs on the snow, as it rolled on to its inevitable destruction.

Suddenly Iron Mike sat down in the snow, all energy drained out of him as if a tap had been opened. He pushed back his helmet from his sweat-lathered face. 'Let 'em go,' he breathed out wearily. 'They've had enough for the time being.' He gulped in a breath of cold air gratefully. 'But don't worry, guys,' he said without enthusiasm, 'they'll be back.'

Limey nodded his agreement grimly. 'Yer can say that agen, sir. In this ruddy world, there's no peace for the wicked...'

'*Gentlemen, the Führer, Adolf Hitler!*' The gigantic black-clad SS adjutant made his announcement at the top of his voice, as if he were addressing a parade and not a handful of senior officers. The generals stiffened to attention, and in the great Gothic hall of Ziegenberg Castle the harsh crunch of their polished boots echoed and re-echoed among the remoter recesses of the timbered roof. Apparently worked by some rusty spring, their eyes turned as one to the huge arched door, both sides flanked by SS men with machine-pistols slung across their black-clad chests.

Slowly and shakily, Adolf Hitler entered, supported by his adjutants, looking a good twenty years older than his real age. The forty-odd pills he took a day, the numerous injections, and the effect of the bomb attack on his life the previous July, had all taken their toll. The man who had once commanded the destinies of 300 million Europeans was a very sick man.

'*Heil* Hitler!' Colonel-General Jodl called without enthusiasm, his pale, cunning face expressionless, revealing nothing that was going on in that clever head of his.

'*Heil* Hitler!' the adjutants cried with full lungs, making the dark rafters in the grey Gothic gloom above ring with the cry.

Hitler flipped up his hand in weak acknowledgement and allowed a seat to be pushed underneath him. Gently he broke wind, as he did constantly as a result of his vegetarian diet and the anti-gas pills he swallowed by the dozen. The adjutant who had placed the chair beneath him backed off hastily, his face nauseated.

Jodl waited until the rest of the staff had taken their seats, now that the Führer was settled, and then turned to the map of Belgium covered with its blue and red china-pencil marks. The squares and the triangles indicated the corps and divisions which were flooding into the great counter-attack, already dubbed by the yankee press the 'European Pearl Harbour'. He took one last look at the man in front of him and wondered if Germany's fate in this, her eleventh hour, could really be entrusted to such a trembling wreck. But he knew that to seek the answer to that overwhelming question could only result in death. Himmler's police *apparat* was still all-knowing, all-powerful. Generals who didn't toe the line ended kicking their heels suspended on a length of wire from a hook in a Gestapo cellar, being slowly garrotted to death.

He dismissed the thought and concentrated on his briefing. 'On Day Five of the offensive, *meine Herren,* we can say that our new offensive has been *conditionally* successful. On both our northern and southern flanks the original impetus has been slowed down, especially in the area of the Sixth SS Panzer Army.' Jodl gave the representative of the Armed SS a cold stare, as if he were making him personally responsible.

In his turn the *Standartenführer* flashed a look of protest at the Führer, but Hitler did not seem to notice. He continued to sit there, apathetically staring at nothing, his hands trembling, constantly breaking wind in one long rumble.

'However, in the centre which, of course, is most important,' Jodl went on, 'we have achieved considerable success. Our armoured spearheads are within striking distance of the Meuse at Dinant – here – and Huy – here. Though,' he raised his finger in warning as he spotted the smiles of triumph beginning to dawn on his listeners' faces, 'I must warn you that we have information from our sleeper organization behind enemy lines that the Tommies further north have been put on the alert. It could be, therefore, that Montgomery will begin moving his men south to man the line of the Meuse as a stop-line if the Americans break altogether.'

Field Marshal Keitel, Hitler's Chief-of-Staff, wooden-jawed and wooden-headed, guffawed loudly. 'By the time the Tommies get moving, Jodl, our brave fellows will be in Antwerp. Everyone knows just how slow Montgomery is!'

Jodl's face remained impassive. He knew the weaknesses of both the Americans and their British allies, but he knew, too, that they were learning, and learning fast. They had invaded Europe the previous June, rank amateurs for the most part; now they were almost as good as the best of what was left of the once great *Grossdeutsche Wehrmacht*. Keitel was a fool who had not heard a shot fired in anger since 1916. What did he know of modern war?

He cleared his throat and continued. 'So in the centre everything is going relatively well to plan, save for here at Bastogne.' He flashed a quick look at his notes. 'As of twelve hundred hours this day, we have achieved some success on its eastern flank. The villages of Wardin and Bizory have been captured. Further south the Second Panzer has captured Noville and this night will advance westwards to Ortheuville – here. At midnight it is the intention of its commander General Lauchert to seize a bridge intact over the Ourthe River. Now, gentlemen, the question is whether we continue our attempts to capture the place or to by-pass and contain it, with Bayerlein's *Panzerlehr* heading for St Hubert – here – 25 kilometres to the west? After all, our main objective is the River Meuse.'

There was no emphasis in Jodl's voice. He was simply stating facts as a good German general staff officer should, not making decisions or attempting to sway his listeners one way or another. He sat down, his briefing over, that enormous question which might well settle the fate of those 9000 unknown American soldiers trapped in the little Belgian town unanswered. Slowly all eyes began to turn to the 'Greatest Captain of All Time', as the Führer was known contemptuously behind his back in the staff.

Hitler took his time, his bottom lip quivering and trembling like that of a very old man. 'You all know my original plan,' he commenced, his voice low and husky with none of that old guttural fire that had once carried away even the most sceptical of his listeners. 'We capture the major Allied supply port of Antwerp, divide the British and the Americans and give them such a severe blow that we will be able to discuss a separate peace, while we deal with the Russians.

130

As you know, the Americans have no heart for a real fight and the British are already scraping the manpower barrel. That was the original plan with the emphasis on speed and the need to by-pass centres of strong Allied resistance.' He paused and coughed in his hand. Sallow face dull, he looked at his palm. It was tinged pink. He was coughing blood again.

His listeners nodded here and there, but otherwise there was no comment. Time was too precious and they didn't want the Führer to go off on one of his hour-long lectures. 'However, *meine Herren,* there is *no* by-passing Bastogne. All roads and railway lines leading through the Ardennes to the Meuse which we will need urgently for supplying the second half of our drive to Antwerp pass through it.' He raised his voice with an effort. 'The place *must* be captured. The question is *how;* for remember this, gentlemen, the battle in which we are currently engaged in Belgium is to decide whether Germany lives or dies. There are no two ways about it. Germany's destiny is linked inextricably with what happens in that pathetic little country.'

For a moment his apprehensive listeners thought he was going to launch into one of those usual harangues of his, but the power vanished from the Führer's voice almost as soon as it had appeared. All the same, the dull glaze had disappeared from his brown eyes to be replaced by something akin to that hypnotic look of old, which had always held and fascinated his listeners.

'Now, *meine Herren,* we all know what our enemies think of us. The Anglo-Americans and their allies regard us as wooden-headed, unimaginative Teutons who never vary from their accustomed pattern of behaviour: cold-hearted, ruthless, unthinking brutes – Huns, I believe they often call us – who have not one spark of phantasy in their bodies. But they forget that the Huns were a highly cunning and treacherous nation, who employed every *ruse de guerre* to trick their enemies to their real intentions. So, I say to you, my generals, why should we not pretend that we are proceeding with our original plan and that this Bastogne is being by-passed, while we make our preparations for capturing it with one supreme overwhelming offensive. The Anglo-Americans are a naïve people – they are easily fooled.'

Jodl, who felt his duty at HQ was not to let the Führer's undoubtedly brilliant imagination run away with him, said sharply, 'But how, *mein Führer?*'

'Yes how?' the others joined in, intrigued to know what Hitler might have up his sleeve.

Hitler broke wind easily, raising one buttock to do so, and looked around at their hard, soldierly faces in the yellow light.

'Simple, *meine liebe Herren,* you show weakness to hide your strength and thus lull the Anglo-American simpletons into a false sense of security that will undoubtedly be their undoing.' He farted again. 'This is the way we are going to do it.' The Greatest Captain of All Time leaned forward spreading the rotten stench of his internal decay through that still, tense room...

Day Five:
Thursday 21 December 1944

'I can't figure it out,' Polack said plaintively, biting off the top of a bottle of Stella Artois that he had found in a wrecked cellar. He spat out the glass, and took a deep, satisfying slug of the beer under the apprehensive gaze of Limey, who said, 'I can. You're guzzling that sodding beer all for yourself. So watch it!'

Big Red grinned and continued his attempts to roast a can of hash over a flickering fire of wet wood, as the thick pearl-white fog which had followed the snowfall of the night swirled through the ruins mournfully, deadening every sound save the persistent rumble of armour to their south.

'What do you make of it, Red?' Dude

asked, warming his hands at the poor fire. 'Hell, they should have clobbered us yesterday or at least last night during the blizzard. I mean, visibility was down to 10 yards. They could easily have sneaked up on us.' His weakly handsome playboy's face creased into a frown.

'Don't know,' Red answered, digging a dirty finger into the hash tentatively and finding it still rock-hard. 'All I know is that that's Kraut armour going south for sure. They're heading for the river, those Jerry panzers are.'

'But what about us here?' Dude objected, as Limey grabbed the bottle of beer from Polack's ham of a hand, wiped the jagged top with exaggerated care and took a delighted swallow. 'After all the effort they put into trying to take Marvie yesterday, you can't tell me that they've laid off us now. It just don't make sense.'

'You're right, there, Dude,' Iron Mike's voice cut into the conversation. 'And you don't need an expensive Yale education to figure out that there's something mighty fishy going on out there.'

Iron Mike strode into the pale-blue circle of flickering light provided by Big Red's fire. His uniform might be ripped here and there and dirty after four days of combat, but his hard, dimpled chin was cleanly shaven, his hair was combed and his face was flushed with rude good-health. Half an hour before, to the amazed cries of the greenhorns and the taunts of his veterans that 'You'll be sorry', he had stripped naked and taken a freezingly cold roll in the snow to get clean. How he was completely, totally alert, every nerve cell tingling electrically.

Iron Mike gazed at his bearded, unwashed Bad Boys looking like the Forty-Niners he remembered from old, yellowed nineteenth-century pictures as they crouched around their flickering fires in the snow, and said, 'Boys, there's only one way we're gonna find out what the Kraut is up to out there, isn't there?'

Limey winked and said, 'Yer, go and have a look-see, sir. But forget about me, I've got a sudden attack of the monthlies.'

'You'll get a sudden swift kick up the keester in one second flat, if you don't knock it off,' Iron Mike answered without rancour.

'Why I didn't think you cared, sir!' Limey simpered in an affected falsetto and fell silent.

'In this goddam mist, they could well be just sitting out there beyond the wire. But I somehow don't think they are.' His face twisted in a puzzled frown. 'That's their armour for sure out there, but I can't just figure out what they're gonna do with it. Big Red says that they're heading for the Meuse. That could be true. But they could be attempting to work their way round back of us, the way they did round Team O'Hara. At all events, I think the CG ought to know a little more of what's going on out there, don't you!' He lowered his gaze.

Big Red cursed softly and dropped his can of hash into the snow. Picking up his grease-gun leaning against the nearest wall, he growled, 'Okay, you guys, you heard what the Captain said. Let's go and have a look... I'm sure the Krauts would appreciate a little social call at this time of the morning. Perhaps they'll offer us a cup of Java,' he sneered. *'I don't think!'*

But Big Red was wrong. On that particular morning, the Germans were prepared to offer the men of the Screaming Eagles something more than just a cup of coffee...

Strung out cautiously at intervals of 5 yards, the men of the little patrol advanced through the rolling mist, pausing regularly to cock their heads in the direction of the sound of the many armoured vehicles. There was something awesome and brooding about the fields through which they passed. Everywhere there was death and destruction. Shattered trucks, burnt-out tanks, mercifully covered by the snow, with here and there long low hummocks of white which had once been bodies.

Big Red raised his hand. They halted. To

their right lay a ghastly tableau of bodies heaped indiscriminately together. Big Red stared at them glumly – a frozen hand striking through the snow, a pair of blue eyes staring up accusingly from a waxen head, the severed stump of a leg complete with jackboot – and told himself that tough as a man was, he could never get used to this, *never!* Then he concentrated again, for he was sure he had heard a different sound than that of the German convoy to the south.

A moment later, Limey heard it too. Everywhere the men tensed where they knelt, grease-guns at the ready, held in palms that were suddenly wet with sweat. Something ... somebody was out there in the grey whirling gloom and whatever, whoever, it was, it was heading straight for their present position! Slowly, very slowly, Big Red, his face dripping with sweat, began to raise his carbine, knowing that what he did next might well seal his fate; for there were just four of them. They wouldn't have a chance if they had run into a standard-sized Kraut patrol; they'd be outnumbered five to one.

The seconds ticked leadenly by as the noise grew louder and louder. Vague shadows were now visible, flickering in and out of the wavering grey mist. Big Red bit his bottom lip, feeling a vein at his temple begin to throb electrically. For Krauts, he told himself, they sure were noisy. Behind him he heard Polack whispering a prayer in Polish and was tempted to hiss him to be quiet. But he knew that the big simpleton was preparing himself for violent death in his own Polack Catholic way. He desisted, and waited.

Suddenly there they were. Only four of them. What looked like a couple of officers and two enlisted men, and even by the poor light of the misty morning, an astonished Big Red could see they were all unarmed. But it wasn't that which made him lower his grease-gun slowly, a look of absolute, complete amazement on his broad, brick-red face. Both the enlisted men had white flags sloped over their shoulders.

'Christ Almighty,' Limey breathed in awe behind him, *'the German Army is coming in to surrender...'*

As the jeep rolled by the line after line of Shermans parked on both sides of the Luxembourg road, the tankers in their leather helmets waving and hooting when they recognized Patton, Sergeant Mims grinned and said, 'General, the government is sure wasting a lot of money hiring a whole general staff. You and me has run the Third Army all day and done a better job than they do.'

Patton – huddled in his parka, a brown Army-issue blanket draped across his knees – acknowledged the cheers with a weary wave of his gloved hand and grunted. 'You

138

might well be right there, Mims. But we sure can't change this goddam awful weather.'

He stared moodily at the swirling fog to their front. Again air re-supply of the trapped Screaming Eagles had been called off this day, which meant that when his Fourth Armored went into action in a few short hours, there would be no TAC Air Force giving them the kind of aerial artillery support they needed if the tankers were going to barrel into Bastogne at double-quick time. 'That goddam Army sky-pilot of mine back in Nancy obviously didn't have it in with God after all.' He spat angrily over the side of the jeep.

Mims grinned as they rolled by a line of Fourth Armored infantrymen, squatting in a bare-bottomed row in a ditch relieving themselves, their white rears turned in an unintentional insult to their Commanding General. Back at Third Army HQ in Nancy everyone knew that Patton had summoned his Army chaplain and told him that he, Patton, wasn't pleased with the way that his troops had to contend not only with the enemy, but also with the weather. He wanted the chaplain to compose a prayer to get rid of the bad weather. If he succeeded, there would be the Bronze Star in it for him.

The chaplain had protested that it would 'take a pretty thick rug for that kind of praying', to which Patton had growled angrily, 'I don't care if it takes a flying carpet! I want you to get up a prayer for good weather.' Now, as they rolled ever closer to Brigadier-General Holmes Dager's Command Post, Mims told himself that the chaplain wouldn't be earning the Bronze Star this particularly foggy December day. It looked as if they were going to be socked in till Christmas Day, the way things were going.

Five minutes later they were ushered into General Dager's CP, set up in the stone-flagged kitchen of a Belgian farmhouse, its sole furniture a wooden table and four high-backed chairs. A long crucifix decorated its bare walls. Patton shook hands with the big bluff commander of the Fourth Armored's Combat Command B and got down to cases immediately. 'Dager,' he snapped, waving his big cigar as if it were a lethal weapon, 'I've picked you to lead the Fourth's drive for Bastogne. Those goddam airborne jerks have gone and gotten themselves surrounded there. It's up to you to get 'em out.'

Holmes Dager, a veteran of Brittany and Northern France, said nothing. He did not dare tell Patton that the old Fourth no longer existed. Its Shermans were falling apart from excess running and its ranks full of replacements, some of whom had never even seen a tank until they had joined the Division. Now, after five months of constant combat, the Fourth was scraping the barrel.

'Now look here at the map,' Patton continued, while outside someone kept saying in a plaintive Mid-Western accent, 'But the goddam joker said, he'd never even seen the inside of a recoil system before – *and he was a goddam gunner!*'

Patton jabbed the map with his gloved hand. 'From the south there are two roads into Bastogne. The Arlon-Bastogne Highway and the black top from Neufchâteau to Bastogne. I'm going to give you the Arlon Highway, Dager. Both will be defended by the Krauts of course, but you're going to hit them so hard and so fast that they're not going to have time to dig their heels in. Envelopment tactics are to be used wherever possible, Dager, with armour, armoured engineers and artillery in the lead, keeping your main body of infantry well back. You are to tolerate no sticking by your commanders. Be ruthless with them, I'll back you the whole way. And you're going to brook no interference by the Boche. Speed is of the essence, Dager. The word is *"Drive like hell!"*'

Dager nodded, as Patton started to rap out order after order. He remembered what had happened when, in the previous September, Montgomery had tried to link up with *his* paratroopers cut off at Arnhem. His armour had advanced down a single elevated road towards the Dutch river town and it had been cut off time and time again by the Krauts

141

coming in from the flanks. The Arlon-Bastogne Highway could be similarly self-sealing. The supply vehicles and their crews, mostly coloured, would be no match for German assault infantry and unless the guys of the Red Ball Express kept bringing up the gas, his tanks would soon bog down.

But Holmes Dager did not dare tell Patton that. In his present effervescent, hell-for-leather mood, Patton brooked no opposition. As he had said only the other day to the commanders of the Fourth at a conference back in Luxembourg City on their arrival from Northern France, 'Gentlemen, let's quit pussy-footing around. The Krauts can still win this war, if we let them. Now it's up to every commander to shoot the works. If those Hun bastards can play tough, then we can play tougher. If they want war in the raw, okay, we'll give 'em it!'

Now Dager accepted Patton's orders without objection. When the attack kicked off, then perhaps Patton would hold the reins loose and let him get on with the task ahead without supervision.

Finally Patton's flow of words came to an end. He drew a deep breath and handed Dager a piece of typed paper. 'I want all your battalion commanders to have that read out to their men before they go into the attack tomorrow morning, Dager,' he said solemnly. 'I composed it specially for you myself. It is a prayer for good weather... The Army chaplain helped me, of course.' And with that he was gone.

Dager waited till he could no longer hear the sound of Patton's jeep and then, as his staff clustered around him, he turned the paper to the light of the little kitchen window. Slowly and hesitantly, he started to read out aloud the most unusual prayer he had come across in his forty-odd years. 'Almighty and most merciful Father we humbly beseech Thee of Thy great goodness to restrain these immoderate rains with which we have had to contend. Grant us fair weather for Battle. Graciously hearken to us as soldiers who call upon Thee that, armed with Thy power, we may advance from victory to victory, and crush the oppression and wickedness of our enemies, and establish Thy justice among men and nations. Amen.'

He looked up at the circle of amazed faces staring at him. 'Wow,' he breathed, 'that is sure some prayer!' And then he began to laugh, the tears streaming down his broad soldierly face. One by one his staff officers joined him until the packed kitchen rocked with derisive laughter.

Outside it had begun to snow again!

Everywhere the weary Screaming Eagles started to crawl out of their foxholes as the strange little procession began to enter the shattered town, the ruins still smoking from yesterday's massive artillery bombardment. In front came the Bad Boys, weapons at the alert. Behind was Captain MacDonald leading in his blindfolded Germans, still carrying their white flag over their shoulders as they faltered their way across the uneven *pavé*. Now the rumour sped from mouth to mouth. *'The Krauts are coming in to surrender... They've had enough... They're gonna throw in the white towel...'* The weary, unshaven begrimed defenders started to clap each other on the back or yell exuberantly to their neighbours. It was all over... They had beaten the Krauts... The siege of Bastogne had ended at last!

MacDonald pushed on through the excited throng, directing his Germans the best he could in the mêlée, determined to say nothing about their real purpose there, flashing warning looks at his men whenever they seemed about to answer the shouted queries of the exuberant, jubilant Screaming Eagles. He approached divisional HQ, a series of red-brick storehouses, their walls pocked with shrapnel fire like the symptoms of some loathsome skin disease. There he halted in front of the colonel waiting for him outside, who had been alarmed by the excited noise breaking the afternoon silence. After an exchange of words, he handed him the note the four Germans had brought with them, and then waited as the other took it into the building.

The staff officers inside eagerly unwrapped the note, holding up the hissing white Coleman lantern so that they could see it better. Quickly one of their number began to read it aloud: 'To the USA Commander of the encircled town of Bastogne. The fortune of war is changing. This time the USA forces in and near Bastogne have been encircled by strong German armoured units.'

The staff officers' happy looks vanished. This did not sound like an offer to surrender by the Krauts. 'Hey,' someone remarked angrily, 'what are those Kraut jerk-offs up to?'

No one answered as the staff officer continued to read aloud, 'There is only one possibility to save the encircled USA troops from total annihilation: that is the honourable surrender of the encircled town... In order to think it over, a term of two hours will be granted beginning with the presentation of this note.

'If this proposal should be rejected, one German artillery corps and six heavy A.A.battalions are ready to annihilate the USA troops in and near Bastogne. The order for firing will be given immediately after this two hours' term. All the serious civilian losses caused by this artillery fire would not correspond with the well-known American humanity. The German Commander.'

The speaker stopped. The cramped underground room, smelling of stale C-rations, ether and human sweat, was very still. In the hissing white glare, the pale-faced officers, their features shiny as if greased with Vaseline, stared at each other, some in shock, some in bewilderment, some amused. 'I think, gentlemen,' the man who had read out the message said finally, breaking that heavy, tense silence, 'we'd better tell the commanding general.'

General McAuliffe stared up at the two colonels, Harper and Kinnard, as if he did not believe the evidence of his own eyes, then he laughed shortly and said, 'Aw nuts! What kind of a game do those Krauts think they're playing? We've given them one hell of a beating and now they dare to come here and ask *us* to surrender. They must be nuts!'

For a while the senior officers chattered and then McAuliffe said, 'I suppose we've got to reply, haven't we?'

The others agreed.

The bluff general, a man of few words, sat down on his bunk, pencil in hand, block on knee, pondering a suitable reply to the German demand. Finally he gave up and said, 'But what in Sam Hill's name can I tell them?'

Colonel Kinnard smiled. 'That first remark of yours could be hard to beat,' he said.

'But what did I say, Kinnard?'

'Nuts, General. You said *nuts!*'

Five minutes later Colonel Harper, tall and rangy, strode over to the blindfolded, waiting Germans. 'I have the American commander's reply,' he said to the one who spoke English.

The German captain asked, 'Is it written or verbal?'

'It is written,' said Harper, then he said to the German major, 'I will stick it in your hand.'

The German captain was then allowed to raise his blindfold to read the message.

The major frowned, perplexed. 'Is the reply negative or affirmative? If it is the latter I will negotiate further.'

The captain also looked puzzled. Again he read out the laconic reply to the offer of surrender; 'To the German Commander: NUTS. The American Commander.'

Harper lost his temper, He did not like the German major's arrogance. It was obvious the Krauts were trying to bluff them into surrendering. They were beat. Young MacDonald had told him about their armour moving south. They were pushing on and trying to hoax the Screaming Eagles into surrendering. 'The reply is decidedly *not* affirmative!' he snapped. 'If you continue this foolish attack, your losses will be tremendous... If you don't understand what "nuts" means, in plain English it is the same as *"Go to hell!"* And I will tell you something else – if you continue to attack, we will kill every goddam German that tries to break into this city.'

The outburst had a sobering effect on the two German officers. They saluted stiffly and the captain said almost sadly, 'We will kill many Americans. This is war.'

'On your way, bud!' said Colonel Harper.

Two hours later the threatened massive German artillery bombardment failed to materialize. The Germans, it seemed, had shot their bolt. They had played for high stakes, trying to bluff the Eagles into surrender, and they had failed. The battle would now move elsewhere. In the 101st's Command Post, General McAuliffe's orderly opened one of his last bottles of precious bourbon. Canteen cups were filled and the officers toasted their victory. Bastogne had beaten off everything the Krauts had thrown at them. Now it was over.

As McAuliffe himself said, face flushed with happiness and good bourbon. 'They were trying it on, gentlemen, and they failed. I guess we can give the Eagles a little rest now...'

Maddeningly the snowflakes whirled round and round below the little light plane, forming an almost impenetrable barrier. Eyes strained to the utmost, the young *Luftwaffe* sergeant-pilot, the steering column gripped between his knees, pressed his nose against the cockpit screen as the wipers flicked back and forth, trying to find the airstrip. Next to him Major von Schlemm, immaculate in his pressed uniform with the broad red stripe of the German General Staff running down the side of his riding breeches, clutching his all-precious briefcase to himself, although it was chained to his right wrist, did the same, cursing silently and fluently with all the inventiveness of the cavalry officer he had once been.

'It must be around here somewhere, *Herr Major*,' the young pilot said, the sweat pouring down his strained young face, '*it must!*' He flung a hasty glance at his fuel gauge. The green glowing needle trembled off and on the frightening letter 'L'. He had gas perhaps for another few minutes.

Major von Schlemm forgot his own danger. He bit his bottom lip as he wondered what his best course of action should be now. 'Do you think we're over enemy-held territory, Sergeant?' he snapped. The pilot shrugged, still trying to catch a glimpse of the earth below.

Major von Schlemm wasted no further

words. He loosened his pistol from his holster with his free hand and thrust it into his belt, then he readied the thermite grenade in his coat pocket. If he were captured with the papers he was bearing personally from Jodl to von Manteuffel, commander of the Fifth Panzer Army, he knew whatever his own fate would be, he could never live down the shame; and for over two hundred years the von Schlemms had always placed their personal honour above their own safety. No, he could not be captured. He must fight off the enemy until he had destroyed the precious orders, cost what it may.

Abruptly the plane gave a thick cough. The engine started to stutter alarmingly. 'Trouble?' von Schlemm rasped, as the Storch started to fall.

'Yessir,' the pilot answered, not taking his eyes off the controls as the banks of needles began to swing frighteningly from left to right. 'I think we've about run out of gas.' Viciously he kicked the right rudder to raise the left wing. Nothing happened. The plane was yawing to the left. Desperately he gunned the engine at maximum power, not caring that he was burning up the last litres of gas. For a moment the Storch's slipping halted. But only for an instant. Abruptly she started to roll. The major gasped. With a curse, the sergeant caught her just in time.

The major breathed a fervent sigh of relief.

Next instant the engine went dead for good. Now there was no sound, as the propeller slowly ceased whirling, save the hiss of the wind in the overhead wing. With great deliberation, as if it were some kind of ritualistic act, the young pilot flicked off all the switches, and announced with strange, almost unnatural calmness for such a young man who might well be dead in a matter of minutes, 'Major, I'm going to have to crash land.'

'*In this blizzard?*'

'It's the only way.'

Now they were coming down in a silent, shallow dive, the snow-flakes beating at the cockpit window like vicious tracer, both men craning forward, trying to be the first to spot the ground.

'Come on … come on,' the pilot said suddenly, as if urging the earth to make an appearance. 'Give us a shitting chance!'

'There!' von Schlemm cried.

'Cover your face!' the pilot yelled with alarm. '*Quick, man!*'

Major von Schlemm threw his free hand across his face protectively. Not a moment too soon. The Storch was going into a steep dive. Down below the ground loomed up through the whirling flakes, only metres away.

With a sickening thud that sent a shock wave racing through the major's body, the hot vomit flooding his throat, the light plane hit the ground. It rose high in the air and hit the ground again. Its right tyre burst with the sound of a shell exploding. Crazily it shimmied from side to side while the pilot fought the plane bravely, eyes wild with excitement and fear.

'You're doing it … *doing it!*' von Schlemm cried in praise, lowering his protecting arm, as the plane careened through some trees, skidding ever onwards, the pilot fighting with all his strength and skill to prevent her from overturning.

A rending sound. Metal bits flew behind the plane in a glittering wake. Next moment the undercarriage collapsed. A terrible, shrieking, tearing sound as the ground ripped the plane's guts out. Metal howled unbearably. They slithered forward at over 100 kilometres an hour, enveloped in a huge cloud of snow, bits and pieces of the plane flying high in the air, on and on, as if they were never to stop, fated to go hurtling forward like this to the end of time.

Then it was over. Almost gently the snow-covered hedgerow embraced them in its tough grip and they had stopped, the two of them wet with sweat, collapsed momentarily in their seats, gasping harshly, as if they had just run a great race.

The pilot spoke first. 'Holy strawsack, Major ... we've ... we've done it!'

Major von Schlemm shook his head violently and drove away for good that whirling world of howling, rending metal. With his elegantly booted foot, he kicked at the door. It flew open at a crazy angle. He peered outside, eyes narrowed against the driving snow. There was nothing to be seen but a flat, white plain of snow reaching to the leaden horizon.

The pilot raised himself out of his seat beside him, and dropped down to the ground.

'Well?' Major von Schlemm queried anxiously, the sudden stillness somehow unnerving him, he did not know why.

'Nothing!' the pilot said miserably. 'For all I know we could be the last people left alive.'

Major von Schlemm followed him out, shivering in the sudden cold. He turned slowly, straining his ears, attempting to find the thunder of the permanent barrage. Without success. There was no sound save the soft beat of the snowflakes into the hedge. As the young pilot had just said, they might well have been the last people alive on the earth.

'What are you doing?' he asked suddenly, breaking the tense silence, as the pilot started to unscrew the cap to the gas tank, a roll of lavatory paper in his free hand.

'Standing orders, sir. We are supposed to

153

destroy our crates if we are not sure where we have crash-landed. To prevent them falling into the hands of the enemy,' he added, seeing the major's puzzled look.

Dipping the end of the roll in the gas tank, he began to walk backwards with difficulty through the deep snow, unrolling the paper, fumbling in his pocket for matches.

Hastily the major joined him. 'Don't you think the fire will give our position away?'

'That's what I'm hoping, sir,' the pilot answered, stopping now that he was satisfied he was far enough from the wrecked Storch.

'How do you mean?'

'*If* there is anybody out there and *if* they come looking for us, we can check them out. *If* they are our people we're in luck. *If* they are the enemy, we're off like the proverbial bat out of hell.'

As the pilot fumbled to strike a match with fingers that felt like clumsy sausages, Major von Schlemm considered for a moment, his mind full of his precious documents.

'Isn't that a bit risky?' he said at last.

'What other way is left open to us, sir?' the other man countered, holding the flickering blue flame to the paper. 'Look at this snow and the terrain,' he added, glancing at the major's elegant, thin uniform, as the first little flame began to burn on the paper, 'and you are not exactly dressed for an Arctic trek.'

'I suppose you're right,' Major von Schlemm agreed, 'but we must take proper precautions... For reasons that I can't explain to you Sergeant, I cannot allow myself to be captured.'

The pilot shrugged as the flame became more powerful and it began to run down the paper towards the crippled plane. 'I'm easy, sir... It's been a long war and I've already got enough tin to set up a scrapyard.'

Von Schlemm did not answer. His eyes were searching the area for a suitable place of concealment from which the two of them might well observe their would-be rescuers, if there were to be any in this wintry wasteland.

'The barn,' he said finally, 'half hidden by snow over there at two o'clock next to the patch of firs. We–' He stopped suddenly, as the pilot dropped the paper which was well alight now and cried, 'Come on, let's run for it, sir! She'll go up in thirty seconds flat!...'

The Death-Merchant stared moodily at the burning plane, his greedy, red-rimmed eyes searching the wreckage strewn all around for something that he could sell on the black market once the Eagles were taken out of the line again, while his comrades from the gliderborne infantry chattered excitedly among themselves about the Kraut plane which had appeared so mysteriously out of nowhere, just in front of their foxhole line.

'Silly cunts,' the Death-Merchant muttered to himself, bending down and picking up a piece of glittering metal with the dentist's forceps that he always used to pluck gold teeth out of dead men's mouths, his sleeve riding up to reveal the half-dozen wrist-watches strapped about his brawny arm. In disgust he dropped the metal. It wasn't worth anything. 'Nothing's worth a plug nickel here,' he cursed to himself. 'Hell, I could have just as well stayed in my goddam pit.'

Near the plane, Perkins, the troops sergeant, was shouting, 'Okay, youse guys, let's start getting organized... We're 50 yards into no-man's land. Now let's get on the stick...'

The sergeant's words were borne away by the snow-laden wind. For suddenly, directly at his feet, the Death-Merchant saw two sets of footprints, fresh and clearly imprinted, as if they had only been made a few minutes before. He bent awkwardly on one knee and stared down at them, noting immediately the marks of the nails, which told him that the boots did not belong to any Screaming Eagle. 'Hell, they're Kraut,' he whispered to himself in the fashion of a man who is cut off from his comrades and talks a great deal to himself. 'Kraut officers!'

Inside his head a sign bearing the label '25 dollars' popped up, as if on the top of a cash register. Kraut officers had Luger pistols and back in Paris's Pig Alley black market, a

Kraut Luger easily brought that from some sucker of a COMZ guy who wanted to send home a souvenir of the Big War to his Ma. The Death-Merchant ran a wet circle of red around his thick sensualist's lips. He clicked off the safety catch of the German Schmeisser machine-pistol hanging around his neck and then, as an afterthought, drew his razor-sharp machete. Face set in a wolfish grin, mind racing with the hot knowledge he was going to earn himself a large number of greenbacks in the next five minutes, he started to follow the trail, while behind him Sergeant Perkins desperately tried to get his men away from the warmth of the burning plane.

The Death-Merchant spotted the barn, half-hidden in the snow, and grinned. That's where they were. Other men would have crouched apprehensively, knowing that there were armed enemies in the place. Not the Death-Merchant. He remained erect and confident, a knowing grin on his black-bearded, lupine face. It was part of his stock-in-trade: to look absolutely, totally confident. The trick had worked time and time again when he had stalked his prey in these last six months of combat. Once when the CO had sent him back to the head-shrinkers on account of his persistent looting of dead bodies, he had heard one of them say to his colleague with a shudder,

'That creep frightens the pants off'n me! He seems to exude the very odour of the grave!'

'Jewish faggot,' had been the Death-Merchant's cynical comment at the time and he had gone back to his necrophiliac robberies uncured. Now he strode into the kill.

A sudden hard crack like a dry twig breaking underfoot in a hot parched summer. A spurt of snow shot up a dozen feet away. The Death Merchant did not pause. He continued his steady determined pace, as if nothing could stop him, knowing that this would rattle his unknown assailant. Slowly and deliberately, taking his time, that same cold smile fixed on his wolfish face, the Death-Merchant unslung his machine-pistol. He pressed the trigger. As always, his aim was perfect. Slugs ripped the length of the barn, striking up bright-blue, angry sparks as they hit the stone wall. Glass shattered. Someone screamed. The Death-Merchant smiled slowly, as if the howl of agony gave him real pleasure. 'All right,' he yelled, 'come on out now – hands up! You'll be okay... *Raus... Mak schnell... Raus!*'

His answer was a burst of machine-gun fire. But it didn't come from the barn. The high-pitched, hysterical burst of fire came beyond the field. He swung round, just as Perkins yelled in a frenzy of fear, 'Come on, guys... Beat it... *Kr – auts!*'

Two hundred yards away a long line of

men in field-grey, their rifles held at the port, were advancing towards the scene of the wrecked plane like ponderous, weary farmers.

The Death-Merchant hesitated. He knew the Krauts wouldn't hurry because they were scared of anti-personnel mines. That's why they were so slow and kept their eyes down all the time. Still, the rest of the guys were running back to the safety of their own foxholes. Should he follow? His dark killer's face contorted into a sneer. Why should he? He'd be in that barn and snatch his Luger long before the Krauts reached him. He raised his voice again, 'Okay, *raus...*' he bellowed in his crude broken German, *'mit der Hande hoch!'*

The door lurched open. A bareheaded blond German staggered out, a great pink stain on the front of his grey tunic. The Death-Merchant grinned evilly. He waited till the German, his hands raised weakly, came out completely into the open. Almost without sighting, he pressed the Schmeisser's trigger. It chattered frantically. The slugs ripped the German's guts apart. Bone and gore sprayed up in a scarlet welter. The pilot slammed against the dirty white wall and began to sink weakly down it, trailing blood behind him.

The Death-Merchant leapt forward. The Kraut infantry were only 100 yards away and they were firing wildly in the direction of the fleeing Screaming Eagles. 'Couldn't hit a barn door,' he cried exuberantly, preparing to loot the man he had shot in cold blood. A pistol barked. Just in time he twisted to the left, as a tall, elegant figure came rushing out of the barn, pistol in one hand, what seemed to be an expensive leather brief-case in the other. 'You swine,' the German officer cried in English. 'You killed–'

The Death-Merchant's Schmeisser burst into action. The German screamed. His face disappeared like a soft-boiled egg cracked by a too-heavy spoon. Desperately Major von Schlemm groped for the thermite grenade. Too late. The Death-merchant's machete hissed in a silver sweep through the air. In his dying agony von Schlemm's spine curved like a taut bowstring. The pain in his arm was absolutely unbearable. Then, with the severed forearm clasped tightly to his chest, the brief-case still attached to it by the handcuffs, the Death-Merchant was running in a crazy zigzag across the snowy field, the German slugs stitching a pattern of death at his flying heels, laughing like the mad man he was...

Book Two:
BLACK CHRISTMAS

'So they've got us surrounded again, the poor dumb Kraut bastards!'

Anonymous GI in Bastogne,
22 December, 1944

Day Six:
Friday 22 December 1944

'For God Almighty's sake!' General Mc-Auliffe snorted, 'Will somebody *please* get that goddam horror out of here!' The staff officers, crowded together in the confined, stuffy Command Post to hear his decision, hesitated. The pale-faced orderly went even paler, his prominent adam's apple working itself up and down his skinny throat rapidly as he approached the gruesome object lying, still attached to the brief-case, on the table.

Suddenly the Death-Merchant, already high on the bourbon that the general had presented him with for his find, guffawed hoarsely, and shouldering the orderly out of the way, sneered, 'Out of the way, sonny-boy! You don't need to cream ya skivvies! Gimme it!' He grabbed the severed hand, the wrist already black with congealed blood, and swaggered out with the grisly object, chuckling contemptuously. 'Fags,' was his last word as he disappeared for good, 'a bunch of goddam fairy fags!'

McAucliffe mopped his brow although it was freezing in the evil-smelling cellar, crowded as it was with officers who hadn't washed for forty-eight hours or more. He tapped the blood-stained papers that had been taken so cruelly from Major von Schlemm and said, 'So the Krauts played us for suckers, gentlemen. That surrender bit was a bluff, okay, but we misinterpreted its meaning. We thought the Krauts were going to quit here at Bastogne and that's *exactly* what they wanted us to think, the cunning so-and-sos!' He glared around the circle of unshaven, pale faces in the white light of the petroleum lantern. 'And we fell for it. Now,' he slapped the sheaf of papers, 'here's the proof of their real intentions.' He nodded at Colonel Kinnard, as if he were too upset to continue himself. 'You tell 'em, Kinnard.'

The big colonel crossed to the map pinned on the cellar-wall by four bayonets and took up a suitably dramatic pose, the cellar completely, utterly silent now, save for the hiss of the lantern.

'Shoot the works, Kinnard!' McAuliffe urged. 'Don't pull ya punches. Give 'em the unvarnished truth.'

'Yessir. All right, gentlemen, it's bad, very bad. We thought the other fellah was running out of steam. In truth it's everything else but that. According to the plans taken from the dead German officer by – that … er–' He didn't finish, but everyone could guess what he thought about the Death-Merchant. 'The other fellah has been steadily building up his strength all around Bastogne ever since the night of the 20th and is *continuing*,' he emphasized the word as if it were of special significance, 'to do so…' He let his statement sink in for a moment, then continued. 'To the south here, one whole corps of General Brandenberger's Seven Army is blocking the roads up from Neufchâteau and Arlon in the south so you can see that Old Blood an' Guts is not going to have an easy time of it when he kicks off his attack this morning.'

'Tough tittie for Georgie,' someone muttered unsympathetically, and Captain Iron Mike MacDonald standing on the fringe of the staff officers told himself that someone wasn't particularly fond of the flamboyant commander of the US Third Army.

'But that's not the only bad news, gentlemen,' Kinnard continued. 'While we've been sitting here, congratulating ourselves that the worst was over – I've heard that some of the line battalions were even starting to cut Christmas trees for a nice quiet Christmas Day party – the other fellah has been engaging in a massive build-up on the Bastogne front. According to the captured documents, he now has the following outfits out there. The 15th Panzer Grenadier Division, the 26th Volksgrenadier Division, elements of the 2nd Panzer Division, Panzerlehr…'

As Kinnard reeled off the list of German units being assembled on the Bastogne front, the staff officers turned and stared at each other, faces white with shock, mouths slightly open, as if they could not believe the evidence of their own ears.

'And according to those captured documents, the German High Command is also going to release armoured units of their Sixth SS Panzer Army from the north, as soon as they become available, which is expected to be on 24 December, at the latest. So a rough calculation gives us a German strength of some four to five divisions, plus another two armoured divisions, by – say – Christmas Day.'

'Happy Christmas,' someone sighed hollowly.

No one laughed.

Kinnard waited for a moment. 'Now what have we got going for us?' He answered his own question. 'Two things. George Patton – and a break in this goddam awful weather so that we can get air support when the other fellah's attack comes in, which it will do either on the 25th or the 26th.'

'But surely, sir,' someone protested, 'the Krauts will change their plans now they know we know what they're up to?'

Kinnard favoured the officer with a cold smile. 'We have tried to play it cunning. As soon as the find was reported to HQ,. General McAuliffe ordered that all proof that we had the plans should be removed.

The Germans who attempted to recover the bodies from the crashed plane area were driven off. Then a patrol went out, placed both bodies back in the wrecked ship, and re-lit the blaze. So far the other fellah has not made another attempt to pull in the bodies of the dead pilot and the German staff officer. But when – and if – they do, we're hoping all they'll find is charred skeletons and assume that the documents perished in the blaze.'

'Smart thinking,' somebody muttered and another voice exclaimed, 'Now that's what I call real downright Yankee cunning.' But the officer who had first objected that the Germans would change their plans persisted. 'But if we attempt to conceal from the Krauts that we know their dispositions and intentions, sir, how are we gonna get the news to the outside – to General Patton and Supreme HQ? We don't possess a high-level code. The one we've got, the Krauts can crack in half-an-hour. There is no other means of signalling the information to the outside, and it goes without saying that we are completely cut off, with as you say, sir, a whole Kraut corps between us now and the Third Army...' His voice faltered away into nothingness, as if his own realizations were proving too much for him.

Kinnard opened his mouth to answer, but McAuliffe realizing the sudden mood of despair that had spread over the cellar at the staff officer's words, said quickly, his voice full of fake, forced hope. 'Now, gentlemen, now, now, now.' He extended his hand at Iron Mike standing at the fringe of the suddenly very sombre, downcast group of officers. 'We ain't got our dongs in the wringer *that* bad. After all, gentlemen, we have got Captain MacDonald and his Bad Boys squad, haven't we?'

Suddenly, as all eyes turned curiously in his direction, Iron Mike MacDonald had a sinking feeling that he and his men were being sweet-talked into yet another mission for the Screaming Eagles. 'We're ready for any assignment you propose, General,' he heard himself say, as if speaking from a million miles away. *'Any...'*

A thin yellow sun peeped over the grey December horizon. It hung there a few minutes, trying to struggle higher. Finally it gave in, as if exhausted or beaten by the bitter, icy greyness of the morning. A minute later it disappeared for good.

General Dager sighed, as if it was yet another thing sent to try him. This morning, obviously, he would get no support from TAC Air; they simply wouldn't be able to fly.

To his front all was silent. To left and right of the village road that led out of the hamlet of Habey-la-Neuve, his start-line, the Shermans waited expectantly, buttoned down already, their commanders tensed for the signal to start, the gunners already crouching behind the breeches of their big 75mm cannon, the drivers worried that their engines might not go in the freezing cold.

All was quiet out in the snowy no-man's land that lay in front of Habey, though the scuffed snow was still littered with the debris of the great retreat of Middleton's Corps: smashed ammunition boxes, shattered vehicles, abandoned weapons, rusting wires, the shallow, white mounds from which protruded upturned rifles hung with helmets, – the graves of the many young Americans who would never see the 'last Christmas of the war', as the papers back home were calling it.

Dager focused his glasses yet again and took in the scene. Earlier that day Patton had assured him over the radiophone that it was going to be a walkover. 'You give those Krauts a real old bloody nose right at the start, Dager and they'll reel back from your start-line all the way to Bastogne!' But the brigadier-general had not been impressed by Patton's exuberance. Somewhere, out there, according to Intelligence, there were elements of the Fifth German Parachute Division, and Dager knew from past experience that the 'green devils', as the German paras called themselves fought like the very devil; they were better than the SS in a defensive situation. He sighed and lowered his glasses reluctantly.

'What is it, sir?' his aide asked, doing the same, apeing his general in everything, like all aides did.

'Don't know, Charley,' Dager replied. 'It looks too damn peaceful out there – for outlaw country. Christ on a crutch, if only some Kraut would pop off with a machine-gun or they'd give us a little bit of harassing fire with their mortars, then I'd feel okay. I'd know what to expect. But this silence–' He shuddered, whether with the freezing cold or something else, the aide didn't know. 'It's kinda unnerving, weird.'

'Oh, I expect it'll be all right on the day, sir,' the aide said loyally, as aides were expected to say in such situations, though he knew as well as his commander that Combat Command B was attacking into unknown territory, along secondary roads that could easily be cut off by counter-attacks from the flanks, and separated by a gap of 2 miles from its neighbour Combat Command A, attacking along the Arlon-Bastogne Highway where the main German resistance was expected to be.

'I hope you're right, Charley.' Drager turned and strode back to his command car, where the radio operator waited expectantly for the great order. 'All right, damn it,' he snapped, his breath fogging on the air. 'Let's not waste any more time! Give the signal...

Crank up … *and roll 'em!'*

Hastily the operator spoke into his mike while Dager turned to stare at the Shermans waiting in the field on both sides of the narrow road.

There was a low, ominous grinding, a series of backfires. Then abruptly, one after one, nearly 150 tank engines broke into life, shattering the heavy, brooding silence of the morning. Slowly the first company started to waddle forward like a group of monstrous steel ducks, belching thick blue smoke, their aerials whipping back and forth in flashes of dull silver.

Immediately Dager flung up his glasses. He knew where the trouble would come, if it were to come. The thick, snow-heavy firewood to the right. The trees slid into the gleaming circle of calibrated glass. They were perfectly still. Not a breath of wind disturbed their peace. Slowly he swept the line from right to left as the tank at point clattered onto the road, the driver gunning the engine as the Sherman took the slight rise, showering the tank behind it with dirt and snow. Now it began to accelerate, moving ahead faster than the rest of the company.

Dager could visualize what was happening in its green-glowing interior as its commander surveyed his front through his periscope in tense anticipation, knowing that he was the fall-guy – the one who was going to be sacrificed for the safety of the others. If he were hit, they would back off and wait for the combat infantry to come barrelling up to tackle the opposition; but by that time he and his crewmates might well be dead.

Suddenly Dager groaned through clenched teeth. A solitary flare flashed from the forest, burst into a ball of bright, blood-red light, bathing the snow below an eerie sheen. He caught his breath, knowing exactly what was going to happen next.

It did. A small figure in the rimless helmet of a German paratrooper burst abruptly from the firs immediately to the right of the lone Sherman at point. The gunner saw him too late; he was virtually in the dead ground as far as the tank was concerned. The turret hissed round. The para beat the American to the draw. He dropped to one knee, long tube balanced awkwardly on his shoulder. He pressed the trigger. A harsh crack and in the burst of scarlet flame Dager could see the ugly black projectile wobbling its way towards the Sherman. At that range the German couldn't miss.

The *panzerfaust* rocket struck the Sherman squarely on the side, exactly where the turret was joined to the chassis. There was a thunderous roar as the hollow-charge rocket exploded within the tank, chopping the crew to bloody pulp in an instant. Next moment the 10-ton turret sailed slowly into the sky and the Sherman was sprawled right across the road, blocking it completely, burning furiously. The battle of the Bastogne Highway had commenced, and Brigadier-General Dager's Combat Command B was stalled almost from the very start...

A shadow darted from behind the wrecked peasant cottage. 'All clear, Captain,' he reported, his soot-blackened face glistening with sweat, the whites of his eyes big and staring, making him look like one of the nigger minstrels MacDonald remembered from his youth. 'The Krauts still seem to be hitting the hay up there.'

'Thank you, Corporal,' Iron Mike hissed back, keeping his voice low although the nearest German was 200 yards away down the narrow, winding country road.

The corporal in charge of the Screaming Eagle outpost at this northern and quietest point of the 101st's perimeter touched his blackened hand to his helmet and went back to join his men squatting in their freezing foxholes.

Iron Mike turned to Dude, Limey, Kovalski and Big Red, the ones he had selected from his Bad Boys for the bold mission. 'Okay, guys,' he said quietly, looking from face to face and finding only resolution and perhaps a little resignation there. 'You'd still have a chance to back out if you want... You know I can't make you go along with me and I guess you guys have got enough medals as it is to make a decoration no kind of incentive.'

'Broads, booze and a nice soft bed, skipper, that's the kind of bribe I like to hear about,' Big Red growled.

'Yer,' the little cockney agreed, wiping a dewdrop off the end of his red, pinched nose, 'that's the kind of grub to give the troops. Ere, couldn't I just do with a great big Flemish whore with tits like turnips at this very minute! By Christ, I'd pull her knockers right over me ears and never be frigging cold agen!'

Big Red laughed, Iron Mike grinned and the Dude shook his head in wonder. Only Polack looked puzzled. 'How are ya gonna do that, Limey?' he asked, a look of bewilderment written all over his broad Slavic face.

'Forget it,' Iron Mike said hastily. 'Okay, fellahs, you're on. If you guys pull this one off successfully, I'm going to apply to the divisional recreational fund for dough enough to give you guys seventy-two hours leave in Paree – the works!'

'Now that is a war aim worth fighting for,' Limey exclaimed. 'Old Winnie with his bleeding blood, sweat an' tears never did much for me. But broads, booze and beds – that's something else!'

'All right, now let's get down to cases,' Iron Mike intervened swiftly. 'These frontline Joes will make the diversion on the road. While the fireworks are going on, we'll double to the right, through that little wood over there. With a bit of luck, all attention will be concentrated on the road. If,' he paused significantly, 'we do bump into opposition, there's to be no survivors, I repeat, *none* at all. No one's to know that we've passed this way, for obvious reasons. Clear?'

The others nodded their heads, their joking mood of a few moments before completely vanished now; for their captain's remark had reminded them again of just how vital their mission was. If they didn't get through to Patton to tell him what was going to happen in three or four days' time, it might well be the end of the 101st Airborne Division. The responsibility was almost too much to bear.

'Okay guys, the best of luck, and remember this, too – if anybody gets hit, nobody is to stay behind him to help out the guy who's bought it. *Let's go!*'

Like grey timber wolves stalking an unsuspecting quarry, the five Bad Boys started to skirt the rough stone wall that fringed the road to the right, making hardly a sound on the new snow. What noise they did make was muted by the mortar barrage which McAuliffe had ordered specially for this vital break out of the Screaming Eagles' perimeter.

Now they were only 150 yards from the unsuspecting Germans' positions ... 100. To their left they could see the pale faces of the Screaming Eagles in their foxholes watching them file by, their dark, sunken eyes clearly revealing what they thought: the Bad Boys were as good as dead. This was a suicide mission.

Iron Mike bringing up the rear raised his thumb. The corporal in charge nodded his understanding. This was the signal. He raised his flare pistol. He pressed the trigger. The red flare exploded in a blur of garish light above no-man's land. Almost immediately the men in the foxholes opened up with their BARs and MIs, pouring a tremendous hail of fire into the German positions, grouped around the stone barn further up the road.

'Alarm ... alarm!' Faintly Iron Mike could hear the surprised cry of some German NCO or other as he roused his men to meet whatever was coming their way. The captain waited no longer. 'Okay,' he hissed, 'let's move it, guys.'

Crouched low, the Bad Boys, with Big Red in the lead and Iron Mike bringing up the rear, started to skirt the road, merging into the snowy landscape thanks to the new white coveralls that McAuliffe had personally ordered for them. Any sound they made was drowned by the hammering of the Screaming Eagles' heavy machine-guns.

Now they were coming level with the German positions grouped around the barn. Iron

Mike had reasoned that soldiers everywhere, even German ones, were chronically lazy. With the temperatures below zero and the ground iron-hard, they wouldn't waste their energy digging in deeper than was absolutely necessary into the fields on both sides of the road; and it seemed he was right. Apart from a tangle of barbed wire, the German defences appeared to be concentrated around the road.

They pelted on. Before them loomed the security of the woods. Once they were there, they were home and dry. A rest to regain their breath and they could then commence the long swing around the 101st's perimeter till they hit the road network leading to the south and Patton's men.

'Look out!' Big Red's voice cried in sudden alarm.

Iron Mike flashed a look to his front. His heart sank. The Germans had been more thorough than he thought. Up ahead there was a log-covered dug-out, the logs heavy with snow so that it appeared to be part of the field, and at the entrance a man in that familiar coal-scuttle helmet, fumbling with his Mauser.

Big Red didn't give him a chance to complete the job. His grease-gun chattered noisily. The German screamed thin and high like a woman. He reeled back, his face ripped to a pulp.

'Nobody's to get away!' Iron Mike gasped.

Behind Big Red, Dude pulled out a thermite grenade, and even as the dying German sunk to the bottom of the dug-out, he flung the spluttering grenade inside. It exploded in a blinding flash of white light. Burning pellets of phosphorus sprayed everywhere. A screaming German came tumbling out of the chaos, trying to pluck the pellets that burned ever deeper into his face away with hands that were a sheet of flame themselves. Limey's heavy boot lashed out. The German screamed again, thickly. His nose spurted scarlet jets of blood and he sank back into the burning interior.

A German stick grenade came winging its way to them. *'Grenade!'* Iron Mike yelled urgently. Without even seeming to pause, Big Red bent down as he ran, grabbed it and tossed it back in one and the same movement. It exploded with a thick crump. A body, all flailing arms and legs, sailed high into the air and lodged in the skeletal branches of a great oak like some obscene human bird.

'Keep going... For Chrissake, don't bog–' He almost fell, as a pair of arms grabbed his right leg. He looked down.

An old man in field-grey was staring up at him, a look of terror in his sick yellow eyes, mumbling incomprehensible words from slack lips that quavered with absolute fear.

Iron Mike hesitated. To his front Big Red fired a quick burst from the hip. A German staggered back, his hands fanning the air. He fell down, gurgling horribly. As he ran by, Limey kicked the man in the face. His head clicked back, his neck broken, and his moaning ceased at once.

'*Bitte, nicht schiessen, Herr Amerikaner,*' the old man quavered, the tears streaming down his raddled cheeks, a look of imploring in his eyes. '*Bitte!*'

Iron Mike swallowed hard. The German could have been his father – and he was unarmed. Obviously he had been so surprised by the sudden attack that he hadn't had the time to arm himself. What was he to do?

New hope started to dawn in the old man's eyes. He could see the doubt mirrored in Iron Mike's face. He pressed the American officer's legs fervently. '*Danke,*' he croaked. '*Danke, mein Sohn. Ich wüsste, dass du mich er–*'

His words ended in a shrill scream, as Iron Mike smashed the brass-bound butt of his carbine into the old man's face. Something snapped like a dry twig. The old man stared fleetingly up at Iron Mike, a look of absolute, complete incredulity on his face, his yellow false teeth bulging stupidly from his slack mouth. Next moment, Iron Mike pressed the muzzle of his carbine right to the centre of his forehead, pulled the trigger and blasted him to eternity. Seconds later he was racing after the others, vomiting wretchedly as he ran at what he had been forced to do.

Behind him the old man died sobbing like a child in the blood-stained snow...

It was unearthly cold. The icy wind raced across the flat Belgian plain at fifty miles an hour. It lashed their faces with razor-sharp particles of snow. Their eyelashes and brows were white with hoar-frost so that they looked like very old men. Every fresh breath was like a sharp blade to the lungs. With their shoulders bent, as if in defeat, they stumbled and slid across that never-ending, blinding waste, each new step a tremendous effort.

Only habit and the iron discipline of Mac-Donald's Bad Boys kept them going – and that flickering, ever-present desire to stay alive in this hostile, white world. For even Limey, the born and eternal optimist, had no illusions about what would happen to them if they were captured now. In their white coveralls and white-painted captured German helmets, their captors wouldn't hesitate. They'd line them up against the nearest wall and shoot them as infiltrators or spies. Hadn't Eisenhower recently ordered that his GIs should do the same to any German dressed in US uniform? Now it was either, as Dude had put it in his affected, upper-class way, 'Marchez ou crevez, which for the sake of you jerks means in American – *march or croak!'*

But Iron Mike in the lead, trying to follow his chosen compass-heading the best he could in a bitter winter landscape where there were no landmarks, knew that even his veteran Bad Boys couldn't continue much longer. They needed a warm meal and a roof over their heads, for soon it would be dark and no one, not even the hardest of men, could survive a night in the open under these conditions.

Polack, in the centre of the column, had been keeping himself going for the last hour by thinking of those wonderful meals his *Matka* had used to serve him before cruel fate in the form of the draft board had whipped him away from the comfortable, stuffy, warm atmosphere of his mother's apartment with its highly coloured religious pictures and Polish gymnast club calendars. There had been steaming mounds of red cabbage and great heaps of breaded veal cutlets, home fries reaching to the kitchen ceiling, pickled gherkins by the barrelful, washed down with beer, pitcher after pitcher of it – for all that his mother was so severe and religious, she certainly liked her beer of an evening in summer. In spite of the biting cold and the rumbling of his stomach like a motorcar barrage, Polack's big face formed into a smile at the memory. Suddenly his expression changed.

He stopped and let Dude and Limey stumble by him. His nostrils twitched – and twitched again. Slowly, very slowly, he turned his head like a human radar antenna beaming in on the direction from which the smell was coming. For there was no mistaking it. Someone out there, somewhere, was cooking!

He licked his wind-cracked lips, narrowed his eyes against the howling, snow-laden wind, and tried once more to locate the source of that delightful odour.

To the right, glimpsed vaguely through the snow, he caught sight of a thin stream of blue smoke distorted and made jagged by the wind before it disappeared again. Out there, someone lived and cooked.

Polack waited no longer. He struggled forward after the others.

'Limey,' he called, 'Limey, I've seen it!'

Limey paused in the midst of his umpteenth rendering of *This is number one and I've got her on the run, roll me over, lay me down and do it again,*' and looked at the excited giant. 'Have yer now,' he said sourly. 'And did it have hair on it, mate?'

'No, no,' Kovalski said, not understanding what the little Englishman was talking about; but then, he mostly didn't anyway. 'There's somebody out there – *cooking!*'

Limey looked up at his excited brick-red face. 'This snow's getting too much for you, mate. You'd better wat–'

In his excitement at his discovery, Kovalski reached down and lifted Limey up as effortlessly as if he were a baby, grunting, 'Look, Englishman, over there. Can't you see it?'

'Blimey, what a turn up fer the books! Yer right, you big pudden, you. There *is* something over there…'

Patton pressed himself closer into the doorway of the ruined shop as the ex-cook raced for the abandoned anti-tank gun in the centre of the square. Its crew sprawled around it in the crumpled, awkward angles of the violent dead. Another GI, perhaps a clerk this one, followed, head bent, arms working like pistons as he pelted for the gun. German machine-gun fire sent sparks of brilliant blue the length of the cobbles at his flying heels.

The cook flung himself behind the shield. With his shoulder he heaved the long-barrelled 57mm gun round. The clerk, if he were one, joined him an instant later, flinging himself to the right of the breech and wrenching a gleaming shell from the three racked there behind the shield.

Patton breathed out his admiration. 'Holy shit, Mims, if all the goddam cooks were like that guy in the Third Army, I'd have won the goddam war back in Brittany last fall. I–'

The rest of his words of fervent praise were drowned, as the cook pulled the firing bar. The trails rose high in the air and came crashing down on the cobbles the next instant. The empty shell case clattered after it. Hot air blasted backwards and hit Patton in the face. He gasped for breath as the shock drove the air from his lungs.

To their front, further up the village street, the lone Mark IV which had been holding up the Fourth's advance all afternoon lurched to a stop, flames already pouring from its crippled engine. Immediately the crewmen began to drop from their various escape hatches. It was too tempting a target for Patton. Before Mims could stop him, he had stepped out into the street. Crouched low, face contorted into a killer's sneer, like some Western gunfighter in the final shoot-out at the end of a B-feature, he whipped out his twin, pearl-handled .45s.

'*Sir*,' Mims protested.

Too late. Patton aimed and fired from the hip. The tank commander slammed against the side of the burning Mark IV, blood trickling from the corner of his mouth. The driver came crawling from underneath the stricken tank. He didn't get much further. Patton's slug caught him squarely in the face as he peered out from beneath the tracks, as if from between prison bars. He reeled back howling in agony. Systematically Patton picked the Germans off, one by one, until finally all the fight had gone from him and, as if realizing that a sixty-year-old commanding general does not engage in hand-to-hand combat with enemy soldiers who could have been his grandchildren, he allowed himself to be led back inside the building next to the store where at last General Dager had finally arrived to make his situation report, the one Patton had been anxiously waiting for all day.

Dager looked at the Old Man and thought he looked grey, sick and very tired; tired enough for him to risk what he was going to say now. 'Sir, I'd like to register a protest – a very strong protest – at what you have done just now. You can do what you like in the command area of anyone else, but in my territory, sir, with the greatest of respect, I do insist that you never again do anything foolish like that. What would the Supreme Commander do if he heard that I'd allowed you to engage in a fire-fight with enemy troops?'

Dager's staff held their breath.

But the usual blistering Patton outburst didn't come. Instead the Old Man said, 'There is no better way to go, Dager, than with your boots on, while your blood is hot with battle.' He took his helmet off with a hand that trembled and wiped the sweat from the puckered rim of red it had left on his high, balding forehead. 'Sorry... I won't do it again, son. Now what's the sitrep?'

Dager indicated that an aide should shove a

chair under Patton's backside, and without objection the Old Man sat down with a little weary sigh. Outside, now that they had finally been driven from the village square by the hurriedly thrown-together company of cooks and clerks, the Germans had begun to mortar their former positions. The air was full of the sobs and sighs of the bombs, punctuated by the brittle crack and crash of falling masonry.

'It's not good, sir,' Dager snapped. 'Not good at all. The Kraut is fighting back like the very devil. It's tooth-and-nail the whole way.' He waited, but Patton said nothing. So he nodded to his operations officer.

The major unrolled the map and held it up for Dager to continue. 'We are being held up – here, here and here. If not by the Kraut,' he said a sudden bitter note in his voice, 'then by the weather or our own goddam demolitions.'

'Laid by Middleton?' Patton asked wearily, smoothing down his thin white hair.

'Yessir. They slowed the Krauts down last week. Now they're slowing us down too. Over at Martelange, for instance, CCA is held up by a crater covered by a mere squad of German paratroopers. The same thing is happening to us all along the goddam line.'

'What's your next objective, Dager?' Patton asked, his mind seemingly on something else.

'The village of Burnon, sir, here. We know the bridge has been blown over the River Sûre there, but I've got bridging equipment standing by, so that's no problem. The problem is capturing the place.' He sighed like a sorely tried man. 'If we only had TAC Air to support us!'

Patton raised his bare head wearily and looked through the shattered, glassless window. The day was as grey and overcast as ever. A few idle snowflakes were drifting down. 'Air,' he echoed. 'My God, when will they ever be able to fly again? They've been socked in for days now.'

'The prayer-man you've got, General,' Dager said with wry humour, 'ain't got the kind of "in" with the Lord that you must have thought he had.'

Patton nodded his head grimly. Then he reached for his lacquered helmet and placed it firmly on his head. 'Dager,' he said, a note of resignation in his voice, 'then it'll have to be a slogging match. But you've got to get to Bastogne soon, cost what it may. For every infantry company you lose, I'll give you a new one. But slog away.' At the door, he paused and looked straight at the younger general. 'Dager, there's something going to happen up at Bastogne – I can feel it in my bones – soon. We've got to get there in time.' And with that he was gone, the siren on his staff car already beginning to howl outside, leaving Dager staring at the closed door. He knew all about Patton's claims to have lived in other ages and to have visions, and had scoffed at them as yet another example of Ole Blood an' Guts' constant need for self-dramatization. Yet this grey December day there was something about Patton's face which worried him, made him uneasy, a kind of brooding apprehension. Dager shivered suddenly, feeling a cold finger of fear tracing its icy way down the small of his back. What was going to happen at Bastogne?

'*Carbonnade,* the Belgies call it,' Dude explained, dipping his canteen cup into the big, steaming cauldron bubbling merrily on the white-tiled stove that almost filled the kitchen of the cottage. 'Bits of beef and pork boiled in a stew with beer added.' He crumbled a C-ration cracker into the thick, rich stew and blew on it, the steam wreathing his red face.

'Tastes good, just like my *Matka's* cooking,' Polack agreed, and belched appreciatively.

'Listen, while you two characters are filling your guts,' Limey said, putting down his own empty canteen, 'has it ever struck you that somebody must have made the bleeding thing?'

'Yes, Limey,' Dude answered easily, 'one has a certain modicum of brains, you know.'

'And what does *one's* brains tell *one?*' Limey

188

sneered, maliciously imitating Dude's accent.

'That some humble peasant or other made the stew, set it off cooking while he went out to attend to whatever chores humble peasant folk have at this time of the year.'

'Go ferk me with a ferking flute!' Limey groaned. 'Pull the other one, mate, it's got bells on it.'

'What do you mean?' Dude asked, slightly aggrieved by Limey's attitude.

'What do I mean? Where in hell's name does your *humble* peasant get his *humble* beef and pork from when the ferking stuff is going for twenty bucks a kilo on the black market? What is yer *humble* peasant doing in the middle of a bleeding battlefield? And finally, what *ferking* humble tasks is he engaged on on a day like this with it cold enough to freeze the goolies off'n yer and the snow right up to your ass, eh?' He glared at Dude, his skinny little chest heaving with the effort of all that talking.

They were the same sort of questions that were going through Iron Mike's mind as, together with Big Red, he explored the cottage's out-buildings, a series of ancient tumbledown barns and sheds, smelling of stale white cabbage, animal droppings and human misery.

'Well, one thing is for sure, sir,' Big Red said, lowering his machine-pistol, as they passed from a barn into the yard again.

'What's that, Red?'

'There's been somebody hereabouts – and not so long ago.' He pointed the muzzle of his grease-gun at the footprints in the snow.

'Krauts, do you think?'

Big Red shook his head slowly. 'Don't think so, sir.'

'Why?'

'Well, you know the Kraut army? They'd skin a guy alive if he didn't have the correct, regulation number of studs in his boots. Look at those. There are studs missing in the prints everywhere. No, sir, those boots belonged to civilians, not soldiers – at least, not German ones.'

'Yes, I suppose you're right, Red.' Again Iron Mike sniffed, as he had been doing all the while out here in the freezing cold. Underlying the typical smell of a farmyard, there was another scent, heavy, cloying, slightly sweet. But for the life of him, he could not identify it. In the end he gave in, leaving the mystery of who inhabited this lonely cottage in the middle of nowhere unsolved for the time being. 'Okay, let's get back inside again, Red. It's cold enough to freeze the nuts off'n you out here. We'll grab a canteen of that stew and then bed down for the night.'

'Sentries?'

'Yeah, I guess we'd better take turns standing guard, but *inside*. Kay?'

'Kay.' Red grinned in spite of the cold. *Inside* it is, sir. Standing guard outside in this kind of weather could turn a guy into a singing tenor, right quick!'

Thirty minutes later they were all fast asleep, save for Dude who was taking first turn, no sound disturbing the heavy silence except their own snores and the faint hiss of the wind around the snowbound house. They could well have been completely alone in this remote wintry world. But they weren't...

'What the hell–' Iron Mike caught a glimpse of a broken-nosed, brutalized face, only inches from his own, peering down at him in the flickering yellow light of the candle. Beyond, Limey lay slumped at a strange angle in the chair, his rifle dropped to the ground. He tried to rise, fighting the weight on his chest.

Next instant a hamlike fist smashed into Iron Mike's face. Blood spurted from his nose. Desperately he wriggled his head to one side. To no avail. The civilian hauled back his fist once more. A whiff of garlic-laden breath flooded his nostrils. The civilian laughed coarsely. The fist struck him again like a pole-axe. Stars exploded in front of his eyes. He tried to fight off the blood-red mist which threatened to swamp him at any moment. But it was no good. The last thing he saw before everything went black was Big Red on his knees, doggedly trying to rise, as another giant in shabby civilian clothes rained blows down on the back of his big red head with a club. Then he was gone, his nostrils again assailed by that strange sweet, cloying smell...

Day Seven:
Saturday 23 December 1944

'*Nuts!*' Hitler exclaimed, his narrow brow under the dyed lock of black hair set in a puzzled frown, '*Was heist das, Jodl?*'

Colonel-General Jodl nodded to the English-speaking SS adjutant. 'Explain to the Führer,' he snapped.

The tall, blond young man flushed. Everyone knew that the Führer was an ascetic, who lived only for his people and had no interest whatsoever in the baser side of human nature. He hesitated.

Hitler looked up at him. 'Well, Heim... You are our English-speaking expert. Out with it, man! What does it mean?'

The young SS officer's blush grew ever deeper. 'Well, *mein Führer,*' he stuttered, 'it is a little difficult to explain. Basically it means the fruit of the nut-tree.'

Hitler looked from him then to Jodl's cunning, pale-as-death face. 'I am completely at sea,' he said.

'But sir, it also means in their American slang ... er ... the male sexual organs,' the adjutant blurted the explanation out. 'Like our soldiers would say – eggs.' He hung his head. '*Testicles* in other words.'

Now it was Hitler's turn to flush, but in his case, with anger. 'You mean to say,' he cried with some of that old fire in this throaty, guttural Austrian voice, 'that an American general answered a perfectly honourable demand with an obscenity like that?'

'Yes sir,' the adjutant replied in a small voice, still hanging his head, as if he could not bear to see the Führer suffer like this.

'*Himmel, Herr Gott!*' Hitler cursed, 'what kind of soldiers are these Americans?... Have they no concept of the honour of war ... the norms of civilized conduct between human beings?'

Jodl looked at the high-timbered ceiling of the medieval baronial hall, face set in a look of complete boredom. Amis were Amis, he told himself, why should they play European games? The main thing now was to give them a hard kick up the arse and send them flying back across the Atlantic to where they belonged in their remote country peopled with rough, tough cowboys, and probably Red Indians, too.

'Well, that is the limit, Jodl,' Hitler

addressed himself to his chief planner.

Jodl lowered his gaze. '*Jawohl, mein Führer*,' he said dutifully.

'Now we must show them *speedily* that they cannot treat German officers like that, in spite of the fact that the surrender offer was only a trick on our part. We must attack immediately. Bastogne must be in our hands by nightfall.'

For a fleeting moment, Jodl thought of Major von Schlemm, his courier, who was still reported missing, although the whole of Manteuffel's Fifth Army surrounding Bastogne had been alerted to be on the lookout for his plane. Yet Manteuffel's listening service which had cracked the trapped Amis' regular code had not reported any plea for aid from the paratroopers: a plea which would certainly have been winging its way across the airwaves by now if they knew what was going to hit them soon. 'There is a hitch, sir,' Jodl said deliberately keeping his voice cold and expressionless.

'Hitch?'

'Yes. Berlin reports that a high is on the way – temporarily. It will last only twenty-four hours. But unfortunately, with the tremendous air superiority the Allies possess it would be unwise to launch our great attack today. Besides, we haven't assembled the overwhelming strength, *mein Führer*, which you personally insisted we should have for the attack on Bastogne. The two SS panzer divisions won't arrive until Christmas Eve.'

Hitler's face revealed all too clearly the struggle which was going on inside him as he absorbed the new information. In many ways he was like a spoiled brat, Jodl thought, always wanting to have his own way, brooking no hindrance. But in the end he contained himself. 'Well,' he said, 'I suppose you're right, Jodl. But,' he raised his forefinger in warning, 'those Americans up there in Bastogne must be taught a lesson this very day. I will tolerate no further delay.'

'But how, sir?' Jodl asked, puzzled now.

'If *they* can fly, so can *we*,' Hitler answered. 'I want all fighter-bombers available on the Western Front assembled for a raid on the place.' A look of cunning swept into his brown, faded eyes. 'Let the Allies have their day, fly all they wish, then just before evening, when they start to return to their bases further west and will have no time for re-fuelling, we will strike them with all we have got. It must be a swift sharp lesson to those impudent cowboys!'

Hitler yawned happily. It was three o'clock, his usual time for bed. Jodl nodded to the waiting medical orderly. He hurried across with the silver tray full of the Führer's pills – anti-gas tablets, liver pills, vitamins, sleeping draughts, the whole range of drugs with which he doped himself day and night. Suddenly Hitler raised one cheek and farted violently. Jodl quickly excused himself and hastened outside into the night, sucking in great gulps of the icy fresh Hessian air. He stared up at the immense sweep of velvet, studded by the cold silver of the stars, and wondered again, as he always did these days what fresh terrors and surprises the new day would bring. Suddenly he shivered violently, but not with the cold. With the clarity of a vision, he knew abruptly that whatever happened this day at Bastogne, Germany had lost the war; it was just a matter of time...

'Good morning, General,' Sergeant Meeks, Patton's coloured servant said in his soft southern accent.

'Is it?' Patton snapped from the bed at the far end of the big hotel room.

Outside in the corridor of the Hotel Alpha, just opposite Luxembourg City's main station, soldiers were stirring and Patton told himself that the Group staff were again preparing to take off at the first sight of a Kraut. All week it had been the same. The nervous nellies of General Bradley's staff, with jeeps packed and gassed-up, suitcases stacked in the hall, were prepared to bug out at a moment's notice.

'Open the blackout curtain, Meeks,' Patton ordered and began to sip the cup of coffee that his servant had placed on the old-fashioned night table that came complete with chamber-pot, standing next to the big double-bed. 'Jesus Christ, at least, you could have gotten me a blonde, Codman,' he had complained to his aide at the sight of the bed. 'Something alive to keep me warm in that barn of a bed!'

Meeks did as he was ordered. Patton blinked suddenly. The high slate roofs opposite glittered with new snow, but it wasn't that which had made him start. It was the sun. The sun was shining a bright winter-yellow from a flawless, hard-blue December sky!

'I'm seeing things, aren't I, Meeks?' he cried excitedly, sitting up and spilling his coffee. 'That's … that's *not* the sun out there, is it?'

Meeks beamed at his boss lying old and white in the big bed. 'It sure is, General. It's been shining ever since I done got up at seven o'clock this morning, General, sir. Now, General, what you gonna have for your breakfast. There's powdered egg–'

'To hell with the powdered egg, Meeks,' Patton cried happily, flinging himself out of bed. 'Get me my uniform … and get someone to get Chaplain O'Neill on the horn at once.'

Half-an-hour later, the first flights of silver B-29s started to drone over Luxembourg City, trailing hard white lines behind them across the clean blue sky on their way to the front. As the shabby Luxembourgois cheered mightily in the streets below, Patton was talking on the phone to a surprised Chaplain O'Neill in far-off Nancy. 'Chaplain,' he barked in high good humour, 'I want you to rush over here forthwith.'

'But why sir?' the flustered clergyman asked.

'Because you're the most popular man in Third Army HQ at the moment. God damn! – excuse me, Chaplain, but I'm so damned excited – you sure did some potent praying. I guess you must stand in right good with the Lord after all.'

'But what have I done, sir?' O'Neill finally managed to break through the torrent of excited words.

'Done!' Patton echoed. 'Why, man, you've made the sun shine – and saved Bastogne... Get your ass down here at once. I want to stick a medal on you...'

'Sales cons ... mangez pour la dernière fois ... jambon ... pain ... bière...' The giant, flanked by two other civilians, both armed with British sten guns, flung the bits and pieces he had brought with him on the straw-covered floor of their place of captivity, while the eyes of the bloated corpses which lined the end of the barn stared at him in silent reproach.

'One minute,' Dude said in French. 'Why

198

are you keeping us prisoner like this? You are Belgian... We are your Allies, aren't we?'

'Are you?' the giant growled in his surly bass.

Behind him the other two clenched their free fists in the communist salute, and Dude fell silent as if the gesture symbolized for him the futility of speaking any more.

The red-faced giant with the ugly mean eyes placed the litre bottle of beer on the floor and growled *'bon appétit'* before turning to allow the other two to bolt the door behind him. Seconds later they were marching across the cobbled yard, their boots crunching on the frozen snow, leaving the five captives staring at each other in awed silence, and the food on the barn floor untouched. The corpses behind them seemed to be brooding too.

Iron Mike rubbed his chin which was red and sore where the giant had battered it with his fist in the night and said, 'Well, Dude, you're our brains, what do you make of them – and those?' He indicated the ten bodies lying in the straw. He realized now the source of that sickly cloying smell he had noted for the first time the day before.

'Well, without belabouring the point, Captain, for the last four years or so Hollywood and the papers have accustomed us to think that apart from a few quislings, occupied Europe is full of patriots burning with hate for Hitler and the Nazis. Of course, as we all know from what we saw in France, that isn't the case at all.'

'Hell, those Frogs back in Normandy last summer hated us with a passion,' Big Red said bitterly, reaching for the bottle of beer. 'They had a nice cosy thing going with the Krauts and we came along and upset the apple cart.' He flipped open the cap and took a deep, disgusted pull at the weak Belgian beer.

'Agreed,' Dude continued. 'The Jerries actively encouraged Europe's minorities and those guys out on the make for their own purposes. Why, at this very moment, there must be hundreds of thousands of so-called Allied citizens serving in the *Wehrmacht*.'

Gloomily Iron Mike nodded. Since Normandy, they'd fought Russians, Poles, Italians, even Frenchmen in German uniform. In a way Dude was right. They had become victims of their own propaganda. 'But what about these guys?' he asked, indicating the two men in field-grey among the dead Americans, their throats slit horribly from ear to ear. 'That doesn't make it look as if they are fighting for the Krauts, so why jump us?'

'You saw those guys give the clenched fist salute, sir. So that makes them just one thing.'

'Communists?'

'Yeah.'

'But the Russians are on our side, Dude,' Iron Mike objected. 'I mean, forget all those minorities who were fighting against us in France. The commies were our strongest allies in the Resistance.'

'*Were,* sir, that is the operative word,' said Dude.

'What do you mean – were?'

'Well, your guess is as good as mine, sir. But I should imagine that the word is out from Moscow not to co-operate with the Western Allies any more now that the war is as good as won.'

Limey laughed hollowly. 'As good as won... *I don't think!*' The others ignored the little Englishman, concentrating their attention on Dude, who seemed to have some explanation for the strange thing which had happened to them this day.

'Last month, the Belgie government ordered the men of the communist resistance to surrender all their weapons to the Belgian authorities. The result? The commies threatened a general strike and the British had to bring back an armoured division from the front and quietly surround Brussels, the capital, just in case of serious trouble. It didn't materialize, but you can see from the British sten guns those other guys were carrying that they didn't hand over all their weapons.'

'So you're saying,' Iron Mike said slowly, while Polack reached for the bit of air-dried blackened ham and started to gnaw on its iron-hard surface, as if hardly aware of what he was doing, 'that these guys belong to the commie resistance who aren't co-operating with us, the Western Allies? Are they working for the Krauts then?'

'I doubt it strongly, not with those poor joes there with their throats slit. I don't think that would be well looked upon in the enemy camp, do you?'

Iron Mike nodded. 'Well then in Sam Hill's name, what *are* they after?'

'Weapons, is my guess, sir,' Dude answered.

'*Weapons!*' the others echoed in astonished unison.

'Why not? What better place for a resistance movement which is aiming at armed takeover and is without its main source of supply, London, to find weapons than a battlefield! Hell, we all know what a battlefield looks like after a battle. The place is lousy with abandoned rifles, machine-guns, cannon and the like. After Normandy was over, you could have equipped a small army with the stuff lying about everywhere.'

Iron Mike and the others nodded. 'Sure, you're right enough there, Dude. So now they've got our goddam weapons, what's gonna happen to us, do you think?'

Dude did not answer immediately, his gaze wandering to the ghastly lifeless figures lying in the gloom at the far end of the barn.

'That,' he said slowly.

Polack gasped and crossed himself hastily, mumbling something in Polish, his mouth filed with bits of hard ham.

'Ferking hell!' Limey said, his humour deserting him for once. 'You can't mean that, can you?'

'I can.'

'But why didn't they do it last night?' Iron Mike objected. 'They could have done it then and had finished with it.'

'Yeah,' Big Red agreed, 'I was out cold when the bastards snuck up on me and hit me over the head. They could have croaked me easy for sure.'

'It was too quiet is my guess,' Dude answered. 'Let's say one of us started putting up a fight and kicking up a racket. At that time of the night sound carries for miles. A Kraut patrol might have heard and that would have been that.'

'So what are they waiting for?' Limey demanded. 'Come on, Dude, piss or get off the pot, man!'

'Gunfire, is my guess, or any large amount of noise. After all the ugly bastard did say that this was out last meal... I hate to say it fellers, but once the barrage starts again, they're gonna come for us...'

With a groan, Limey dropped lightly from Polack's shoulders to the floor of the barn.

'Not a hope in hell that way, sir,' he reported, indicating the hole he had made in the red-roof-tiles of the barn. 'They've got a bloke posted out there with a machine-gun. He's watching this place as if his bleeding life depended on it.'

'Shit!' Iron Mike cursed and slammed his clenched fist at the wall in frustrated fury. 'The damned red bastards have thought of everything.'

It seemed they had. First they had tried the dirt floor of the barn. But it was frozen iron-hard and their fingers had been powerless against it. It had been the same with the barn walls. They were composed of the typical mix of the area, loose slate, with a stone-dressing to the front; but try as they might with the penknife that Limey had concealed in his blouse, they had been unable to work their way through the mortar that bound the stones of the outer layer together. Now the slates of the roof, apparently their last hope, had proved disappointing too. There was no easy way out of the barn.

Iron Mike slumped abruptly down on his haunches and stared moodily at one of the German corpses at the far end of the room, his mind blank. It was as if every idea, every plan, every spark, had poured out of him. He was numb, powerless, unable to think. Fate, it seemed, had overtaken him and his Bad Boys at last. There was no way out.

Idly he listened while the others chatted about the usual subjects soldiers all over the world chat about: women, drink, and what they would do once they had left the Army. As if there would be something *afterwards* now.

How long he sat there, he never knew. It could have been a few minutes or even a whole hour. But it was only when the distant rumble of artillery started to impinge on his consciousness that he snapped out of his mood of black despair. They *couldn't* just allow themselves to be slaughtered like dumb animals, *they couldn't!* He sprang to his feet. 'Listen guys,' he snapped. 'If they're gonna kill us, they've got to get in here, haven't they?'

Limey's eyes flashed. As usual he was quickest off the mark.

'You mean barricade the door, something like that, sir?'

'Yeah,' Iron Mike answered, throwing a glance around the interior of the barn, searching for something to seal off the door, as the rumble of gunfire grew ever louder. 'They'll be coming for us soon, if that gunfire keeps up. So let's get on the stick. Let's start off with those stiffs. Drag 'em over to the door. Now, move it!'

Polack gulped, crossed himself hastily and then took hold of the first dead American. 'Sorry, buddy,' he said, and with a grunt lifted him as if he were a child.

The thunder of the guns rolled nearer and nearer and from the yard outside they could hear the first excited cries in French. The killers were coming for them...

In the cellars of Bastogne that evening they celebrated. The gliders and the supply Dakotas from their bases in France had come sailing majestically in just after midday. The German flak surrounding the town had opened up immediately. Here and there planes had been hit and gone streaming down, trailing smoke and supply parachutes behind them in their final dive. But most had gotten through. The bright-blue sky had been full of multi-coloured parachutes, bearing food, medical supplies and ammunition, cheered on by weary, begrimed Screaming Eagles.

Now deep under the frozen earth in the stout cellars of the shattered Belgian houses, they drank and sang, toasted one another, wives and sweethearts, departed friends, shrugging off the brooding melancholy of the last days, the knowledge that imminent death was waiting for them again on the morrow, becoming happily more and more confused as the bottles passed from hand to hand with increasing speed.

'Gentlemen,' someone would say, 'the King!'

They would rise and drain their drinks.

'To Marshal Stalin!'

Again the glasses would be drained.

Toast after toast followed, but always the same proud one cropped up after every few drinks, the one to their bold new name, *'The battered bastards of Bastogne!'*

Even the civilians who shared their cellars with them, living on lice-infested mattresses, carbolic acid mixed with water sprinkled everywhere on the floor to counteract the nauseating stench of human excrement, could raise a weary sad smile at that particular toast.

Thus the hard-pressed Screaming Eagles snatched a few hours away from the war, young men fated to die, feeling immortal for a little while as the alcohol took hold of them – but only for a little while.

As the full moon began to rise above the ruins, it started. Everywhere the signal gongs and the hand sirens began to shrill their urgent, stomach-churning warning. At 400 miles an hour, flying at tree-top level, the German fighter-bombers came screeching in, dragging their evil black shadows behind them over the snow-fields. Violent blue lights crackled the lengths of their wings. 20mm shells streamed towards the men suddenly flooding the streets everywhere. Great gaps appeared in their ranks. Then, when it seemed that the fighter-bombers had to crash into the first line of buildings, their pilots jerked back their sticks. The planes with their yellow and blue spinners soared high into the silver sky chased by the jagged burning lines of tracer, a myriad evil little eggs dropping from their blue bellies.

They couldn't miss. An aid station was hit and the screaming survivors, some of them minus legs and arms, crawled out into the snow to die writhing in agony. Houses on both sides of McAuliffe's headquarters vanished in a burst of crimson flame. A 500-pound bomb cut right through the roof of McAuliffe's own house, penetrated four floors and lodged in the ceiling of his command post, but didn't explode.

For one long hour, the German planes howled up and down the length of the burning town, arrogantly deigning not to notice the handful of anti-aircraft guns still firing. And then they were gone, leaving behind a sea of flames, the streets filled with men, women and children sprawled out in the melting snow like bundles of wet rags; and in the skeletal ruins the sickly-sweet odour of the untended dead. The battered bastards of Bastogne had had their few happy hours out of the battle. Now the greedy God of War had reached out his gory, blood-stained claws once more...

'Here they come!' Limey called from his

observation post under the tiles.

'How many of the bastards are there?' Iron Mike asked urgently.

Limey did a rapid calculation. 'About twelve of them, armed with stens and the other one with the m.g. But he's sticking to his post, covering the door with his pop-gun.'

Iron Mike nodded. They would have to act now, for the rumble of the guns at Bastogne – if that's where they were firing – was beginning to die away. 'Now fellahs,' he said, 'we've got to hold them. I don't think there is any chance of our getting out. You heard what Limey just said. They've still got that m.g. posted out there. They'd cut us down – *like that!*' He snapped his fingers together, as the key turned in the rusty lock of the barn's door. 'Okay, let's get to it!'

While Limey remained on lookout duty, feet braced against the rafters, the other four flung themselves behind the pile of corpses and the wood-frame wagon they had braced in a primitive kind of barrier behind the door. Big Red and Polack held the centre ready to exert their massive strength when the time came.

'*Ouvrez la porte,*' someone commanded angrily. '*Allez vite, sales cons!*' There was a series of grunts from outside as the communist partisans put their shoulders to the door and tried to push it open.

'Take the strain,' Iron Mike urged through

gritted teeth, for the pile of corpses had begun to move under the pressure. 'Here they come!'

Polack and Big Red heaved, their shoulder muscles rippling through their thick combat jackets, the veins standing out at their temples an ugly purple as they put all their weight behind the farm cart.

'*Un ... deux ... trios... MAINTENANT!*' As the partisans hit the door it opened a little. Iron Mike caught a glimpse of the ugly giant's dark, straining face, gleaming beads of sweat hanging on his bushy eyebrows. Freeing one hand, he used all his strength to fling the bottle at him they had found at the back of the barn. It was filled with their own urine. Struck squarely in the face, the giant went reeling back screaming obscenities, urine dribbling down his chin. Up in the roof, Limey yelled happily, 'Good for you, skipper. You certainly bowled that bastard a nice old googlie!'

Captain MacDonald neither knew nor cared what a googlie was. All he knew was that the pressure had been relaxed and, they had a few minutes' respite while the enemy re-thought their tactics. 'Keep your eyes peeled, Limey,' he warned.

'Like a skinned tomato,' sir,' the little Englishman answered cheerfully from his perch. Suddenly his voice changed. 'Grenades, sir!' he cried in sudden alarm. 'Jerry stick–'

'*Hit the dirt!*' Iron Mike yelled, as the first stick grenade came sailing through the gap in the door to explode with an ear-splitting roar at the far end of the barn. Splinters cut the air, ripping the woodwork apart, but passed harmlessly over the heads of the men who were hugging the dirt floor.

Polack and Big Red reacted. Just as the next grenade came hurtling their way, they flung their combined weight against the cart. It budged. The corpses tumbled against the door. It slammed shut. Next instant the grenade exploded harmlessly against the massive oak door and there were muffled yells and curses from outside as the steel splinters from the potato masher struck some of them. Above them in the ceiling, Limey called down. 'Sir, they're buggering off … a couple of them were wounded… I think they've had a bellyful – for the time being anyhow.'

Iron Mike nodded sombrely. They weren't out of the wood yet by a long chalk, he knew that. 'Keep a good lookout, Limey… They'll be back, the bastards.'

'Yessir,' the little Englishman answered. 'But one thing's in our favour though.'

'What's that?'

'The gunfire It's stopped!'

General Dager fumbled in the pocket of his parka and brought out the fruit bar from a D-ration pack. He chewed it in between drags at the fortieth cigarette he had smoked that long December day, his throat raw with nicotine. Down below in newly captured Chaumont, the weary survivors of the infantry attack which had cost the lead company sixty men were heading to drag in the stalled Shermans.

The sunshine of the day had been a mixed blessing. Although his hard-pressed men had at last had air support from low-flying 'tank busters', the winter sun had thawed out the fields and his Shermans had bogged down everywhere in the sudden mud. Almost immediately the concealed assault guns of the 5th German Parachute Division had cracked into action, knocking out tank after tank. Now, it didn't take a clairvoyant to know what they were going to do this moonlit night. As soon as they had gathered the infantry together, they would counter-attack and attempt to re-take Chaumont.

'General, sir,' his aide's voice cut into his moody reverie, as he saw the first green flares begin to sail up from the heights above Chaumont. 'It's General Patton.'

He took the radio-phone from the officer's hand. 'Dager, sir,' he snapped, trying to put professional iron into his voice, though he had never felt less soldierly; he was so tired and depressed.

'There's too much piddling around, Dager,' Patton cried in his thin, too-high voice. 'By-pass those damned towns and clear them up later! Tanks can operate on that ground now.'

Dager waited in silence. From the heights came the first squeaky rumble of tank tracks. He had guessed right. The German paras were coming back.

'Do you know, Dager,' Patton continued angrily, 'you've been going exactly thirty-six hours now and you're only a couple of miles further on than you were at dawn on 22 December. Don't you realize that those guys up at Bastogne are bleeding – and by Christ, I'm not going to have an Arnhem on my hands like Montgomery did last fall. The Krauts are not going to take out one of my airborne divisions, no sir!'

On the heights a German mortar opened up with an obscene snarl. The first bomb came trailing through the moonlit sky to explode directly on top of one of the stalled Shermans, swiping away the GIs working on it as if by magic. Dager winced. 'Sir,' he interrupted Patton's angry tirade, 'my Joes are doing their best. But they're not supermen. The terrain, the conditions, the roads are all against them, not to mention the other feller.' He waited. Down below the first white-clad infantry were beginning to appear, grouped tightly behind the leading German tanks. Even at this early stage Dager could see that this was a maximum effort. The enemy was determined to recapture Chaumont.

'Excuses ... excuses, Dager,' Patton snapped, his voice bitter and icy. Instinctively Dager knew what was going to come. It was Patton's ultimate weapon. 'Dager, if you think you can't handle the assignment, you know you can–'

The rest of Patton's threat was drowned by the chatter of 20mm cannon as the enemy fighters came sweeping in low in front of the attacking infantry, guns blazing. 'Christ on a crutch,' Dager yelled, *now this!*'

Next moment the Commanding General of CCB was cowering in the snow, hands clasped to his ears to cut out the roar, watching helplessly as his infantry broke down in Chaumont, and started to run heavily for the rear. He had lost Chaumont again...

Iron Mike sniffed suspiciously. Outside there was no sound save the steady drip-drip of some leaking tap. He sniffed again. The others did not seem to notice. They lay behind the barricade, eyes closed, heads on their chests, as if they were asleep, though Iron Mike knew that was not the case. All of them were too tense for that.

'Limey,' he called softly, not wishing to disturb his men unnecessarily, 'can you see anything out there?'

'No sir,' he replied. 'I think they're somewhere round the back. But I can't see them... Why sir?'

Iron Mike hesitated, wondering whether he was imagining the smell or not. 'I don't know, Limey, but I can smell something... I think burning...'

Limey flashed him a look, his smart little face suddenly very pale. 'You don't think.' He bit his bottom lip, as if he could not bear to pursue the thought to its end.

'I wouldn't put it past them.'

'What's that, skipper?' Big Red growled, opening his eyes and sniffing suspiciously too.

'Smoking us out!'

Polack and Dude opened their eyes with a start. 'Oh my God,' Dude exclaimed. 'Not *that!*'

Now Limey had begun crawling carefully along the rafter to the other side of the barn. With his penknife, he dug out the ancient cement between the tiles. From below a single rifle shot rang out. Limey started back, brick chippings flying into his face as the slug broke the tile he was working on. But through the hole it had created, the first sinister wisp of grey wood-smoke trickled into the barn, and Iron Mike knew with a desperate sinking feeling that his suspicions had been correct. The communist partisans were going to smoke them out into the open or burn them alive here within the barn!

For what seemed a long time the five of them froze there in silence like characters in a cheap nineteenth-century melodrama at the end of the third act; then Limey broke their stupor by dropping to the ground. 'Well, sir we know the worst, what do we do?'

Suddenly the other four were staring at Iron Mike with looks of such passionate intensity on their faces that it almost hurt. They had reached the end of the road; he was their only hope. Iron Mike hesitated no longer. Already the smoke was beginning to trickle in through the gaps in the stonework, writhing insidiously across the floor. 'There are only two ways out of here – the door and the roof. Obviously they've got them both covered.'

They nodded, eyes still fixed doggedly on his handsome face.

'Now guys, I'm not offering you much hope, but if we can fool them to our intentions, a couple of us might get away. Some of us, however, are gonna get the chop this time.'

'Better than having our balls roasted off here, sir, and not being able to do anything about it, sir,' Limey said aggressively.

'Yeah,' the others agreed. 'If we're gonna die,' Red added, 'let's kick off on our feet like real men. Sure, we can goldbrick dumdums like them. What do we do?'

'This.' Swiftly Iron Mike explained his hastily improvised plan, listening to himself with contempt as he did so, knowing it wouldn't work, *it couldn't;* that they didn't have a chance in hell of getting out of the barn; but knowing, too, that there was no other way unless they wanted to let themselves be slaughtered like dumb animals. Now they set to, making as much noise as possible, clearing away the barricade, while Limey swarmed up on the rafters again, to work on the tiles with his penknife, clearing away the mortar to an area of two square feet, enough for a man to squeeze through, but not yet removing the tiles. Then, quickly moving on, he started on another square.

As they worked they coughed dry and harsh like men who smoke too much do on first waking in the morning, blinking occasionally as more and more grey, choking smoke filtered through the gaps in the stonework and the temperature started to rise.

Now the sound of the flames crackling outside was clearly audible. Quickly they knotted their webbing belts together and attached one end to the handle of the barn door. 'Right, up you go!' Iron Mike commanded.

They needed no urging. Already the stone was beginning to glow with the terrific heat outside. Hurriedly they clambered up to the roof. Each man positioned himself behind a loosened square of tiles. Iron Mike took a last look at the door then, tucking the end of the rope of belts into his pocket, swarmed up the rafters after the rest. Panting with the effort, he commanded, 'Ready, let's go!' He jerked the belt-rope. The door flew open in the same instant that each of his men crashed through the tiles with their heads to emerge into a night that was as bright as day, the whole scene bathed in glittering, cruel, silver moonlight.

The machine-gunner was caught off guard. The door had worked part of the trick. Crazily he swung his gun up again. A burst of white tracer scythed the roof, stone chippings flying everywhere. Limey yelped with pain and started rolling down the steep roof. The others followed. There were shouts of alarm and rage from behind the barn. Men came running round the corner, fumbling to unsling their weapons, their faces glowing in the flames.

Iron Mike cursed as he slithered down the slippery roof, dodging and ducking instinctively as bullets howled off the tiles on all sides. They hadn't a chance. Once the communist partisans had recovered from their surprise they were sitting ducks on the roof, outlined as they were by the moonlight and the roaring flames – complete, total sitting ducks. Struggling to maintain a hold on the roof, Iron Mike grabbed a tile and flung it in the direction of the cursing, sweating machine-gunner, putting him off his stroke so that his next burst stitched a line of sudden holes two or three feet below the would-be escapers. But the other partisans were not so easily distracted. They started to raise their rifles. With a sinking heart, Iron Mike waited for the inevitable.

Which never arrived.

Suddenly, out of nowhere, came a great howl of racing engines. A huge black shadow swept across the snow, and abruptly the moon was blacked out. Twin cannon spat white flame at the barn. The leading partisans were galvanized into violent electric action as the first burst of cannonfire slammed into their ranks. They went spinning round, dead and ripped to red gore even before they hit the ground.

The Bad Boys did not wait for a second invitation. As the Messerschmitt zoomed high into the sky, trailing white smoke after it, prior to swooping in for another attack, they dropped into the snow below. A partisan tried to stop Polack. The big paratrooper rammed his boot into the man's crotch. He went reeling back, howling with pain, vomit spurting from his mouth as he clutched his ruined testicles. Next moment they were running into the night, as the Messerschmitt pilot, gaze fixed hard and intent on the burning barn, an ideal target, came howling in once more for the kill…

Day Eight:
Sunday 24 December 1944

'I'm dreaming of a White Christmas ... like all the Christmasses...' Limey sang the Bing Crosby song softly as they crouched there, on either side of the icy Belgian road, in the freezing pre-dawn gloom, shivering with cold.

To the west the sky flickered a faint purple in the direction of Bastogne and there was the muted rumble of heavy guns, the permanent background music to war. But the road remained obstinately empty.

An hour before, hearing the drone of a heavy motor, they had speedily prepared their trap. But the approaching vehicle had turned out to be a lumbering German truck, its back packed with sleeping infantry obviously going up the line for the day's battle – too many of them for the five Screaming Eagles to tackle. Hastily dismantling their lethal trap, they had crouched low in the frozen white undergrowth out of sight of the unsuspecting Germans as they drove by.

Now it would be light in thirty minutes or so and an anxious Iron Mike knew that if they didn't spot a likely vehicle soon, they would have to abandon their attempt. By day it would be impossible to spring their trap on the Germans.

'Christ,' Big Red moaned softly to Dude, whose face had turned a delicate shade of blue with the cold, 'why didn't I volunteer for the greens instead of the paratroopers. Hell, now I could be toasting my nuts off in some Pacific island with a couple of hula-hula gals to fan me if I get too hot. I've never been so goddam cold!'

'You get yer share of it, mate,' Limey hissed, breaking off his jungle. 'You Yanks don't know what cold is. Now if you'd have been up with us in Norway back in '40 then–'

'Knock it off,' Iron Mike commanded urgently, head cocked to one side. 'Something's coming.'

Dude said a quick prayer that it was the 'wheels' they so urgently required, anything to get out of this tremendous cold, while on the opposite side of the road, Polack, their anchor-man on account of his tremendous strength, raised the steel hawser that they had found abandoned two hours before.

Iron Mike raised his thumb and Kovalski started to wind it round the thick oak tree at his side. Now the hawser barred the road at a height of some five feet. Iron Mike seized it with his hand. It was nice and tight, and decidedly lethal. All he hoped now was that the vehicle coming down the road would be the right kind and that its driver would not know about the particularly dirty trick they were about to play on him.

'It's a jeep,' Dude whispered, straining his eyes in the gloom, just able to make out the familiar boxlike shape above the twin slits of the blacked-out headlights.

'Yeah, you're right,' Iron Mike agreed tensely, straining too to make out if the driver was armed against a trick of this kind. 'What do you think, Dude ... has he ... or hasn't he, eh?'

Dude, who had the sharpest eyesight of them all, hesitated for a fraction of a second; then he said, 'No, skipper, he hasn't... He hasn't got a bar at the end of the hood.'

'Hot shit!' Big Red chortled in delight. 'A guy can lose his head over a thing like that.'

'That you can say again, mate,' Limey agreed. 'And it couldn't happen again to a nicer bloke.' He laughed evilly.

'All right,' Iron Mike cut into their excited whispers. 'Stand by now – and remember this is our only chance. They'll be armed – the others – so we've got to clobber them as soon as the vehicle stops. Right in and at them.' He gripped his own crude club made from a piece of wooden fencing.

'Don't worry, skipper,' Big Red growled, clenching a fist like a small steam shovel. 'Those Krauts up there are as good as dead.'

They all fell silent as the jeep crawled closer

and closer, feeling its way cautiously on account of the icy road surface. Dark hooded figures could be seen outlined in its open cab. The tension increased by the instant. Iron Mike felt a nerve tic start up at the side of his mouth. He swallowed hard, his throat suddenly very dry. But still the nerve continued.

The jeep was only yards away now. Over on the other side of the road Polack, hawser gripped in both hands, thrust his right foot against the trunk of the oak around which it was wound, to give himself greater leverage. Opposite him, Dude muttered another silent prayer that the German driver would not spot it. For his part, Big Red gripped his fistful of five franc pieces and prepared to launch himself onto the jeep once it had hit their trap.

It was almost upon them, its windshield wipers ticking back and forth, as the driver tried to keep the screen from freezing up. Only a couple of yards separated the vehicle from the hawser. Then the driver did a fatal thing – for him. In order, presumably, to get a better view of what lay ahead, he thrust the windshield flat down onto the jeep's hood. Next moment he ran straight into the cruel hawser stretched tightly across the road. He gave a single scream of absolute agony as it cut deep into his throat. Instantly the jeep went out of control, and the driver, his head rolled to the ground, slumped onto his wheel. One second later the Bad Boys had risen from their hiding place. Dude grabbed the controls. Big Red slammed his fist into the face of the first German. He went reeling back, spitting out teeth from a mouth that was suddenly filled with hot blood. Coming round the rear of the stalled jeep, Limey grabbed the back of the other German's helmet. Instinctively the German dropped his rifle and grabbed for Limey's hands. Too late. The little Englishman dragged the helmet down so that the chinstrap cut deep into his throat. He hadn't a chance. Limey, his foot levered against the back of the jeep, exerting all his strength, slowly garrotted the German to death. The others quickly dealt with the other one.

Five minutes later they were on their way again, leaving the cruelly murdered German boys sprawled out on the road, already beginning to stiffen in the dawn cold...

Colonel Kinnard walked briskly into the Screaming Eagles' operations room. A corporal at the switchboard was beating time with his feet as he hummed to himself *'Santa Claus Is Coming to Town'*. He stopped and straightened up as he saw the young colonel.

'At ease, Corporal,' Kinnard said with a laugh. 'Hope you're right about Santa Claus... Is the general in?'

'Yessir, Colonel. Go right in.'

Kinnard saluted and then handed the general the message he had laboured on most of the morning. 'The Christmas message to the men, sir,' he said.

McAuliffe, hollow-eyed from the strain of the last week, nodded. 'Read it Kinnard, please,' he said.

The colonel cleared his throat somewhat pompously. 'Merry Christmas,' he began. 'What's merry about all this, you ask? We're fighting – it's cold – we aren't home. All true, but what has the proud Eagle Division accomplished with its worthy comrades of the 10th Armored Division, the 705th Tank Battalion and all the rest? Just this: we have stopped cold everything that has been thrown at us from North, East, South and West... Allied troops are counter-attacking in force. We continue to hold Bastogne. By holding Bastogne, we assure the success of the Allied Armies. We know that our Division commander, General Taylor, will say: "Well Done!"

'We are giving our country and our loved ones at home a worthy Christmas present and being privileged to take part in this gallant feat of arms and are truly making for ourselves a merry Christmas.' He looked up, but McAuliffe's dour expression had not changed. 'Don't you like it, General?' he ventured.

McAuliffe forced a weary smile. 'Oh, it's

very good, Kinnard. You ought to have been a writing man instead of a soldier. And I'm sure our poor battered bastards will like it. But,' he shook his head, 'I wonder how many of them will survive to see another Christmas with their loved ones back home?'

'News bad, sir?'

'Yes. Patton's Fourth has been stalled again, it seems. Intelligence reports the Krauts are really massing now, with new armour moving up from the north – SS, Intelligence thinks. And, of course, the crappy weather is acting up again. There'll be no air cover for us here for the next twenty-four hours. The fields in Northern France are socked in again. I don't know, Kinnard,' he said hoarsely, 'it's a damn hard row to hoe.'

'Do you think they realize the urgency of our situation here, sir?' Kinnard asked, as outside the sirens indicating a new German artillery bombardment started to wail and a shrill voice cried in alarm, 'Incoming mail, guys!'

'No, I don't. It looks as if MacDonald's Bad Boys have not gotten through to Patton, or he'd put more pep into his drive north to relieve us. My God, Kinnard, time is running out fast! If Patton's boys don't get to us soon, it'll be curtains for the good old 101st.'

As if to emphasize the urgency of the Screaming Eagles' position, three great explosions outside slammed into the side of the combat post, making it tremble and quiver.

'155mm,' Kinnard guessed the calibre of the German guns shelling them correctly.

McAuliffe nodded and wiped away the plaster that had drifted down from the ceiling onto his uniform. 'It's the softening up, Kinnard, believe you me. The Krauts are getting us ready for the kill.' He looked up at the younger officer, naked appeal in his worn face. 'For Chrissake, let MacDonald's guys get through...'

The Bad Boys reacted like the seasoned veterans they were. The clumsy German half-track started to work its way down the hill towards them and the driver cursed as the 5-ton vehicle slipped and skidded alarmingly on the ice, causing the men in the back, wearing the camouflaged tunics of the SS, to hang on for dear life. Dude calmly eased the jeep to one side at the foot of the hill as if getting out of the way. Behind him, Big Red, Polack and Limey, squeezed tightly together, brought up their captured weapons, con-cealing them behind the backs of the other two in front. The young SS driver bravely fought the big awkward half-track down the hill, not knowing that he was driving straight to his death, grinning – between gasps of fear – in triumph at the waiting men in the jeep, proud of his ability, and ready, when it had reached the bottom, to accept the tributes of his comrades in the back.

Limey, crouched behind Dude, raised his Schmeisser slowly.

'If you want the sarnt-major, I know where he is,' he sang in a harsh undertone, *'I know where he is... I know where he is... If you want the sarnt-major, I know where he is ... he's hanging on the old barbed wire.'*

'Ready!' Iron Mike hissed in the seat next to Dude, smiling wildly at the sweating young SS man, only a matter of yards away now, knowing as he did so that the youngster would spot them at any moment now. 'Dude, when I shout – *duck!'*

'Wilco, sir,' Dude snapped, eyes narrowed to slits, as the great armoured monster slithered ever closer. There were at least twenty young SS men in the back of the half-track. Their every slug would have to count. They wouldn't get a second chance.

'Now!' Iron Mike yelled. *'Duck, man... Duck, man, now!'*

As one the two men in the front of the jeep ducked. Instantly the other three rose, weapons blazing. The young SS driver screamed. A knife of scarlet flame stabbed the midday gloom. The driver reeled, his eyes ripped out, blood jetting a dark ugly purple. With a bone-jarring crash, the half-track slammed into the off-side ditch and tilted crazily to one side.

The three Bad Boys knew no mercy. They

poured a tremendous hail of fire onto the trapped SS men. Screams, curses, yells, cries of agony filled the air. Iron Mike, still crouched low so as not to obstruct his men's field of fire, could hear them gasping harshly as if in the last throes of sexual excitement. The young Germans screamed for their mothers, for mercy, for help. None were forthcoming. They died where they lay, unloved, untended, unknown...

Sombrely Iron Mike watched his Bad Boys walk from corpse to corpse, checking if they were really dead, pausing here and there, when they found otherwise, to press the muzzle of their weapons against the dying man's skull and blast him into eternity. Iron Mike didn't like it, but he knew it had to be done. Technically, he supposed, he and his men were committing a war crime; but there could be no survivors who might talk later.

Then it was done and Limey and the rest started to loot the bodies piled in the back of the half-track for food, drink, and above all, cigarettes. 'Gaspers', as Limey called them, were more important than chow at times like these. In the face of such mayhem and wanton killing, they were the only things, Iron Mike knew, which kept his veterans sane.

He gave them time, although he knew it was vital they got away from the scene of their crime before more enemy vehicles came this way. He waited until they settled down among the heaped dead, stuffing cold German rations into their greedy mouths between grateful puffs at the coarse black cigarettes, before he made his announcement. 'Okay fellers, listen to me. I'm gonna make a suggestion. I think we'd better take some of these guy's uniforms. I know the risk. We can be shot as spies, but I doubt if they're gonna treat us with kid gloves if they catch us anyway – especially after this.' He nodded at the slaughtered young men, most of them rosy-cheeked youngsters who looked hardly older than seventeen. 'It's a risk we've gotta take, if we're gonna clear their lines.' He paused momentarily. 'Are you with me?'

One by one they nodded, their mouths too full for them to speak, save for the little Englishman, who was as cocky as ever. 'Why not, sir. Only hope I can find one my size which ain't lousy.' He poked his finger into the back of the dead driver, still slumped over his shattered wheel. 'This one looks like a clean sort of lad, who wrote home to his mother every week and didn't play with his John Thomas too often.' He made an explicit gesture with his free hand. 'Five against one, or the one-handed widow, eh!'

The others laughed coarsely and once again Iron Mike, suddenly sickened by it all, wondered if his Bad Boys would ever be able to return to any kind of normal life

when all this was over; the war had brutalized them too much…

'Abrams and Jaques,' Patton snapped, his
breath fogging in the icy afternoon air, 'it's
now up to you two.' He looked down at the
two colonels, one small and squat, the other
tall, lean and bespectacled. 'If you don't pull
it off, Tony McAuliffe and his Eagles up
there in Bastogne won't get the Christmas
present I promised them on the 22nd.'

Abrams, the commander of the 37th Tank
Battalion, flashed a quick look out of the
side of his eye at Jaques, CO of the 53rd
Armored Infantry Battalion. Jaques read the
look immediately. It meant that CCB had
failed and that General Dager was out of the
running. Now Patton was throwing in his
last reserve, the Fourth Armored's CCR to
which they both belonged.

'This is good Kraut-killing weather,' Patton
went on, 'and I want you two guys to do exactly that – *kill Krauts!*' He glared at the two
colonels almost angrily, showing his sawn-off
dingy teeth. 'Now I'm moving your command to the west of Dager's CCB. You'll
group this evening near Cobreville. You'll get
the support of two 105mm howitzer battalions and a battery of 155mm howitzers, and
I don't need to tell you *that* is real muscle.'

The two colonels nodded in unison.

'The route you will take, is as follows,

gentlemen. Due east to Cobreville. From there to Reconville. Thence north in the direction of Remichampagne. After that on to Clochimont. In order not to cut into CCB's lines of communications, you will turn north-west to Sibret, entering Bastogne from the south-west. Is that clear?'

Abrams, one day to be commander-in-chief of a US Army himself, opened his mouth to object; then seeing the hard, mean look on Patton's face thought better of it. 'Clear,' he said, followed a second later by Jaques.

Patton wasted no further time. Mims was already gunning the engine of the White scout car they were travelling in now since small bands of wandering German paratroopers had taken to ambushing lone 'soft' vehicles on the roads leading back to Luxembourg. 'Gentlemen,' he barked harshly, 'I'm expecting results from you, *or else*. Good afternoon.' With that unmistakable threat, he strode back imperiously to the waiting armoured car. Seconds later he was on his way again to ginger up yet another unfortunate subordinate, sirens howling, leaving the two colonels staring a little morosely after him.

'Shit!' Abrams cursed, 'I'd never thought I'd see the day when an army commander briefs two lowly battalion commanders on tactics. Things *must* be bad!'

Jaques grinned, eyes gleaming mischievously behind his steel-rimmed GI glasses. 'You know, the Krauts have a saying, old buddy, that the soup is never eaten so hot as it's cooked. We screw this one up and we're out on our necks. We succeed and believe you me, Old Blood an' Guts is not gonna ask if we stuck to the tactics and routes he prescribed for us. So what do we do?'

Abrams answered the rhetorical question for him. 'We do it our way.'

'Exactly, so let's get the lead out.'

'Yeah, let's get the lead out!' Abrams echoed enthusiastically.

Like two excited schoolboys just released from school after a long, boring day, they ran back to their command cars, while their men stared at them apprehensively, knowing that such enthusiasm could only mean battle and danger...

'Holy Jesus,' Big Red breathed as Dude braked the crowded jeep behind the cover of a grove of snow-heavy firs, 'willya get a load of that!'

Polack gasped and Limey whistled softly through his dingy front teeth. 'Cor ferk a duck, there must be half the Jerry army down there!'

Iron Mike raised the binoculars he had taken from one of the slaughtered Germans and focused them, shading the glass so that it did not reflect in the weak yellow afternoon sunshine. He swept them the length of the armoured columns below. Camouflaged with fir-branches and netting, or painted a bright white to blend in with the snow, was tank after tank: the loot of half the armies of Occupied Europe, Russian T-3s, Skodas, the Char Bs of the French Army, plus the latest productions of the Reich's war factories, row upon row of Panthers and Tigers, hedged in by the great lumbering Ferdinand self-propelled guns. Iron Mike did a quick calculation and reckoned there were at least two whole German panzer divisions sheltering in that tight valley below.

'Wow!' Big Red breathed, leaning over the windshield, naked longing in his red-rimmed eyes, 'what a target that would make for the tank-busters! I've never seen so much Kraut armour crowded together in one place like that before.'

Iron Mike nodded glumly. Big Red echoed his own unspoken thoughts. It *was* a tremendous target, one that every fighter-bomber pilot would have given his eye-teeth for the opportunity of hitting. But they hadn't seen a single plane all day ever since they had captured the jeep. Presumably the Allied air-fields back along the coast in Northern France were socked in again.

Limey spat angrily into the snow over the side of the jeep. 'You know what those Brylcreem blokes are like. They're probably trying to get up some Frog popsy's knickers at this moment, or getting plastered in the mess. What do they care for the ferking infantry?'

Iron Mike grinned. He had never heard an infantryman say a good word for the Air Force yet, British or American. He supposed it was partly due to envy. After all, the average pilot could go back to base for a warm meal and into a warm bed after his few minutes in combat; the infantry just stayed in place in his freezing miserable foxhole.

'Well, fellers,' he said, putting his binoculars back in their case, 'there's nothing we can do about it – at the moment.' His grin vanished at the sudden thought. 'But one things is for sure. Those panzers down there mean one thing only.'

'What's that, sir?' Dude asked.

'They're massing for the big attack – on Bastogne. If we don't get through and inform General Patton what's going on up here–' He left the rest of that unpleasant thought unspoken.

For a while they lapsed into a heavy brooding, silence while below black-clad German tankmen busied themselves with their vehicles. Some were preparing tar-pots to place under their engines to warm them up for the moment when the order to move came; others were stacking fresh ammunition inside the turrets; thrusting brushes down the barrels of the long, overhanging 75mm and 88mm cannon, or slinging 50-gallon drums of fuel into their metal decks – carrying out all the hundred-and-one tasks to make them ready for the big push. In spite of the freezing cold, for the most they looked hard and confident, their smooth, young faces flushed with good health. Iron Mike noted gloomily the contrast with the bearded, worn looks of his own men who bore a haunted – even hunted – aspect in their red-rimmed eyes. Veterans though they were, even they were slowly reaching the end of their tether. They wouldn't be able to stand much more.

'Fellers,' he said breaking the heavy silence, 'this is the drill. My guess is that we're about a dozen miles from our own guys.' He indicated the flickering pink lights on the horizon to the south-west. 'That can only be the Third Army. Now, if we've still got enough gas,' he looked at Dude and the latter nodded to signify they had, 'we should be able to reach the Kraut line by evening. There we abandon the wheels. From there on in we hike.'

They gave a collective groan, but Iron Mike knew they realized, too, that they hadn't a hope in hell of getting through the frontline in the jeep. The 'front swine' as the German footsloggers called themselves, were no different from their American opponents; they shot first and challenged afterwards. That way you lived a little longer in the line.

'You know the ordinary routine of the line, fellers. As soon as the front quietens down – say, around midnight – the usual Joe tries to get a little shut-eye, even the ones who are supposed to be awake and on guard.' He looked piercingly at Limey, whom he had twice caught sleeping at his post in Normandy.

'Sleeping sickness, guv,' the little Englishman said quickly, 'caught during my long service for King and Country in the Empire 'pon which the sun never sets.'

'My ass,' was Iron Mike's unfeeling comment before he continued. 'So the way I see it we've got between midnight and the usual pre-dawn stand-to to get through their lines. It's going to be hairy, I know. One slip and we can find ourselves in real trouble – and, of course, it's going to be colder than a witch's tit out there in the open tonight. There could be mines too – ours and theirs. Then–'

'Hold it, hold it,' Limey pleaded in mock misery. 'You'll be having me pissing meself in a minute, sir, you're laying it on so thick.'

Iron Mike grinned. 'Yeah,' he admitted, 'I suppose I am.' Then his grin vanished again and his men watching him could see that even Iron Mike was beginning to feel the strain of this terrible trek through a winter wasteland where every man's hand was against them. 'I kid you not, guys, it's going to be tough, plenty tough, but–' he indicated the massed panzers down in the valley below, already beginning to vanish in the late afternoon gloom – 'we're gonna do it. We've got to, if we're gonna save the good old 101st. Okay, hit the rubber.'

Obediently Dude slammed home first gear. Iron Mike took one last look at the Germans and their machines of death and then they were gone, labouring their way up the narrow path into the fir-covered hills beyond.

Von Manteuffel, neat, determined and aristocratic, firmly in charge of the tall divisional generals of his Fifth Panzer Army who crowded around him in the hall, despite his diminutive size, nodded to the orderlies. Hastily they began to draw the heavy, felt blackout curtains, while others started to light the candles stuck in the necks of empty champagne bottles. Impatiently the little corps commander, who had once been a gentleman jockey in another and happier age, waited for them to depart. He nodded again at the burly, steel-helmeted chain-dog at the door, the silver crescent of his office glistening in the candle-light. He unslung his machine-pistol and strode out to post himself outside the door.

Manteuffel breathed out. 'Gentlemen,' he announced in a solemn voice, as befitted the occasion, for he knew better than most that the future of the great counter-offensive in the West, on which the fate of the Third Reich rested, would be decided in the next forty-eight hours, 'the moment of decision has come. Tonight we attack.'

He allowed his generals a moment or two to absorb the news, noting automatically – experienced commander that he was – that there was no fear in their eyes at the decision; they were confident, not only the SS generals who were always confident (because they were usually brave fools), but also his *Wehrmacht* commanders, many of them men like Bayerlein, who had been chased halfway across Western Europe by the victorious Anglo-Americans.

'*Meine Herren,*' Manteuffel continued, breaking into their excited chatter, 'to the south, as some of you know, General Patton's Third Army is attacking, attempting to break into the pocket, but Heilmann's Fifth Parachute Division is doing an excellent job of holding off that cowboy general of theirs. However, there are reports that Patton is attempting to put a whole US corps into the drive. These reports shouldn't alarm us unduly because of the scant road network in the area Arlon-Neufchâteau-Bastogne, for – as we all know – the Americans can do

239

nothing without wheels – and wheels demand roads. It is my considered opinion that we have nothing to fear from that quarter for the time being and by the time Patton wakes up to what is happening, we shall have captured Bastogne.'

'Hear, hear, hear,' several of his listeners muttered enthusiastically, and the SS commander's eyes sparkled with that arrogant fanaticism of theirs. For a moment Manteuffel, the traditionalist, feared they might well click to attention, shoot out their stupid right arms and bellow '*Sieg Heil*' as they seemed wont to do at the slightest excuse.

He hurried on. 'Now, gentlemen, I think that I have convinced Jodl to accept the small solution for the time being. That means we postpone the drive for Antwerp and concentrate on crossing the Meuse and the capture of that damned place, Bastogne. Mind you, the Führer will be on our tails immediately he becomes aware of what we are about. He will change our orders immediately, but for the time being I think we shall be able to continue to fool him, at least long enough to lance that festering spot up there.'

Lammerding of the 2nd SS Panzer Division flashed an angry and inquiring look at Priess, his corps commander, but the hard-faced SS general showed no emotion. Lammerding flushed and told himself that these days *Wehrmacht* generals could get away with rank treason with impunity.

'So, gentlemen, I am giving you exactly twenty-four hours to deal with the problem. You all have your orders already,' he looked at Bayerlein whose men would bear the brunt of the great attack, but said nothing. Instead he clapped his hands. The chain-dog opened the door. White-jacketed orderlies bearing silver trays started to file in, as if they had been waiting out there in the cold all the time. Immediately they began to fill glasses with ice-cold Schlichte out of the well-known stone flasks, handing a glass to each general with an elaborate bow.

The little corps commander in his riding boots waited till each general had a glass of the potent Westphalian gin, then he raised his own, a sudden cautious smile on his taut, clean-shaven face. '*Meine Herren,* a toast,' he barked, the complete Prussian now.

The generals raised their glasses with the precise formality of the old Imperial Army, in which they had all served as young lieutenants, glass level with the third tunic button, elbow set at a right angle, head thrown well back.

Manteuffel flashed a quick glance around their tense, hard faces. Satisfied he rapped, 'Bastogne – by Christmas!'

'Bastogne – by Chrismas!' they cried in unison.

'Prost!'

'PROST!'

As one, they bent their shaven heads to their glasses, took a great draught, throwing their heads back to do so, and drained the glasses without a pause for breath. Next moment glass after glass shattered against the nearest wall, flung by the generals with the same vigour and enthusiasm they had displayed as young officers in another war.

Manteuffel took one last look at their suddenly flushed faces, their eyes sparkling with the potent spirit. He told himself if anyone could do it on the morrow, it would be these men, the victors of battles over three continents. The fate of Bastogne had been sealed. Nothing would stop him now. He touched his hand to his shaven head. 'Gentlemen, you attack at midnight...'

It was a sound unlike any the Battered Bastards of Bastogne had ever heard before. As the weak yellow ball of the winter sun started to slide over the grey horizon, there was a dull roaring like the groan of some primeval monster in abject pain. Once ... twice ... three times. A flash of hard pink light stabbed the grey. In their foxholes and from among the shattered ruins they stared in wonder, rubbing their unshaven chins. What could it be?

Now the sound became a high-pitched howl, elemental in its fury. Everywhere the sky was streaked with fiery-red bolts of light. Suddenly they came plunging down, and the very earth shook under the impact of one tremendous explosion after another. The bombardment of the whole length of the 101st's perimeter had commenced. Being thrown against them was the most terrible weapon in Hitler's armoury – a full artillery brigade of captured 'Stalin Organs', as the German soldiers called these awesome rocket-launchers.

The American paratroopers quaked before the most terrifying onslaught they had experienced in six month's combat, cowering in their holes in abject fear as the ground reared and bucked like a wild horse being put to the saddle for the very first time. The shelling merged into one continuous cyclonic roar as rocket after rocket plunged down on the perimeter, each curving a glowing frightening parabola before exploding like a volcano spewing forth flame and fire.

On and on it went. Some men went mad, babbling like crazy children. Others killed themselves. A blessed few lapsed into unconsciousness, soaked with their own urine and faeces. But the rest, trapped in the heart of this fiery cauldron, had to endure it. Huddled together, trembling with fear, tightly clenched fists pressed in their ears, mouths wide open to prevent the blast waves from smashing their eardrums, eyes wild and staring with overwhelming, unreasoning terror, they stuck it out.

Now closer at hand, the German mortars added to the fury of the bombardment, their bombs reaching high into the burning sky before plummeting straight down on the foxhole line, churning up great steaming craters in the earth like the work of some monstrous mole.

A dozen miles away, the Bad Boys crouched in the frozen undergrowth, awed even at that distance by the tremendous barrage; but frightened, too, of what lay ahead of them.

They had abandoned the jeep an hour before. In single file, fingers clutching the triggers of their weapons, they had marched across what appeared to be empty countryside, and Iron Mike had guessed that they were approaching the front. For the front was a lonely place, where the number of men to be found thinned out rapidly the closer one got to danger. Still, he was glad of the emptiness, for a full moon had begun to rise, flooding the snowy fields with a hard, cold silver light, and the wind had dropped so that sound carried for miles.

Twice he had stopped and placed his ear to the ground to see if he could pick up any sound apart from that of the bombardment falling on the dying town to their right; and twice he had heard nothing. It seemed that

they were quite alone in this vast, danger-
ous, snowy landscape.

But now all that had changed. About eleven
o'clock, with a weary Limey muttering that
this was a 'bloody fine old Christmas Eve ...
not even a ruddy pint of ale to celebrate
with', they had spotted the long line of dark
figures on the skyline and recognized the
squat, stark silhouettes of massed vehicles.

'Ours?' Dude queried anxiously.

Iron Mike shook his head grimly. 'Not a
chance,' he said. 'They're Kraut all right,
moving up for the attack on Bastogne. All
right, off the track... We'll make less noise
that way.'

That had been fifteen minutes before.
Now, shivering with cold and perhaps fear
too, they crouched behind a row of firs,
probably planted as a snowbreak along the
side of the highway on which the German
column now waited. As they wondered how
to get across, they listened to the Germans
chatting softly, glowing cigarettes cupped in
their hands, occasionally leaving the road to
urinate in the ditch in a hot hiss of steaming
liquid.

Iron Mike was taking his time, although he
knew the biting cold was sapping the will of
his hungry, exhausted men. But he knew
haste would be fatal. Somehow or other
they had to cross that road through the
German line, for the column extended as far

as the eye could see; the detour would be too great for his Bad Boys. They were about at the end of their strength as it was.

'Dude,' he whispered, not taking his eyes off the dark figures of the Germans only 100 yards away or so, 'you still got a time pencil and some sticky?'

'Time pencil, yes... Sticky I don't know... Hang on,' Dude fumbled in his pockets with clumsy fingers. But even before he replied in the affirmative, Iron Mike could smell the familiar acrid odour of bitter almonds. 'Yessir, it might be about an ounce or so.'

'Enough,' Iron Mike said. 'You other guys, did you take those Kraut stick grenades in the jeep?'

'I got one in my boot, sir,' Big Red growled.

'Me, too, Captain,' Kovalski said.

Iron Mike gave a weary smile. At least that was a start. 'Now listen, we can't wait here all night until they decide to move. We've got to get across. Now we're in Kraut uniform so I don't think we're in trouble right at the start. But once we get close enough, somebody is going to challenge us. I mean what the Sam Hill are we doing wandering about the countryside at this time of the night?'

'That's what I've been asking myself all along,' Limey said miserably.

Iron Mike ignored the comment. 'So for that exact moment when somebody up there challenges us, we need a diversion. Then it's every man for himself. Go like a bat outa hell for that wood over there, where – God willing – we'll meet up again.'

'But what kind of diversion, sir?' Dude asked.

'Give me that plastic and the grenades and I'll show you,' Iron Mike answered. Quickly he bundled the grenades together and clapped the sticky brown explosive, which looked like a piece of kids' modelling clay, against their side. Holding up the time pencil, he gritted his teeth.

The timing of pencils was notoriously difficult to get right. In the factories where they were made, the workers always made minute differences in the amount of acid with which they filled the devices; or the thickness of the metal which separated the acid and the explosive varied slightly; so that one could never set them for a certain number of minutes with complete, reliable accuracy.

Iron Mike made a quick calculation. It would take them three minutes to reach the embankment below the road, going at a leisurely pace. Thereafter there would be, perhaps, another minute before the Krauts challenged them and they replied, still plodding up the steep side like the weary patrol they would pretend to be. With luck they would be on the road itself when the thing went off. He said a quick prayer and set the pencil for exactly four minutes. He thrust it into the plastic mass and said, 'Right, let's go.'

Strung out in single file, spaced at 5-metre intervals, weapons at the port, to give the appearance of a returning reconnaissance patrol, the five Screaming Eagles plodded straight for the German positions, their hearts beating furiously. Their faces were bathed and greased with sweat in spite of the freezing cold, for each man knew he was a perfect target in the hard silver light of the full moon.

Time passed leadenly. On the road, the Germans continued to chatter. No one seemed to have noticed them yet. Now they could hear the crunch of heavy nailed jackboots being stamped on the frozen ground as the Germans tried to warm their feet. Up front some officers were gathered, nightglasses focused on the burning fires on the horizon which were Bastogne. Iron Mike swallowed hard and thanked God for that small mercy, in spite of the fact that their comrades were dying over there; at least it made sure the Germans' attention was not directed elsewhere. Now they were 25 yards away from the road. The lumbering outlines of the white-painted Tiger tanks with their huge, overhanging cannon were clearly visible. Still no one challenged them.

Ten yards… Another few steps and they would be at the foot of the embankment. Behind Iron Mike, Polack, who had been born in Austria-occupied Galicia and had spoken German as a child before the family had emigrated to the States, wet his lips and cleared his throat nervously. Iron Mike, for his part, curled his finger around the trigger of the German Schmeisser, just in case.

Now they started to climb the embankment, slipping and slithering on the frozen snow. Heads began to turn in their direction, idly curious. Iron Mike swallowed hard. They were getting away with it. Now everything depended upon that damned English time-pencil. He said a quick prayer that it had not been made on a Monday after a weekend on the booze in the local pubs, spending the inflated wages that weapons factory workers made these days.

'*Halt … wer da?*' The challenge cut into him like a knife. He jumped with shock, his breath fled, as if someone had just punched him in the guts.

Still his men reacted automatically. Like men too worn out to react swiftly, they continued the climb as if nothing had happened. Somewhere a rifle bolt snapped back with a metallic click. More and more of the German tankmen were turning to look at them struggling up the embankment.

'*Was machen Sie da?*' a harsh official voice, used to giving commands and having them obeyed, snapped. '*Wer sind Sie, Mann?*'

'*Patrouille, Feldwebel ... wir waren dadruben,*' Kovalski tried in his strangely accented German. Even though Iron Mike spoke only a few words of the language he knew that Polack was not going to pull it off. More and more weapons were being raised and pointed threateningly in their direction. In a minute he knew the Krauts would order them to halt or they would shoot. Still they kept on, every nerve tensed, ears cocked, waiting for the noise of their diversion, and then they would break and run.

'*Bleiben Sie stehen ... oder wir schiessen!*' The harsh voice barked again and instinctively Iron Mike knew that this was it. Another step and the Germans standing all round would fire. What was he to do?

Then it happened. From their former hiding place behind them came a loud crump followed a second later by a blinding sheet of flame as the two grenades and the plastic explosive detonated. Iron Mike waited no longer. 'Run for it, boys!' he yelled, as the Germans started to shout and somewhere a whistle shrilled. In a flash they were up and onto the road. A big man tried to stop Iron Mike. He was too close for the American to fire. Instead he jerked up his Schmeisser. The steel frame butt collided with the man's chin. His knees sagged like those of a newborn colt. Big Red blundering up behind Iron Mike thrust out his big paw like a footballer warding off a tackle. The sagging German slammed against the side of the nearest Tiger.

Now there were shouts, curses, cries, orders, counter-orders everywhere. In the confusion some of the German soldiers knelt and started to loose off wild volleys in the direction of the explosion. It was an opportunity that the Bad Boys could not waste. Kicking and lashing out at dark figures on all sides, they broke through the line of tanks. In a flurry of snow they pelted down the other side. Arms flailing like pistons, heads tucked well down, waiting for the hard thwack of tempered steel in their backs, they tore across the snowy fields in crazy zigzags, tracer cutting through the air behind them, slugs chopping up the snow on all sides, heading desperately for the safety of the dark firs...

In Bastogne the shelling had ceased, but its echo lingered on as the dazed survivors crawled out into the smoking streets to assess the damage. Some still tried to forget what must soon come. In the vaulted chapel of Bastogne's seminary, soldiers and officers stood in the transept. Slivers of silver moonlight slid through the holes in the great

251

sheets of canvas covering the broken stained-glass windows. Snow drifted sadly from the cracks in the shattered roof. Together they sang.

O, little town of Bethlehem
How still we see thee lie

Wounded Screaming Eagles lying on the icy floor, wrapped in the multi-coloured parachutes of the supply drop, listened in silence; even the combat fatigue cases had ceased their crazed babbling.

Yet in thy dark streets shineth
The everlasting light;
The hopes and fears of all the years
Are met in thee tonight.

The carols went on. '*Silent night, holy night,*' the impromptu choir sang, and here and there a grievously wounded paratrooper attempting to join in in a quavering broken voice. Near the altar, a boy with both legs severed who wouldn't last the night wept silently for himself and his mother.

As the clock of the great seminary began to sound the strokes of midnight on Christmas Eve 1944, the hard-boiled joking in the foxholes of the perimeter ceased. Men shook hands solemnly and in silence. There was no bravado, no pathos, only an unspoken agreement among men who had fought, whored and drunk together these many years that this might be their last night on earth...

Day Nine:
Monday 25 December 1944

Now the night silence, disturbed only by the muted roar from Bastogne, had taken on a new character. It possessed a strange, brooding quality which gave Iron Mike the eerie sensation that someone was just behind him, stalking the Bad Boys on silent feet. More than once he fought the desire *not* to look behind – and lost every time.

They cleared some German positions which had been abandoned perhaps only hours before. The dampened fires were still smoking fitfully and the cans they scooped up just in case there was anything left to eat in them were still warm.

'They must have taken off in a hurry, skipper,' Big Red who was bringing up the rear with the officer, growled.

'Yeah,' Iron Mike agreed, 'I think it's the big push. They're probably thinning out the line holding back Patton, or perhaps they're attacked in the opposite direction. Let's

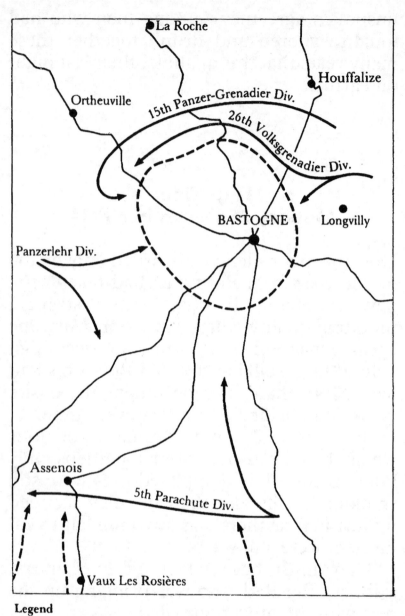

La Roche

Houffalize

Ortheuville

15th Panzer-Grenadier Div.

26th Volksgrenadier Div.

BASTOGNE

Longvilly

Panzerlehr Div.

Assenois

5th Parachute Div.

Vaux Les Rosières

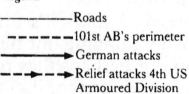

Legend

——————— Roads

– – – – – – 101st AB's perimeter

———► German attacks

– –►– –► Relief attacks 4th US
Armoured Division

hope so. It means our chances of getting through the Kraut lines are increased.'

They plodded on. Now the sounds of battle to their front were getting louder. There was the rapid hiss of machine-guns, punctuated by the snap-and-crack of rifle fire and the heavy, stomach-churning thump of mortars.

They started to move through a wood of firs, hugging the side of what was probably a pre-war logging trail, reinforced by thin boughs laid horizontally to take heavier wartime traffic.

'Looks like the kind that our engineers put down,' Dude in the lead observed. 'Perhaps we're nearly there now.'

'Perhaps,' Iron Mike echoed without enthusiasm. He didn't want to raise the Bad Boys' hopes. 'Just keep your eyes peeled up there at point. We could soon be running into their second-line positions.'

Time passed. Now Iron Mike knew they were definitely getting closer to the fighting line. At regular intervals, green, red and white signal flares sailed into the hard night sky, summoning help, ammunition, reinforcements. It seemed as if the Krauts holding Patton back were under heavy attack.

They had just crossed a large fire-break carved in the forest, the kind of place where the enemy usually set-up his deadly fixed-line machine-guns and his trip-wires attached to those fiendish 'bouncing Betty' anti-personnel mines which peppered a man's crotch with a dozen cruel steel balls if he were unlucky enough to step on one of them. Just then Dude called out softly, 'Engines ... tank engines, sir!'

As one they dropped into the snow-filled ditch at the side of the road, hearts thumping, ears cocked to the sound.

But it did not increase in volume, continuing to throb steadily with none of the sudden roars and bellows that tanks make when they are being steered round corners and the like.

Iron Mike rose to his feet cautiously. 'I think it's a tank motor idling ... somewhere ahead of us up the track.' He clicked off his safety catch. 'Come on.'

In single file they edged their way down the line of spiked, intensely black shadows cast by the firs, moving like grey ghosts. They turned a bend.

Parked in the middle of the trail, protected from observation from above by the interlocking of the trees' top branches, were two white-painted tanks, engines running. A little to the side stood a small group of men warming their hands on a primitive earth-and-gasoline fire that was flickering fitfully in a can.

'Brother,' Big Red hissed, clicking his safety catch on, 'those tanks are a sight for sore eyes – they're Shermans, skipper!'

'And those guys at the fire are GIs,' Polack agreed enthusiastically.

'Perhaps from the Fourth Armored.' He made as if to walk forward.

Limey held him back in time. 'Hold it, dumbo,' he hissed. 'You never know these days. Besides those guys could shoot first and ask questions later. Let's do this scientific.'

'Yeah,' Iron Mike said, 'if they heard your accent first, Limey, they'd shoot us as spies for sure. Remember we *are* dressed in German uniform. Okay, now let's get these helmets off – and open those camouflaged smocks so that they can see the US gear underneath... Dude, you go first, we'll cover you. Sling your grease-gun and walk nice and slow. Shout loud and clear – and don't take any chances... Okay, off you go.'

As casually as he could, Dude stepped out from the shadows and began to walk slowly down the trail to the flickering fires, while in the shadows the other four edged ever closer. 'Hi, you guys,' Dude called when he was within 50 yards of the tankers, 'don't shoot! I'm American.' He held his hands up high. 'Don't shoot... I'm from the 101st, guys ... honest!'

The men grouped round the fire jerked round violently, hands falling to their pistols, then as Dude continued to advance, their hands dropped away again and Iron Mike felt a wave of relief surge through his body. They had made it. They had linked up with the Fourth. These were their own fellows.

A big sergeant in a leather tank-helmet left the circle of the fire. 'Did you say you were from the 101st?' he asked in what appeared to Iron Mike to be a Chicago accent.

Dude lowered his hands gratefully, a big smile spreading across his peaked, unshaven face. 'I certainly did, Sergeant,' he answered joyfully, 'and boy, I could do with a cup of that java you've got—'

The words died on his lips. A figure in a dark un-American uniform was clambering from the turret of the second Sherman wiping his greasy hands on a piece of cotton waste, as if he had just completed a repair.

'*Krauts!*' Iron Mike yelled in sudden alarm. '*Beat it, Dude!*'

In that same instant, he raised his Schmeisser and snapped a quick burst at the group around the fire. The can went over, spitting blue flames everywhere. A German fanned the air with frantic hands. Another slammed into the side of a Sherman and slumped there, a line of bloody button-holes stitched the length of his chest, while the others scattered crazily, fumbling for their pistols.

The wild burst of fire had alerted someone in the second tank. As the man with the cotton waste ducked inside the turret, slugs ripping the length of the armour, it started to swing round with a soft electric purr. The Sherman's long 76mm cannon was being brought to bear down on the Bad Boys.

Iron Mike didn't wait for the inevitable to happen. 'Run for it,' he screamed urgently. 'Back into the trees... *Quick!*'

Not a moment too soon. As they blundered frantically back the way they had come, fighting the clinging embrace of the firs, stumbling and slipping in their haste on the frozen roots, the 76mm fired. A shell roared through the trees like an express train. It seemed to pass only inches above their bare heads. Next instant it exploded 50 yards away.

Iron Mike was swept off his feet. He slammed against a fir, gasping for breath, the air snatched from his lungs. Like a choking asthmatic he staggered on, following the trail of broken branches and snapped firs wrought by the explosion, the cries of rage and alarm behind him getting ever less...

Ever since midnight, Abrams' tanks, laden with Jaques' armoured infantrymen, had been zigzagging up and down the Belgian lanes and forest trails. Time and time again they were just about to congratulate themselves that finally they had found a clear run, when there was the quick burr of a German MG 42 from the trees on both sides, and yet another roadblock held by the German 'Green Devils' had loomed up out of the glowing darkness. Once again they began the weary, bloody business of trying to break through or back off in an attempt to find another route to Bastogne.

CCR's progress was bitterly costly. Behind the lead companies, Abrams' force left a burning, blackened trail of knocked-out Shermans and White scout-cars filled with dead men. Jeep after jeep bearing its wretched cargo of human misery bumped its way back down the shell-pitted icy roads to the forward dressing stations, where the harassed sweating surgeons operated like automatons in the light of hissing gasoline lanterns, slicing, hacking, sewing, binding, while the orderlies fed them black coffee and dabbed the sweat from their glazed foreheads.

Christmas Day 1944 was the coldest day of one of the worst European winters in living memory. Inside the stations blood plasma and morphine syrettes froze up. Outside, so did the weapons, their lenses clouding over. Windshields became sheets of ice. Men on foot were needed to push the tanks and trucks up the slippy slopes of inclines. Some simply could not stand it. They broke down completely under the strain of the battle and the extreme cold, tears streaming down their agonized faces to freeze on their twitching cheeks.

Still the two colonels allowed their hard-pressed men no respite. The tall lanky infantryman and the short burly tanker who affected a big cigar in the fashion of his chief Patton were here, there and everywhere that night, pleading, cajoling, threatening, keeping their men moving through the freezing gloom. They tried not to see the wrecked vehicles that lined the roads and fields, or the dead lying like broken dolls in the verges.

'*Take it out!*' Abrams would bark angrily as his tanks stalled yet once again in front of some hamlet or hastily erected barricade. 'Come on ... stop piddling around, willya!'

And his Shermans would line up like a battery of guns for some ceremonial parade and plaster the hold-up with massed fire, but always there would be another barricade – and another; and the whole bloody, time-consuming business would have to commence yet again.

'In God's name,' Abrams cursed at dawn, eating his Christmas dinner – tinned turkey and potatoes, cold, washed down with luke-warm black Nescafe – for breakfast because it was the only food handy, '*will* we never reach that lousy place?'

And his exhausted staff knew what that place was. It was Bastogne.

Now Bastogne was fighting for its life. It was being attacked along the length of US ever-narrowing perimeter by four whole German divisions with elements of at least three more. Their white-clad infantry supported by massed tanks attacked over and over again across the snowy plain. With the fervour of youth they cried *'Heil Hitler'* and *'Alles fur Deutschland!'* to be stopped only at the very last moment before they swamped the Screaming Eagles' foxhole line.

Casualties were mounting alarmingly. The lightly wounded volunteered to stay behind and help out their buddies, and back in Bastogne itself, staff officers combed the cellars for deserters and cowards, forcing them at pistol-point to pick up a rifle and go back into the line. Every man who could fire a Garand was needed in the line. 'Cooks, clerks, canteen commandos,' a harassed exceedingly worried McAuliffe urged time and time again, 'send the whole goddam shoot up the line!' His gaze constantly flashed to the south, the direction from which Patton's men would come. But the blazing horizon remained obstinately empty of Patton's tanks.

Back in his cellar HQ that midday, as the walls trembled with the explosions of enemy shells, he stared up at Kinnard, face set in a look of uncharacteristic despair, and said in a hollow voice, 'Kinnard, the finest present anyone could give me this Christmas Day is relief by the Fourth Armored Division!'

Five miles away General von Manteuffel was eating his Christmas dinner, consisting of cold captured US K-rations, washed down with cognac, standing up in the freezing hall of his château HQ. Just then an aide came running the full length of stone-flagged corridor crying, *'Herr General... Herr General ... der Führer am Apparat!'*

Von Manteuffel dropped his spoon and can and ran too. One did not keep Adolf Hitler waiting, not even a general who presently commanded the destinies of nearly 200,000 soldiers.

Hitler wished the panting little general a merry Christmas, for the dictator was still a typical sentimentalist who joined wholeheartedly in the Christmas trees and candles and all the other cloying traditions of the seasonal celebration.

Manteuffel barely remembered to do the same before broaching the reason for having asked to speak to the Führer at his castle HQ in the far-away Hessian hills. *'Mein Führer,'* he barked, 'the Americans are proving a tougher nut than we imagined yesterday. We are pushing them back and our attack in the south-east is doing particularly well, *but'* – he emphasized the word – 'I would like to request permission to stop the 2nd Panzer's and the Panzerlehr's drive to the Meuse *temporarily,* and use them to wheel north on *this* side of the Meuse. This way I will trap all

Allied troops east of the river and be able to deal with the problem of Bastogne with more time at my disposal.'

The general, who was trying to hedge his bets, just in case Bastogne did not fall this freezing Christmas Day, waited expectantly. Soon one of the Führer's celebrated outbursts must come.

In didn't. Instead, his voice almost gentle, Hitler said, 'I understand your problems down there, Manteuffel, but we must continue our drive westwards and *at the same time* take Bastogne. I do not want just a tactical and strategic victory, I want a political one, too. I want that old sot Churchill and the Jew Roosevelt coming to me on their knees crawling for mercy – and I can only achieve that aim if we reach the coast. Bastogne is secondary to that objective.'

'But *mein Führer*,' Manteuffel objected, 'I cannot do both under present circumstances. If I concentrate my forces, I can take Bastogne and then continue to the river. If I don't concentrate, then I could fail in both objectives.'

Hitler chuckled, a surprising sound. 'Don't get cold feet, my dear General, on account of a few minor setbacks this morning. The reports we are receiving from your front and those of the Sixth SS Panzer Army and the Seventh Infantry Army indicate that satisfactory progress is being made. All captured enemy prisoners show a remarkable lack of spirit and despondency. Their morale is at a new low. Besides, I have a few surprises up my sleeve, you know, Manteuffel.'

The general wondered what new white rabbit Hitler would produce out of the top hat now; for the Führer loved to spring surprises on his commanders.

'Firstly I am sending you three completely new divisions on the morrow.'

Manteuffel was genuinely surprised. Where the devil, he wondered, had *they* sprung from?

But Hitler was not finished yet. 'Something else. I am sure you are worried by Patton's army on your left flank, especially as our Seventh Army is not adequately equipped to deal with a highly mechanized army like Patton's. Well, I have a nasty surprise for that American cowboy. In exactly six days from now – on the night of 31 December – I shall launch a completely new offensive in the Alsace – *to his rear!* Two whole corps, one of them SS, will fall on the Anglo-American front like a bolt out of the blue, and I can leave it to your imagination, Manteuffel, just how horrified and shocked Patton will be at that. It will be the end of his attack.'

'*Himmel, Herr, Gott!*' the little general exclaimed.

Hitler chuckled again. 'I thought you would be surprised. Now, my dear Manteuffel, go to it with renewed energy. Give me Bastogne with what you have, and I promise you, you will be celebrating the New Year in one of those expensive restaurants you favour in Brussels' *Grande Place*. And now to the attack... *Auf wiederhören*...' Suddenly the phone went dead in Manteuffel's hand.

In a daze he put the instrument down, his ears still hearing of the total confidence in the Führer's voice. He had made it sound all so easy. For a moment or two he felt the old magic, the magic of 1940, when they had swept through France, driving all before them, the French and the English running, a broken rabble of pathetic creatures whom they did not even bother to take prisoner.

Could they do it again four years later? Suddenly Manteuffel's narrow Prussian face under the shaven scalp hardened with new resolve. Perhaps they might not achieve the successes of that heady summer of the great *blitzkrieg*, but by God, they'd take Bastogne this day – or else...

Iron Mike wiped the scum off his cracked lips with the back of his hand; he had never felt so cold, hungry or tired. But as he peered at the miserable collection of ruined houses, huddled around the grey Gothic church, its steeple gone, he knew he couldn't let up one bit. This was the front. Further down the road that led out of the hamlet, he could hear the distinctive slow chatter of an American BAR. Now their own guys were only half a mile away.

'What do you make of it, sir?' Big Red asked softly, the blood from the scalp wound he had suffered that night already caked and dried a hard black the length of his right cheek.

Iron Mike did not answer for a moment. Instead he kept his red-rimmed, weary eyes fixed on the hamlet.

Nothing moved in that miserable place. No smoke came from the chimneys. There was not even the usual stray dog left behind by the refugees, and adopted by the soldiers, to bark hysterically every time strangers approached. The hamlet *seemed* empty. But was it?

Up in the remains of the church steeple, which stuck out like the stump of a broken tooth, there could be an enemy artillery observer, concealed in his camouflage cape, surveying the fields to his front for the least sign of movement. In the cellars of the ruined houses, weary but keen-eyed infantrymen might well be dug in, waiting for the first sign of an attack up that straight, deserted road.

In the end the captain broke his heavy silence. 'Well, Red, I'm not taking any chances – not at this stage of the game. If that dump weren't occupied, you'd think our own boys would have already taken it.'

'We skirt round it, sir?'

'Bit difficult, sir,' Limey answered Red's question for him. 'If that steeple – or what's left of it – *is* a Jerry OP, they've got the front pretty well covered. They'd soon spot us.'

Iron Mike agreed glumly. None of them, except Dude, had come away unscathed from that mad scramble through the German panzermen's positions. Limey had been hit in the calf and now he hobbled along supported by a fir branch. Polack had been struck in the shoulder. Though the bullet hadn't lodged and he made light of wound, he could no longer fire his rifle from that position. As for Iron Mike himself, a bullet had entered the upper part of his left arm, leaving it completely numb and useless, so now he was keeping it strapped within his belt. As Limey had commented as they had re-grouped after that mad dash, 'The sick, the lame and the hungry – what a ferking mess!'

'Once I ate roast dog when I was stationed at Schofield Barracks before Pearl Harbor,' Polack said apropos of nothing. 'The natives think it's a delicacy.'

They all looked at him, as if he had suddenly gone off his head. 'Is there something wrong, Polack?' Iron Mike asked, forgetting their problem for a moment.

'I'm just plumb hungry, sir,' Kovalski hung his head, as if ashamed of himself.

'Sorry, I mentioned it.'

Iron Mike's heart went out to the big simpleton; it went out to all of them as they crouched there, pale and shivering and wounded. They had suffered a lot these last terrible days and still they were as loyal as on the very first day. Somehow that knowledge gave him new resolve; he knew he must lead them to their own lines that very day. 'This night,' he swore to himself, 'my guys will be eating steak and french fries, washed down with enough hot coffee to fill a bath-tub.' But he didn't tell them that. Instead he said, 'We've got to make this one last effort, guys. I know you're all beat to the wide. But there's no other way.'

Limey looked at the straight road that led through the village towards the American lines, a look of almost passionate, sexual longing in his faded eyes; then he stumbled to his feet and tucked the impromptu crutch under his arm. 'Ready, when you are, sir,' he said.

Big Red slung Limey's weapon over his broad shoulder next to his own. 'I'm with you, skipper.'

Iron Mike looked at Polack and Dude. Both of them nodded and Dude, the only unwounded Bad Boy, said, 'I'll take point, sir.' He unslung his grease-gun. 'Give me ten yards, sir.'

'Good, thank you.' Iron Mike knew he was

over-tired and when a man was over-tired he grew emotional at moments like this, but there was no mistaking the tears that welled into his eyes and the sudden lump in his throat. He swallowed hard and brushed his bruised dirty knuckles across his eyes. 'Come on guys,' he said huskily...

They had been trudging around the tracks which skirted the front-line hamlet for nearly half an hour and were beginning to move south again in the general direction of the American line when Dude at point groaned and held up his free hand urgently for them to stop. The others crouched down, hearts beating like trip hammers, while Iron Mike went forward to where Dude had concealed himself behind a bush. 'What is it?'

By way of an answer, Dude pointed forward, face set in a look of complete disappointment. 'Ten o'clock, skipper,' he whispered.

'Oh shit,' Iron Mike moaned. Up front just next to a tumble-down wooden barn with a heap of frozen straw peeping out of the upper storey, a German 57mm anti-tank gun was dug in, with a white camouflage net draped over the pit. There was no mistaking the white smocks and coal-scuttle helmets. The men standing about behind the barn were Krauts all right!

Dude looked at the officer and, his voice

very worried now, said, 'The men won't be able to take any more, sir. They can't go on detouring and detouring…'

'Oh, for God's sake, knock it off, Dude,' Iron Mike cut savagely into the other man's mournful words. 'Don't you think I've got eyes in my head, man. I can see they're tuckered out.' He bit his bottom lip and did a quick count of the Germans down below. There were at least a dozen of them. His Bad Boys, in the shape they were in, wouldn't be able to tackle them; they didn't even have the fire-power to frighten them off. At last they were between the devil and the deep blue sea. They could go neither forward nor backwards. This it seemed, was the end of the road.

Dude sensed what was going through the officer's head, for he said, 'We can't surrender … not in these Kraut uniforms. Hell, they'd have us up against that barn wall in no seconds flat.'

'We're not going to surrender, Dude,' Iron Mike said. 'But we can't just hang around here much longer. Hell, it's colder than a grave-digger's arse!' He shuddered violently.

For what seemed an age the two of them crouched there, unable to react or make a decision, listening to the Germans chatting, apparently quite happy in spite of the cold, stamping their feet every now and then. Two of them, with their helmets off, were cooking over a couple of bright-blue petrol fires.

Crouched further back, Polack sniffed the air and said, 'That's chicken, they're cooking down there.'

'Hold ya water,' Big Red snarled, 'you goddam chow-hound, you think only of your Polack guts!'

'But chicken!' Polack protested. 'They're eating real live chicken down...'

Iron Mike let the words slip away, hope slowly dawning on his worn face as a plan started to cross his mind. 'Dude,' he said suddenly.

'Sir?'

'You see those gas-and-earth fires down there.'

'Yeah.'

'Do you think you could hit them with that Kraut grease-gun of yours?'

Dude made a quick estimate of the range and then looked down at the Schmeisser. 'The range is a bit extreme for it, but I could get a little closer without them seeing me, I suppose. But why sir? What good would it do to hit them?'

'Well, you know how they make those fires? Gasoline stirred slowly into a mess of dirt, with holes punched into the can with a bayonet to keep up the draught going. Turn them over and you have gas flames spreading everywhere.'

Dude's face lit up. 'You mean that wooden

barn … and the straw hanging down everywhere?'

'I do,' Iron Mike shared his sudden excitement. 'If we can get that damn place alight, we *might* just be able to slip through in the confusion. Besides there are animals inside the barn still, I can smell the goddam things. Perhaps cows. If they panic and bolt, we've got it made.'

'Then what are we waiting for?' Dude snapped.

'Just to get the other guys in position. Off you go, we'll follow as close as we dare.'

'Roger and out,' Dude said with a grin and a trace of his old devil-may-care pose. He started to crawl forward on his belly, greasegun clasped in his arms. More slowly the others followed, each one of them knowing that if Dude failed and the Krauts didn't stampede they were finished. They couldn't go on much further – and surrender meant death.

Now they were all in position, the air heavy with the odour of frying chicken and burning gasoline. Carefully, very carefully, Dude began to take aim, knowing that this was the most important burst he had ever fired in his life, lining up the ring sight of the Schmeisser with the can on the right, one eye closed, forcing himself to breathe normally. His finger slightly damp with nerves, he took first pressure. The can and the man crouching over it were still ringed by the sight. He said a quick prayer. His finger slid into second pressure. The grease-gun chattered violently. Acrid smoke filled his nostrils. The steel butt slammed into his right shoulder.

Then it happened. The man cooking sat down abruptly, a look of almost comic bewilderment on his face as he started to fold over, while the can sprawled to the rear, flinging burning gasoline everywhere.

The Germans rushed about, crying wildly in alarm, and Dude fired again. Again he was lucky. The second can overturned, flew against the wooden wall of the barn, flinging gasoline three feet high. Almost immediately, as the Germans scattered to left and right, firing wild bursts to all points of the compass, the dry, ancient timber caught alight. The hay began to burn a second later, slipping down in a cascade of fiery sparks, swamping the screaming men below. Inside the barn there was the muffled whinny of a suddenly panic-stricken horse. A thunder of flying hooves. Abruptly the door of the barn splintered, rotten planking flying everywhere. A great heavy Fleming blundered into the open, its flying mane already aflame. It reared high on its mighty hindlegs like a thoroughbred, hooves flailing. A German screamed and went reeling back, face a sudden gory mess. The horse clattered forward, whinnying with terror as the wind caught the flames, engulfing its whole head in them.

It did the trick. Germans fled madly to get out of the way, while behind them the ramshackle barn swayed like a stage backdrop as the flames rose higher and higher.

Iron Mike waited no longer. It was now or never. 'Up!' he commanded. *'Straight through them!'* He grabbed Limey with his good arm. 'Come on, old timer, let's go!'

Limey grinned back at him, in spite of his fear. 'Not so much of the old timer, cock,' he cried above the confused racket to their front, and then they were off hobbling towards the American lines, Dude snapping shots to left and right like a gun-slinger in a B-movie shoot-out...

'Now just hold it there, buddy!' the voice from the other side of the field called.

'Go crap in yer hat!' Big Red called back angrily. 'We've been trying to get to you guys for nearly a week now. So don't screw us about.'

The speaker, a second-lieutenant with a white, weary face under his too-big helmet, peered out of his foxhole again. All along the line of foxholes dug beneath the snowy hedge his men did the same. 'Listen,' he said, 'why the hell do you think we're dug in like this, freezing our nuts off, instead of advancing to where we can get our heads under cover, eh?'

'I don't know,' Big Red answered sourly, 'but I'm sure you're going to tell us, *lootenant.*' He emphasized the rank sarcastically.

'I'm sure as damn will!' the officer answered hotly, his face flushing suddenly. 'On account of the fact that this field is mined and the rear is so screwed up that we can't get the engineers up. Take a gander at that sign to your right.'

The weary Bad Boys turned in the direction indicated. Attached to a rusty iron stake there was the old familiar German sign, a black skull-and-crossbones with the legend *'Achtung-Minen'* stencilled below it.

Dude whistled softly and Big Red cursed angrily.

'It could be a trick,' Iron Mike called, speaking for the first time, just now beginning to regain his breath after that mad dash from the burning barn. 'I've seen the Krauts use it before. A couple of signs – and no mines.'

On the other side of the field the second-lieutenant laughed hollowly. 'Tell that to the two guys I've just evacuated – one with his nuts blown off and the other with his right foot gone. Yeah, some trick!'

'Deballockers?' Iron Mike gasped.

'Yeah,' the other man answered back grimly. 'Nice sweet little Bouncing Betties all over the goddam place!'

'Oh my aching back!' Iron Mike groaned

and sat back on his heels, all fight knocked out of him. It seemed as if luck had been against them all the time these last terrible days. This was the final straw. Dude, who was in the best shape of them all, took in the look of absolute exhaustion on the captain's face and knew he would have to act. He raised himself out of the ditch and called, 'Listen over there, we've got a vitally important message for the commanding general of the Third Army. We've got to get through to him this day. It's about Bastogne...' He filled his voice with all the theatrical urgency he could muster. 'It's a matter of life or death... Can't you guys clear a path for us? We're beat.'

'What do you think we are buddy?' the other man answered cynically. 'Ole Blood an' Guts has been driving us with a whip since the 22nd. We've had it.'

'But I'm the only one not wounded of our group,' Dude protested angrily.

'So you find a way across,' the officer answered coldly.

'Listen, when General Patton finds out,' Iron Mike added his voice to Dude's, 'he'll have you court-martialled for this. He'll have your hide, buddy.'

The second-lieutenant laughed cynically. 'So, I think I'd enjoy a nice quiet rest in the stockade.' His voice rose harshly. 'Listen, whoever you are, we're armoured infantry with a life expectancy of six weeks, shorter even than that for shave-tail second looeys like me. So what do I care about Ole Blood an' Guts?... If you're coming across, we'll give you covering-fire, in case those Kraut paras up there spot you. If you're not going to bother, take off and leave us in peace. We need the shut-eye.' He tilted his helmet over his eyes as if he were going to go to sleep and disappeared into his foxhole again.

The Bad Boys looked at each other moodily. 'Always nice to have a friendly welcoming committee to greet you, ain't it?' Limey quipped like the cheeky, ever-optimistic Cockney sparrow that he was; but no one laughed.

'Perhaps,' Dude began and then stopped.

'Perhaps what?' Big Red asked wearily.

'I could spray the field with the Schmeisser,' he said not very hopefully, 'and explode a path ahead for us ... like a bangalore torpedo?'

Iron Mike shook his head. 'No deal, Dude. You know the Bouncing Betties? Their prongs above the earth are so thin, hardly visible at all until you're right on top of them and then it's too late. You might explode a couple of the damned things but there would still...' He shrugged and didn't finish the sentence, that cynical little voice at the back of his mind already telling him what he had to do, ending with a brisk, 'Okay brother, you're an officer.... Start

278

earning an officer's pay!'

Wearily he staggered to his feet, feeling the numb ache in his strapped arm. The best he could, he removed the glove on his good hand, while the others stared up at him, wonder in their lack-lustre eyes. At last he managed to get it off, flexing his fingers, wondering how long it would take before they froze up and became useless for the tremendous self-imposed task ahead of him. 'All right, guys, I'm gonna have a go.'

Big Red opened his mouth to say something, but Iron Mike stopped him with a wave of his hand. 'Someone's got to do it, Red,' he said without heroics. 'There are a lot of good guys back there in Bastogne depending upon us. If I don't make it–' He shrugged. 'I'll leave it up to you. One of us *will* get across, and guys' – he looked around their weary unshaven faces – 'it's been nice working with you.'

Next moment, before anyone could stop him, he had clambered out of the ditch and was advancing on the field on his hands and knees, everything forgotten now, save what lay ahead.

General Patton looked around the gloomy dining-room of the Hotel Alpha with its Thirties' murals of elegant young men in blazers with pomaded hair and young women with short skirts and no breasts. He frowned. The sight didn't please him. He had always liked women with big breasts. His frown deepened as he looked round the faces of his staff finishing off their miserable Christmas dinner in the flickering light of the candles on the fir-tree that Meeks had fond somewhere or other. The staff officers looked beat although they were, for the most part, a good quarter of a century younger than he was. Over the last five months of combat he had worn them all out; there was hardly one of his original staff left.

Patton took a pull at his cigar. From outside there drifted in the noise of shunting trains at the station opposite. Someone was trying to start up a jeep which obstinately refused to turn over in the freezing afternoon air. 'Gentlemen,' he rasped, 'you look as pooped as an army-post whore on pay-day!' His sally had no effect. His officers' expressions did not change. They stared down gloomily at the remains of their pathetic Christmas meal. Patton squinted down the length of his long cigar, his thin lips set in a savage smile. 'Gentlemen,' he tried again, 'you're letting this battle for Bastogne get to you. Don't forget that battle is the most magnificent competition a human being can engage in. You think the Krauts are supermen just because they are holding us up there in Belgium. But they aren't. The Third Army has licked them before … it will lick them again!'

Still, he could see, he wasn't getting any response from his officers.

'Gentlemen, we Americans are a competitive race. We bet on anything and everything. We love to win. And we're going *to win* this one, too, believe me. But you don't win by pussy-footing around. In the final analysis, attack saves lives. You've got to get the doughs moving and keep them moving. Oh, I know, they tend to stick. Who wouldn't when he's faced with the prospect of having his balls shot off the very next moment?' Patton's voice sank and his faded blue eyes blazed with sheer, naked menace. 'This afternoon, gentlemen, I want all of you up the line. I want you all up there rooting hog. Fire any commander who won't attack, even if you have to fire every goddam officer in the battalion ... and if you run out of officers, then put the noncoms in charge, and if they won't do what you want 'em to do, put a frigging rifleman in charge of the battalions. *But I want action ... and I want action ... NOW!*'

With that he swept out, leaving the officers stumbling to their feet, looking shocked and not a little afraid.

Ten minutes later, while Meeks prepared his outfit for the afternoon's drive to the front, Patton knelt at the foot of the big double bed, eyes closed, hands clasped together, all bravado gone from his voice, as he prayed fervently for the victory at

Bastogne which had eluded him for four long days. In the weak light of the yellow bulb overhead, the silver-haired general who commanded the destinies of half a million Americans looked frail and old as he pleaded with God to deliver him from that final overwhelming fate.

The top-priority phone started to shrill at his bedside. Meeks in the other room heard it, but he didn't dare enter while his master was saying his prayers. On and on it rang until Patton, after what seemed an age, at last became aware of it. He creaked stiffly to his feet and in a bent-knee, old man's walk, crossed over to it and picked it up.

It was Colonel Harkins of his staff who was already up front with the Fourth Armored Division, doing some personal trouble-shooting for his boss. 'Sir … sir,' he gasped, his excitement coming over quite clearly, although the line was very bad, 'we've made contact, sir!'

'Contact with whom, damnit?' Patton barked.

Harkins forgot all telephone security in his excitement. 'With some boys from the 101st, sir!' he yelled.

Patton's faded eyes lit up; had his prayer to the Good Lord been answered so promptly? 'Is it the link-up?' he asked urgently.

'No sir … not exactly,' Harkins answered, his voice suddenly very faint, as if it might well fade away for good at any moment. 'They've been sent through the Kraut lines by General McAuliffe to bring a personal message to you, sir.'

'Well,' Patton snapped, indicating to Meeks hovering by the door to the bedroom that he should bring his jacket,' what is it?'

'The Krauts are putting in a max effort against Bastogne this day. Apparently the 101st captured their plans. It's Bastogne or bust for them this afternoon.'

'Say that again, Harkins,' Patton said, new hope beginning to dawn in his eyes, as Meeks fitted him into the elegant, bemedalled tunic. Harkins did so.

Patton laughed out loud, and cried out of the side of his mouth. 'The helmet, goddam... Why that's tremendous news, Harkins! Tremendous!'

Meeks hurried across the bedroom, while Patton's face assumed a big grin.

'But why tremendous, sir?' Harkins stuttered, 'I don't understand...' His voice trailed away.

'But don't you see? This is the way that Third Army is going to sneak first base. If the Krauts are putting in a max effort up in Bastogne, they're conducting a holding operation against the Third Army, presumably with their line thinned out accordingly, for the big attack on poor old McAuliffe.'

'Yessir, but...'

'No goddam buts! This is the opportunity we have been waiting for all along. Now it's shoot the works! Every man into the line! It's max effort for us, too, Harkins! By God, Colonel, this is gonna be one hell of a scrap,' he chuckled, rubbing his hands together, as if in anticipation. 'But by God, we're gonna win it... *Tell the boys, Ole Blood an' Guts is on his way.*'

Day Ten:
Tuesday 26 December 1944

'Old Blood an' Guts is coming up, did you say?' Abrams exclaimed. 'Hell's bells, that's really torn it!'

Iron Mike, his arm feeling easier now after the shots Abrams' MO had given him, grinned. Patton obviously had an effect on his men.

He flashed a look to their front. Dead German paratroopers were scattered everywhere on the road and in the fields to both sides of it: ghastly tableaux of bodies in mottled green camouflage jackets; a bloody sawn-off stump, already black with caked blood; dead eyes staring accusingly from waxen pinched faces. The 5th German Parachute Division was certainly putting up one hell of a fight,

284

he told himself, even though Patton's new strength was overwhelming. Then he forgot the German dead and his own men, who were now presumably warm and fed and fast asleep somewhere to the rear of Abrams' tank battalion. The benzies were working flat out and he felt as if he had just had twelve hours' sleep, his nerves jingling as if with high-power electricity.

Abrams was going into the final attack and he had his doubts, that was obvious. He, Iron Mike, had to ensure that he kept going; for it was pretty obvious from the ominous orange cloud that flickered off and on over the besieged city up front that the 101st were taking a terrific beating; they would not last long if the great breakthrough weren't made this Tuesday morning.

'Well?' Colonel Jaques asked, posing the question that Iron Mike would have liked to have asked. 'How are we going to do it, Creighton? If Ole Blood an' Guts is on his way up, we've gotta have a plan firm and settled.'

Abrams puffed his cigar and then said, 'There is only one way we're gonna do it in a hurry and that is to take Assenois.'

The tall infantryman looked down at his stubby running-mate in dismay. 'But we can't do that, Creighton,' he protested. 'Div. HQ has got it all worked out. The attack has to go in at Sibret. They've got it worked out

285

to the last detail. You just can't switch plans like that–' he clicked his fingers together. 'They have even got TAC Air on tap for the Sibret attack. You can't change Air just like telephoning for ... er...' he stuttered, searching desperately for the right comparison, 'room service!'

'Why not?' Abrams said, 'especially if you've got General George S Patton Jnr backing you. That's one thing I've learned in this war – generals are Gods, accountable only to themselves. If Patton says it's okay it's okay and even the President of the United States can do goddam nothing about it!'

'Amen,' Jaques intoned, head lowered, hands momentarily clasped together in mock piety.

Iron Mike grinned. The two colonels of the Fourth were cards, but he wondered how they would get on with the redoubtable General Patton, now hurrying up to the point. Would they convince the Third Army commander, or not? If they didn't, or their attack failed, then, Iron Mike knew, the US Army might just as well write off the 101st Airborne Division...

The whole valley to the west of Assenois quaked. From one end of Bayerlein's positions to the other the copper-red lights blinked furiously like the chimney blast of enormous furnaces. The snow-capped hills all around echoed to the tremendous roar. At regular minute-intervals 200 shells from the massed guns of the Panzerlehr Division ripped the sky apart and slammed into the remaining positions of the Ami paratroopers, while Bayerlein's panzer grenadiers advanced doggedly, dark little figures against the white backcloth of snow.

In their cellars and foxholes the Screaming Eagles – what were left of them – huddled together like terrified children, as the hillside shook and swayed as if struck by a tremendous hurricane.

Holes collapsed under the terrific pounding. Screaming hysterically, the wounded fought the soil, clawing their way free of the streaming earth with fingers that ran red with blood. Here and there a cellar took a direct hit. Instantly it was transformed into a red gory mess, pieces of bodies and limbs plastered to the shattered walls like postage stamps, men below drowning in their own blood. Some broke under the strain and ran, mindless and screaming, directly into the German fire. Others fled to the rear, throwing their rifles, helmets, ammunition pouches away as they ran, faces contorted with overwhelming unreasoning terror.

But when at last that terrible bombardment had to cease and the panzer grenadiers loomed up out of the fog of brown rolling smoke, there were a few, very few, left – and they were waiting. Machine-guns pounded, rifles cracked. The first wave of panzer grenadiers was swept away, as if hosed down. The second wave came on bravely, their officers in the lead dramatically flourishing their pistols as in a gallant nineteenth-century battle portrait. But the defenders were still there. Their machine-guns swept the line of young soldiers from left to right, killing them systematically, like cattle in a Chicago stockyard being slaughtered to order, one after another.

Bayerlein, watching through his glasses from the roof of his command half-track, held his breath. The third wave of his brave young men was going in now, stumbling over the carpet of bodies of those who had already fallen for *Volk, Vaterland und Führer.* Would *they* make it?

The third wave went in more slowly, coming in from both flanks, trying to outguess the weary handful of Amis still holding the foxhole line. Now their officers did not make themselves so conspicuous. The pistols which marked them as officers had been replaced by ordinary soldiers' rifles or Schmeissers. They advanced, bent like men going forward against beating rain, their young faces set and ashen, each wrapped up in a cocoon of his own hopes and fears.

Bayerlein tensed. There was no fire coming from the Ami positions. Had they had enough? Would they be coming out in a minute, hands clasped on their heads, waving dirty white rags in surrender? Would he at last break into Bastogne? He had been there from the start; would he now be in at the end? For he had reasoned what that cowboy general of theirs, Patton, would do when he heard that von Manteuffel was launching an all-out attack on the damned place. Patton would assume – correctly – that the line of the 5th Para would be thinned out and would attack it with everything he had available. For that reason Bayerlein had disobeyed von Manteuffel's order to continue the drive for the Meuse with the bulk of his Division. Instead, he had turned his full weight on this key link-up point between the two American forces. Now he *had* to break through before Patton linked up; *he just had to!*

The third wave of panzer grenadiers were less than 150 metres away from the Ami positions, stumbling and slipping over the dead bodies in their way. In a minute, a tense, nervous Bayerlein knew, they would break into their final charge, carried away by that crazy blood-lust of battle, forgetting all fear, motivated solely by the blind desire to kill. When would the Amis react?

Slowly, very slowly, it seemed to the watching German general, a lone figure rose from the centre of the American line. Whether he was an officer or common soldier, Bayerlein did not know; nor did he ever find out, even after the war when he became a prisoner of the Amis. No one was ever able to identify the man who would die so bravely in the next five minutes, although to his dying day, General Bayerlein always insisted that the unknown Ami was the one who saved Bastogne for the United States.

The man in khaki cleared the heap of brown earth in front of his foxhole and stood watching the advancing panzer grenadiers as if he were a spectator at a football match or were watching a newsreel of some event that had taken place on the other side of the globe.

The panzer grenadiers were only 100 metres away now. Bayerlein gasped with surprise. The lone man in dirty khaki was lighting a cigarette calmly. *'Himmel, Arsch und Zwirn!'* Bayerlein exploded. 'What in three devils' name is the fellow up to?'

The lone Ami took a puff of his cigarette. Bayerlein could see the blue smoke ascending slowly into the grey air. Now his men were less than 75 metres away. In a moment they would charge. Now nothing but this strange Ami was between them and success, it seemed. Suddenly the American flipped away his cigarette. It was a melodramatic gesture, a product – Bayerlein guessed – of seeing too many cheap films, but still it was strangely effective. It was an act of defiance.

The Ami straightened up to his full height. Almost casually, he reached for the leather pistol holster strapped low on his thigh and tied to his knee with a thong. He drew out the .45 and, snapping off the hammer, took aim and fired in one and the same gesture.

A panzer grenadier stumbled as if he had fallen over something, but a gaping Bayerlein knew he hadn't. He had been hit by the Ami's bullet. The Ami fired again. Another panzer grenadier fell. Still his men didn't react. Instead they were coming to a halt, as if too startled by the lone Ami's actions to know how to behave. 'Damn fools,' Bayerlein bellowed, although he knew they couldn't hear, *'kill him!'*

Then it happened. The length of the Ami foxhole line erupted into violent life. Rifles cracked, machine-guns rattled once more, as the lone Ami firing from the hip advanced towards the stalled panzer grenadiers – to his death.

One minute later, the third wave had broken and the survivors were stumbling back the way they had come, clawing and fighting at each other in their determination to escape that deadly fire. Behind they left their own dead and that lone Ami, pistol still clutched in his lifeless fingers. Bayerlein dashed his glasses to the ground. Almost instantly the divisional artillery started to smash down on the stubborn Amis – what

291

was left of them – yet again.

It was now just after one o'clock on the afternoon of 26 December. The two colonels, the one tall, the other fat and squat, stood on the hilltop waiting and stamping their feet. Patton had come and gone. He had agreed and made his promises, but he had made one proviso. There would be no side-stepping to attack Assenois instead of Sibret until TAC Air had flown in to support the tank-infantry force. Thus they waited, while down below the tankers in their Shermans, with engines running, already buttoned up, were ready to go. But could the Thunderbolts and Typhoons which Patton had insisted upon arrive in time? The light was bad as it was; soon it would fade altogether. Just behind the two colonels, Iron Mike sucked his teeth anxiously and waited, too. When would they come?

At first it was only one, fat-bellied, 7-ton blob of silver, gleaming in the grey light. It waggled its wings as it saw the recognition panels spread out below. For what seemed an age it hovered over the German positions. Then abruptly a great roar filled the air from the west. Like fat silver ducks, swarms of the tank-killers came scuttling in. Scores and scores of them, already dropping out of the sky, their 20mm cannon thumping, sending brilliant white shells speeding to the ground.

Abrams threw his cigar away with a wild Texan hoot. 'Hot dog!' he cried, 'Patton came through... *Ole Blood an' Guts kept his word!*' He flung a look behind him at Iron Mike. 'Well, MacDonald what are you standing there for like the proverbial spare penis? Let's go, if you want to say happy Christmas to those buddies of your'n up there!'

'Yessir,' Iron Mike snapped and sprang up behind Abrams as he clambered onto Thunderbolt IV, his command tank, his number four Sherman since the campaign had started the previous August. At long last they were on their way.

When it came, it did so almost as an anti-climax. Leading Abrams' point with his three Cobra Kings, a Lieutenant Boggess spotted that the men in the foxholes ahead were wearing what appeared to be US uniforms, just in time to stop his somewhat trigger-happy gunner from opening fire on them. Cupping his hands around his mouth, as he stood there in the turret, Boggess yelled: 'Come on out!'

But the men in the foxholes stayed stubbornly where they were, giving no reply.

'Let me give 'em a burst of HE, sir,' his gunner begged.

Boggess ignored the demand. Others of his crew crawled up into the turret and started shouting at the men in the foxholes. Here and there suspicious faces peered at them. Finally, after what seemed an age, a man in khaki crawled from the nearest hole, carbine suspiciously levelled, eyes wary, and advanced on the Fourth Armored men. 'I'm Lieutenant Webster of the 101st Airborne,' he said, looking up solemnly and unsmiling.

Boggess grinned hugely and thrust back his leather tanker's helmet, revealing the puckered red line around his forehead.

'Glad to meet you, Lieutenant,' he exclaimed enthusiastically.

'My name's Boggess of the Fourth Armored. Bastogne has just been relieved.'

The Screaming Eagle nodded absently, as if the tank officer had just made an everyday remark about the state of the weather. Then he said, completely without emotion. 'You got any water?... We ain't had a drink all goddam day...'

The long siege of Bastogne was over...

ENVOI

'Brave rifles, veterans, you have been baptized in fire and blood and have come out steel.'

General George Patton 1 January 1944

Its 'steamboat trombone' klaxon shrieking, flanked by two motor-cycle outriders zig-zagging on their gleaming machines through the still smoking debris of the great siege, the command car advanced on the waiting parade. In its back stood Patton, upright and imperious like some Roman emperor in a war chariot. His features, under the familiar lacquered helmet with its three outsize stars, were set in his 'war face number one', the one he practised most of all in his mirror, his jaw jutting out pugnaciously. Rolling past the flags of the United States and the 101st Airborne Division, his gloved hand quivered up to his helmet in a precise salute in the French fashion. Patton was pulling out all the stops this fine, bright December morning.

He held up his hand. Mims and the outriders stopped immediately. Behind them the squad of heavily armed MPs in their bright white helmets tumbled out of their scout-car and immediately took up defensive positions surrounding their master. Patton did not deign to notice them. Instead, he swept his imperial gaze around that dreadful landscape. Burnt-out German and American tanks littered the hills like enormous dead animals; newly fashioned birch crosses draped with helmets, marked the graves of both sides; and from a shell-stripped tree a human leg, complete with jackboot, dangled like a piece of monstrous human fruit. Then he had seen enough. He descended from the vehicle and the band struck up, all gleaming silver and brassy blare, the bandsmen's cheeks red and gleaming with effort, their breath fogging the cold morning air. Salutes were exchanged. The Screaming Eagles were stood at ease. They breathed out a collective sigh of relief. Someone farted. The ceremony could begin.

A portly brigadier-general from Eisenhower's staff who affected riding breeches and a crop stepped forward. While the movie cameras whirled and the press photographers, no respecters of person, jostled for position, snapping angrily at each other as they did so, he began to read the statement prepared by Ike's PR staff. Patton, standing next to McAuliffe, watched from the wooden rostrum, a look of disdain on his aristocratic, haughty face; it was typical of Eisenhower: cheap, shoddy, just another attempt on Ike's part to hog the headlines, come what may.

'Thus I say to you, gentlemen,' the fat general droned on self-importantly, his breath grey on the crisp air, 'you battered bastards of Bastogne, heroes one and all,

298

that the 101st has a new watchword ... one belonging to the bright lexicon of the American fighting man which reaches back into the far days of George Washington and Valley Forge' – Patton groaned inwardly and wondered who had written such puerile crap; they'd be bringing in Gettysburg next – 'through Gettysburg and San Juan Hill, the Argonne, the battles of North Africa, Sicily...' There followed phrases like 'Don't give up the ship, Gridley'... 'Don't shoot till you see the whites of their eyes'... 'Praise the Lord and pass the ammunition...' At last the portly brigadier-general raised his head for the punch-line and smiled benignly at the paratroopers who stood all around him. 'From this time onwards,' he declared in a ringing voice, 'wherever American fighting men congregate, that one little word *"Nuts"* will forever symbolize American courage under fire. Gentlemen of the United States One Hundred and First Airborne Division, *I salute YOU!*'

Patton swallowed, as if he were going to be sick, as a bored cheer went up from thousands of hoarse throats, and told himself that the longer the war went on, the more of this sort of crap they would hear. How Tech-Sergeant Joe Zilch from East Overshoe, Maine, stuck his thumb in the dyke and stopped the bridge from collapsing, or how Colonel Wideass from Little Pessary, Ohio, led his men in a suicidal charge – to the rear. *Human interest.* It stank, it was nauseating. Whoever had heard of a general of the United States Army replying to another commander with a word like 'Nuts?', America was becoming too damned democratic. *It had to stop!*

A minute later, however, he allowed himself to be photographed pinning the DSC on a smiling McAuliffe. 'Everybody was worried about you,' he commented as he stooped to pin the medal on the much smaller general.

'Hell, sir,' McAuliffe replied pugnaciously, 'my Geronimos are ready to attack again, just any time you want them to!'

'Well spoken, McAuliffe,' Patton declared, raising his squeaky, thin voice for the benefit of the newsreel cameramen recording what they would later undoubtedly call 'this historic moment'. Then, the ceremony over, Patton said, 'Tony, I'd like to see these latterday Paul Reveres of yours – the ones who brought the message.'

'You mean MacDonald's Bad Boys?'

'Yes, if that is what you call them, Tony.'

Flanked and followed by pressmen and staff officers, the two men walked slowly over to where Iron Mike, immaculate as ever, stood with his arm in a sling in front of his battered survivors. Patton halted abruptly some six yards away. The others stumbled to a surprised stop. For a moment he did not speak. There was no sound save that of the flags flapping in the breeze and the faint drone of the fighters circling high up above in the blue sky to protect the ceremony and the brass from enemy bombers.

'Captain MacDonald, sir,' McAuliffe introduced Iron Mike who had stepped forward three paces and saluted.

Patton looked at him hard – from the strained, handsome face, down the trim, lean frame, to the jump-boots which gleamed as brightly as his own elegant riding boots – and liked what he saw. Facing him, he knew, was the finest type of American officer, concerned only to do his duty, unaffected by all that public relations bullshit dreamed up by the canteen commandos at Ike's fancy Parisian HQ. Instinctively he thrust out his gloved hand and seized a surprised MacDonald's. 'Thank you, Captain,' he said fervently, 'you did a damn fine job!'

His gimlet gaze fell on the handful of troopers behind the tall, young officer, some of them still bearing signs of the recent battle, their bandages tinged pink with fresh blood. 'And *thank you*, fellers, too,' he added.

Again he looked at Iron Mike, standing rigidly to attention, his keen eyes fixed on some distant horizon. 'They tell me, your men are the rejects of the 101st Airborne Division, the Bad Boys ... what they used to call jailbait in my days as a field-grade line officer. Well, Captain MacDonald, let me tell you something,' Patton snapped, a sudden angry note in his voice. 'Most men in today's US Army find a rifle about as useful to them as a pecker would be to the Pope. They goddam well won't fight unless they're forced too.' His voice warmed up again and there was a sudden, affectionate look in his faded eyes. 'I dearly love soldiers who'll dive into a scrap like your guys... Captain MacDonald, if I had only one single division made up of fighting bad boys like yours, I could lick A-dolf Hitler and the whole of the Kraut army goddam single-handed!' He grinned broadly at them. 'MacDonald look after yourself and your boys... America's gonna have need of them again, *soon...*'

And with that he was gone into the History of World War Two...

The publishers hope that this book has given you enjoyable reading. Large Print Books are especially designed to be as easy to see and hold as possible. If you wish a complete list of our books please ask at your local library or write directly to:

Magna Large Print Books
Magna House, Long Preston,
Skipton, North Yorkshire.
BD23 4ND

This Large Print Book, for people
who cannot read normal print,
is published under the auspices of

THE ULVERSCROFT FOUNDATION

... we hope you have enjoyed this book.
Please think for a moment about those
who have worse eyesight than you ...
and are unable to even read or enjoy
Large Print without great difficulty.

You can help them by sending a
donation, large or small, to:

**The Ulverscroft Foundation,
1, The Green, Bradgate Road,
Anstey, Leicestershire, LE7 7FU,
England.**
or request a copy of our brochure for
more details.

The Foundation will use all donations
to assist those people who are visually
impaired and need special attention
with medical research, diagnosis
and treatment.

Thank you very much for your help.